A MAN LIKE AN

Rosalyn told herself not to be deceived by the surface
singularities that seemed to set Mr. Worth Forrester
apart—his strikingly tall stature, his extraordinary
strength, his free and easy manner, his tales of der-
ring-do in the American wilderness across the sea.

He was, after all, just another man.

A man who had joined her rakish brother Gordon
in his London revels.

A man who had stayed the weekend at one of Lord
Whitbourne's infamous debaucheries.

A man who sought to lure her into the odious en-
slavement known as wedlock.

There was only one question she had about him.
Why, if he was like any other man, did she feel so
strangely different when he came so dangerously
near . . . ?

THE WHITBOURNE LEGACY

SIGNET Regency Romances You'll Enjoy

MARJORIE DeBOER

THE WHITBOURNE LEGACY

A SIGNET BOOK

NEW AMERICAN LIBRARY

Copyright © 1985 by Marjorie DeBoer

SIGNET TRADEMARK REG. U.S. PAT. OFF. AND FOREIGN COUNTRIES
REGISTERED TRADEMARK—MARCA REGISTRADA
HECHO EN CHICAGO, U.S.A.

SIGNET, SIGNET CLASSIC, MENTOR, PLUME, MERIDIAN and
NAL BOOKS are published by New American Library, 1633 Broad-
way, New York, New York 10019

First Printing, July, 1985

1 2 3 4 5 6 7 8 9

PRINTED IN THE UNITED STATES OF AMERICA

For Wendell
who made it all possible

∽ONE∾

The post-chaise from London was due at any moment.

Rosalyn Archer awaited its arrival with her two sisters in the upstairs parlor of Torview Hall, their grandfather's country estate in Devonshire, freely admitting to herself that she was in a state. Not, certainly, because their brother Gordon was coming home after an eight month's absence; but because he was bringing a stranger with him.

Due to a delay in the post, they had received the news only that morning. As the minutes ticked by, Rosalyn, trying to knit a wool cap for her grandfather, Baron Clifton, found her fingers growing damp and awkward. It was nerves, of course, but realizing it helped not at all. She simply could not think what Gordon was up to. In his letter he admitted he had only recently met Mr. Worth Forrester, who was, of all things, an American. He had not given so much as a hint of a reason why he had so generously invited this foreigner to stay with them.

It's not fair, Rosalyn silently scolded her brother. You, of all people, ought to have known I'd need to . . . well, *prepare* myself, when I've not met a stranger in years. What a shame that delight at the prospect of seeing Gordon again should be so shadowed by the spectre of this unknown man.

The desultory conversation she and her sisters Olivia

and Evelyn had attempted the past hour had died. Sixteen-year-old Evie, far from being apprehensive, was too excited to sit still and sew as her sisters were doing. She paced impatiently from the fireplace, where a comforting blaze tempered the damp September chill, to the bow window, from which vantage point she kept peering through the mullioned glass onto a tree-lined avenue nearly lost in early evening gloom.

Olivia, sitting at the other side of the fireplace, seemed placid enough as she bent over her embroidery, but her angular face retained a slight frown, reminding Rosalyn how resentfully she had received Gordon's letter that morning. Olivia had taken over the management of the house on their mother's death a year ago, and while she found great satisfaction in wielding her authority and wouldn't for the world have delegated it to anyone else, she made it clear to all—from the least scullery maid to their grandfather Lord Clifton, himself—that her obligations weighed heavily on her thin shoulders. The unexpected need to oversee preparations for two newcomers at the very moment she had been about to go on an errand of mercy with Lady Harriet Whitbourne had put her into a regular stew, until Rosalyn had convinced her *she* could give the servants their orders, just this once.

It wasn't the first time Olivia had been at odds with Gordon. Being three years his senior and of a serious disposition, she had always criticized what she called his "madcap ways," ignoring the light-hearted cheerfulness that made his company such a pleasure. Rosalyn was readier to overlook and forgive his faults. Perhaps because they were closest in age—he twenty-three, she twenty-one—they had confided in each other from childhood, and even when she didn't agree with him, Rosalyn could always sympathize. But now—well, this once, she was inclined to side with Olivia.

She could predict just how it would be with a stranger at Torview Hall. Ever since recovering from the illness that had temporarily paralyzed her legs seven years ago, there were a number of things she could not do, and Mr. Forrester would doubtless wonder why. Seeing her limp, he would ask if she had hurt her ankle recently, or, if he did not happen to notice that immediately, he would expect her to go on riding or walking expeditions. Then the old illness would have to be explained in tedious detail, and Mr. Forrester, if he were like most people, would pity her. She detested being pitied.

The petite ormolu clock on the mantel chimed seven-thirty. Olivia gave an impatient sigh. "I don't know how much longer Mrs. Holbrook will be able to hold back dinner without ruining everything," she fumed. "If she expected to serve dinner at seven . . ."

"Mrs. Holbrook is a marvel," Rosalyn reminded her. "She'll manage if anyone can."

"Indeed," Evelyn added, "Grandfather once said his fondest wish was for Mrs. Holbrook to outlive him, so he'll never have to do without her plum pudding and her manner of fixing a joint of beef."

"I only hope they manage to arrive at all, the way it has rained today," Olivia went on, barely heeding Evelyn. "What if they decided to stay overnight at Chudleigh?"

"Well, they mustn't, that's all!" Evie exclaimed. "I should die of disappointment if they don't come tonight."

Rosalyn suppressed a smile, but the frown line in Olivia's forehead deepened at her sister's excessive language. As if by accord, they returned to their sewing, and the comfortable, old-fashioned parlor sank again into silence. The leap of flames was reflected in the polished black and gold lacquered tables Lord Clifton's father had imported all the way from Japan back when Torview Hall was new, and in the delicate patina of the cherrywood pianoforte—Rosalyn's especial joy. The shadows darkened and enriched the patterned red and blue Turkey carpet, and the brass encircled armillary sphere in the corner, which had always fascinated Rosalyn with its mysterious astronomical measurements, reflected a dark-gold light from the nearby candelabrum.

Then Evie, once more staring out the window, caught sight of a big yellow carriage rolling up the drive, its lamps ablaze, and cried out, "They're here!"

"Softly," Olivia cautioned, looking up but not missing a stitch. "Indeed, Evie, if he heard you hoot in such a fashion, Mr. Forrester would think he was back among the Red Indians."

Rosalyn stuck her knitting needles in her ball of yarn, wrapped the completed portion of the cap about it, and rose to return it to the sewing cabinet. Suddenly, not only her fingers but all of her seemed uncommonly chilled and clumsy.

"How fortunate the rain has ceased at last," Evie said, pulling back one of the blue silk curtains. "And there's Gordie himself, getting down."

"Have you caught sight of Mr. Forrester yet?" Olivia asked, knotting a thread and cutting it off neatly with tiny scissors.

"No. He must still be inside. Oh, wait . . . here he comes. I declare, Olivia, he's tremendously tall!"

"Pray come away from the window, Evelyn. What if he should look up and see you peeping at him?"

"Why, then, I'd wave at him," Evie retorted with a laugh, but she replaced the curtain and turned to look back at her sisters. "Well, aren't we to go down and greet them?"

"I'm sure they'll prefer to settle in first, Evie," Olivia said. She gathered up her needlework and stood. "We'll assemble in the drawing room in half an hour for supper. Meanwhile I must speak to Mrs. Holbrook and let her know there *is* hope that we'll eat tonight."

"And I shall change my dress," Evie decided, flying to the door ahead of her older sister. "Whatever was I thinking of, to put on this old thing?"

Left alone, Rosalyn succumbed to curiosity and went to

look out the window Evie had vacated. The large lantern above the portico cast a golden glow onto the pebbled path where the two men had disembarked. Apparently a problem had developed with a large portmanteau strapped atop the carriage. A corner of it was caught in the much-weathered leather strip on the edge, and the light didn't extend far enough to illuminate the problem. The postboy was teetering precariously on the narrow bar above the forward platform, straining to help Abbot, Gordon's valet, loosen it. Meanwhile the bag trembled half on and half off the roof of the chaise, while Donald, the footman, moved to catch it should it fall.

Gordon held the horses steady while the servants dealt with the problem. The figure behind Donald, cloaked and hatted, must be Mr. Forrester. Silhouetted against the light, he appeared to be at least a head taller than the footman. After watching the struggle with the luggage for several moments, he strode past Donald to the carriage, reached up, and, with apparent ease, released the bag and lifted it down as though it were a box of feathers.

The postboy cheered him, jumped down, and took up the reins. Gordon paid him, then motioned Mr. Forrester toward the house. Suddenly Rosalyn noticed that Donald, who had the stance and shoulder muscles of a bruiser, was having such difficulty carrying the portmanteau into the house that Abbot had to come and help him. Their struggle, coming immediately after the American's effortlessness, made Rosalyn gasp in amazement. The nervousness she had felt at the prospect of meeting Mr. Forrester was compounded. What sort of person would so casually demonstrate such prodigious strength? She tried to make out the features of the newcomer, but his hat brim, viewed from above, effectively hid his face.

Soon afterward, she went to her bedchamber to change for dinner—a simple matter of exchanging one black gown for a fresher one. Unlike Evie, who had abandoned mourning for their mother a fortnight ago, on the anniversary of her death, Rosalyn and Olivia still wore black, Rosalyn because it seemed easier than to change, as she had almost no social obligations.

Now, because Mr. Forrester would soon view her infirmity, it nettled her more than usual that she could not walk in her old even-footed way, no matter how she tried. Usually she was so accustomed to her sedentary life she never questioned it anymore, and continued to be grateful that the frightening paralysis that had gripped both her legs for months had finally left her. But now she could not help regretting the illness that had set her forever apart from others.

Even after the paralysis had gone, she had been beset with frequent colds, which always lingered and left her drained of energy. Her mother insisted she follow the doctor's orders closely: She must not become tired, and she must not use her lame foot any more than necessary. This meant no stair climbing and no walking outdoors, especially when it might entail exposure to wind, rain, or cold weather. She needed a lie-down every day, and an early bedtime whether she was sleepy or not. The strictures seemed endless, and Rosalyn had gradually abandoned some of them. She did go up and down stairs now, and to church on Sunday with the rest of the family, though it meant a carriage ride the five miles into Ashburton. And she did sometimes practice the piano to the point of exhaustion when she became particularly enthusiastic about a number. But mostly she followed the doctor's rules, which Olivia, in addition to taking up her mother's other responsibilities, continually oversaw.

Music and reading, always her primary interests anyway, became Rosalyn's life. *That* was not hard—it was her natural inclination. And it had not been too difficult, after the first shock, to accept her doctor's warning that the stress of childbearing might bring on the paralysis again. It was a good way to avoid what she had long wished to avoid—marriage. Now she had a good excuse, for no man wanted a wife who could not give him children.

Rosalyn had never told Olivia her real reason for accepting her fate so philosophically. Olivia would have considered it unnatural, even though both girls in their childhood had been silent, horrified witnesses to the abuse their mother had endured during their father's drunken rages. Finally, when Rosalyn was nine years old, Lady Archer had fled from her husband, Sir Lionel, taking her four children back to Torview Hall, her ancestral home. A year later Sir Lionel was dead, crushed by a drover's wagon that had been unable to avoid him as he stumbled, drunk, into its path.

When sober, their father had possessed a delightful artlessness and a gift of song that could turn the head of any woman in the county, and Rosalyn was grateful that she, as well as Gordon and Evie, had inherited his musical talent. But most of her memories of him were intermingled with so much unpleasantness that she had long wondered why any woman wanted to marry. Reading Mary Wollstonecraft's treatise on the rights of women only reinforced her decision that men were not worth such pain. She burned with indignation when she pondered male assumptions that women were intellectually inferior to men, the slaves of their passions, and fit only for marriage and childbearing. Never could such theories apply to her!

Yet she had to admit that her own sister had fit only too well into the prevailing notion about women. Once she had met the black-mustached sea captain Samuel Fortescue, Olivia had easily dismissed her mother's experience, succumbed to his lighthearted courtship, and married him. Less than a year later, after she had experienced several days' anxiety over his unexplained absence from their home, he had been found snoring and liquorish in the arms of a harlot at the Golden Lion in Ashburton. When Olivia had exploded in righteous anger, Captain Fortescue had rounded up his crew and sailed for South

America, whose females, he swore, were less judgmental. No one had seen him in the three years since.

Evie had been only five when her father died. She had no real memory of him, nor did she know the true reason for Captain Fortescue's disappearance. She thirsted for new experiences the way Gordon did, and it was, no doubt, perfectly normal that she should look forward with such enthusiasm to meeting a stranger from America. She was already talking of beaux and trousseaus and was excited at the imminent prospect of Vicar Molton's daughter Melinda's marriage to Squire Halburton's son Duncan; she continually pestered Olivia to promise she might go to London to stay with some relatives so that she could be presented to the queen next spring, and have a Season.

Rosalyn was not at all unhappy to miss out on such things. They were, after all, only the alluring bait by which young girls were trapped into marriage. She doubted very much if a man existed who could attract her enough to change her mind. Even Gordon and Grandfather, both of whom she loved dearly, had faults one must overlook.

There was only one man she truly admired—her second cousin, Bernell Mayhew. Bernell was not only a true friend, but was as devoted as she to music. Some two years ago he had founded the Musical Society, a group of six friends who met weekly to sing old madrigals, glees, and part songs, simply for the pleasure of the music and one another's company. Sometimes he even composed songs for them to sing, and Rosalyn thought them wonderful, although Bernell never seemed satisfied with the results.

She guessed Bernell had organized the Society especially for her, who was left out of so many activities, although he would never have admitted to it. Rather than confront him with her thanks, she had, unknown to him, sent the score of one of his songs (which she had copied herself on the pretext of needing a more readable script) to England's leading tenor, John Braham. If Braham recognized his talent, it would help her repay Bernell for the many favors he constantly did for her and everyone else at Torview Hall.

Bernell himself seemed to have no particular use for marriage. At thirty-six he was still a bachelor, and if she occasionally wondered why he had never taken a wife, usually she thought his unmarried state comfortable and right for him. Like Bernell, she saw no reason her own life could not be perfectly fulfilling and serene without it.

Rosalyn had changed into a fresh gown and was brushing her hair, trying to decide how to change the everlasting black of mourning into something more interesting (as though a new face at supper required something equally new from her), when she heard a knock on the door. "Come in," she called, and turned as the door opened.

Gordon stood there, debonair and smiling, his lively brown eyes crinkling with expectation. He had changed his damp traveling clothes for pale gray pantaloons, a dark blue coat with silk frogging and trim on the collar, and a peach-colored satin waistcoat that perfectly showed off his slender elegance and his thick brown hair.

She greeted him with an enthusiastic hug. "Gordon! How tremendous to see you again!"

He kissed her cheek and propelled them both into the room. "Now there's a proper greeting! I'm not sure Olivia really welcomes the prodigal brother."

"Of course she does. It was only that your letter didn't arrive until this morning, and—"

"So I heard," he interrupted ruefully. "The suddenness of it! The mystery of my motives! The unexpected guest! All calculated to overset our poor Olivia."

"So she's conveyed all that to you already?"

"She has indeed, with looks if not with words. I met her on the stairs as I was coming here. And now I've something that will put her into even more of a pother.

Roz, you must help me with this. I know I ought to announce it tonight, but I hardly know how . . ."

"What is it?" Her lips continued to smile, but alarm clouded her eyes. "What have you done now?"

For answer he took a tiny case out of his vest pocket and opened the lid. Inside the locket was a miniature of a pretty young woman, her fair hair done in little ringlets fastened with brilliants. A black velvet ribbon encircled her slender white neck and held an enormous diamond in place.

"Meet Miss Constantia Glynne. We're betrothed," Gordon announced, his voice sounding tentative.

"Gordon, you're positively astonishing! When did all this happen? She . . . she's lovely," Rosalyn added as he seemed, for once, tongue-tied. "What's the problem? Why are you so worried about Olivia's reaction?"

"Miss Glynne's father is a silk merchant."

Rosalyn looked up at him, startled, then burst into laughter. "Oh, Gordon!"

"You may well laugh," Gordon muttered darkly, taking the miniature from her and putting it away. "No one else shall. But I'll marry her nevertheless. Her father is damned rich, and she adores me. And her family has been extremely kind."

He hadn't said he loved her. Rosalyn couldn't help recalling that before going to London, Gordon had spent an uncommon amount of time with the now-betrothed Melinda Molton, even to the point where Olivia had thought it remarkably callous of him to take his share of his mother's inheritance and leave Devon. Only to Rosalyn had he confided that his developing relationship with Melinda had seemed a trap—that he had to see more of the world before he "settled down."

Now, it seemed, he had fallen into a similar trap. Soberly she said, "Yes, you may very well be in for it, then, but . . . Gordon, you know Melinda is betrothed to Duncan?"

"Yes, he wrote me some weeks ago."

"I—I'm glad you know. Are you distressed?"

"Why should I be? I found someone else; Melinda found someone else. It's a relief, actually. I was afraid she'd be wearing the willow."

He looked away from her, a false bravado in his voice, and changed the subject. "Advise me, Roz. Should I tell them now, before supper? Or announce it at table? Or should I tell Grandfather alone, later? He'll probably have my head for considering someone outside our class, but . . ."

"I don't think he means half what he says, Gordon. When he read your letter today, he even admitted it would be interesting to have an American here to talk to."

"That's quite something, isn't it—especially knowing what he thinks of 'the colonies.' "

"I think Olivia's more a problem than Grandfather. Why don't you tell him separately, later on? We don't want to spoil supper, do we?" She gave a little grimace and was pleased to see his face relax.

"Righto! No, by Jove, can't distress our dear sister at supper—at least no more than she is already inclined. Thanks, Roz."

"Now, about Mr. Forrester," Rosalyn said. "Where did you ever find him?"

"Prowling the streets of London," Gordon said with an insouciant grin.

"What?"

"Just a jest. No, he's perfectly respectable, Roz. And quite fascinating. He has come to England expressly to find the family of his father, who died when Forrester was a small child. He has nothing to go on beyond his father's name and the date he left England, some thirty years ago. Apparently the man never corresponded with his family, once he left England, and the only other thing Forrester knows is that he was from Devonshire. So I told him, what could be more logical than to come to Devon and poke around here? Forrester is not that common a name, and there must be—"

"But how came you to meet him?" Rosalyn asked. "How do you know he's—a good sort of person?"

"I just *know*. You aren't going to be like Olivia, are you?" When Rosalyn remained dubious he added, "He came to England with a letter of introduction from some Virginia senator to Mr. Russell, the American attaché in London. But Russell hasn't been able to help him; he's too busy trying to defuse the hostility between his government and ours. You know that Pinkney, the American minister, left in a huff in May because the situation was getting worse in spite of his best efforts. Poor Russell is in over his head—"

"Yes, but what about Mr. Forrester? How did you meet him?" Rosalyn repeated patiently.

"Oh, as to that." Gordon gave her one of his charming, guilty smiles which admitted he was trapped. "I was . . . what you might call 'making a night of it' in Soho. And I saw this poor bloke—I *thought* he was a poor bloke—being positively taken in by—by certain unsavory characters. I could tell he was foreign—cut of his clothes, accent, but especially his utter gullibility. Well, to make a long story short, I interfered and saved Forrester's purse for him, after which he kindly saved my neck for me when aforesaid unsavory characters decided to teach me a lesson for meddling."

She waited expectantly, hoping for further enlightenment about such a fascinating incident, but he only said, "Since then we've been to the theater and the opera together, and to several routs. Also, I introduced him to my tailor. Now, what higher recommendation could I give him than that?"

Rosalyn laughed. "None higher, I'm quite convinced."

"If you're ready, we can go down to dinner together," he suggested, clearly putting an end to the subject.

She recognized the offer as part of Gordon's unassuming kindness. If she appeared on his arm, he secretly helping her bear some weight, her limp would be less obvious to the guest.

Yet, as they filed into the dining room, she on Gordon's arm and Mr. Forrester following with Evie, she could not get rid of the sensation that his eyes were on her. And she wondered why she should hope he had not noticed her limp.

✐⌒ TWO ⌒✐

Rosalyn's appetite, usually poor, fled entirely during the first few minutes of supper. Once she had consumed a portion of the turtle soup, she could do no more than taste the various dishes presented to them by Newton, the butler—the shad with oyster sauce, the joint of beef with creamed peas and potatoes on the side, the roast goose and tongue, the apple tart with the famous thick Devonshire cream.

It did not help at all that she sat directly across the table from Mr. Forrester, who was on Lord Clifton's right. This made it impossible to avoid glancing at him from time to time, and so she must notice again the fascinating contrast of his thick, combed-back, wheat-colored hair to his dark curly sideburns and tanned face. His dark eyelashes and eyebrows gave his gray eyes a distinction and beauty that would have been the envy of any woman, and a decided cleft in his chin softened the strong, well-defined planes of the rest of his face. His clothes were well made but unremarkable—a white, simply knotted neckcloth, a shirt without frills, a brown frockcoat with plain brass buttons, a cream-colored waistcoat of finely woven linen.

Obviously he had not her unruly stomach to put up with, for he ate with obvious pleasure, although he spoke little except when Evie, on his right, attempted to draw him into conversation. For her part, Rosalyn simply let the talk flow about her. Olivia, at the other end of the table, described her visit that morning in company of Lady Harriet Whitbourne, the spinster sister of the Marquess of Whitbourne. They had visited Mrs. Beecham, an elderly seamstress most people considered queer. Lady Harriet, as usual, paid local gossip no mind, but went about in her single-minded way, helping the less fortunate. However, Mrs. Beecham, who suffered from the ague, had refused both Lady Harriet's opium pills and her lavender drops, saying she had her own remedies. In spite of the rebuff, Lady Harriet had, on their return, enthusiastically confided to Olivia her idea of a charity hospital in her brother Lord Whitbourne's village of Blackroy, where the country folk might be introduced to the latest and best medical practices to cure their ailments, and for no fee but what they could afford. Lord Clifton gave a loud "Humph!" of derision and remarked that unfortunately Lady Harriet Whitbourne was ever a meddler, but what could one expect of a woman who had achieved her fiftieth year without the saving state of marriage?

Affronted, Olivia closed her mouth and refused further comment. Eager to change the subject, Evie began telling Mr. Forrester about the Musical Society and invited him to hear its renditions the following day. When Gordon intervened with a mock warning, she quickly suggested he sing with them, since Sir Harry, one of the usual members, would be away.

"Gordie used to sing with us before he went to London," she explained to Mr. Forrester, "and we miss him enormously. He's ever so much better a singer than Sir Harry."

Gordon said quickly, "Uh . . . we really needn't do this, Forrester, if you'd prefer some other activity."

Rosalyn suspected his reluctance stemmed from the prospect of facing Melinda Molton and her fiancé—his old school friend, Duncan Halbarton. Both were members of the Society. But as she considered how to help her brother out of his dilemma, Mr. Forrester said that he was sure he would enjoy the singing very much. He was extremely fond of music; often the only entertainment to be had on the frontier was singing, and his mother had taught him many old songs.

"The frontier!" Olivia exclaimed, as though their guest had just revealed he was really a Hottentot in disguise. Then she added, more calmly, "I thought Americans no longer consider Virginia the frontier."

A gleam of amusement lit Mr. Forrester's gray eyes, but he spoke reassuringly. "Yes, ma'am, and I was born in Virginia. But we removed to Kentucky when I was still an infant, and that's where my father died two years later. My stepfather was a trader, and we just kept going west with the settlements. When he died last year, we were living in Illinois Territory, which is still pretty much wilderness."

"Mr. Forrester is a genuine wilderness scout," Gordon declared. "He can track anything that moves, shoot a squirrel at two hundred yards, and find his way through a pathless forest aided by naught but his wits."

Worth Forrester laughed. "As extravagant a lie as any backwoodsman's, Archer!"

"You're far too modest, man. What of the story Russell told of your exploits in the Indian Wars? How you singlehandedly rescued the families of three settlers who had died in an Indian raid, leading the women and eight children on a two-week trek back to civilization. Shot game for them, built shelters, kept them safe from wild beasts and hostile natives . . ."

"And with all this, you seem remarkably well-spoken," Lord Clifton noted wryly.

This was an amazing observation from Lord Clifton, who, during his long career in the House of Lords, had been noted for his stirring speeches. Now, since his ten-year retirement to the country, his only outlet for this talent was lengthy monologues to his family or to the occasional unwary visitor.

"I was schooled in Lexington until I was thirteen, sir,"

Worth replied. "And my mother was most particular to teach me courtesy. She always said that no matter where or how we had to live, I could never go wrong by acting the gentleman in all circumstances."

"And where did she learn such an ideal of manhood?" Rosalyn was surprised to hear herself say. She had become too interested in his story to remain silent.

He turned his expressive gray eyes on her. "Mother came from the Virginia gentry herself, Miss Archer. But she most particularly held up the example of my father, from as far back as I can remember. To hear her tell it, he was the perfect English gentleman. I reckon she exaggerated a mite, but I doubt I'll ever live up to her image of him."

"Was your father of the nobility, then?" Lord Clifton asked.

"I don't rightly know. Mother said he emigrated to America after a quarrel with his family and never would speak of them. But I've always thought nobility the result of a person's conduct, whether he's nobly born or not." He spoke pleasantly, frankly, with no idea in the world that he might be attacking one of Lord Clifton's favorite shibboleths.

"Hmph!" the old baron muttered into his wine. "Well, I daresay it's all of a piece, you being an American. Like your misled countryman Mr. Jefferson, you probably believe that absurd notion that all men are created equal."

Worth Forrester seemed briefly disconcerted by his host's unexpected challenge. Putting down his fork, as if he thought better without such encumbrances, he said, "Yes, I believe it." When no more than another grunt issued from Lord Clifton, he continued, "You must realize, sir, that Mr. Jefferson's declaration was a political creed. I think he meant that high birth doesn't necessarily make a person fit to govern a nation. Specifically, of course, he meant that King George had no more natural right to decide the fate of the American colonies than did the colonists themselves."

Rosalyn held her breath at this bold retort and was surprised when Lord Clifton did not shoot it down in midflight. Instead, he chose to deliver his favorite sermon. "The ruling class rules because it was bred and trained to do so, young man. Kings rule for the same reason. It's in the blood. We breed horses and cattle and dogs to bring out their best qualities. In the same manner the blood of royalty and of the nobility, when kept pure through proper intermarriage, produces the best rulers." He sat back and wiped his mouth with his napkin triumphantly.

With only a brief pause Worth Forrester said, "With all due respect, sir, it seems then that men have taken less care with their own breeding than with that of their livestock. Or is it just a malicious rumor that King George himself has gone mad and has been declared unfit to rule?"

The startled, chill silence was broken at length by Gordon's short laugh. "He's got you there, Grandfather!"

Lord Clifton's high forehead and wrinkled cheeks grew quite red. He clutched his wineglass angrily, spluttering something about unfortunate circumstances which can undo any man. "We are not gods, sir, not even the best of us!" he roared at last.

Another silence. Mr. Forrester, a bit abashed but deciding he had said nothing to warrant an apology, glanced around the table and returned to his slice of goose. Unable to contain herself any longer, Rosalyn burst out, "As for myself, I have long agreed with Mr. Jefferson's declaration of the equality of men, but he ought to have taken it even further, for he has ignored half the human race."

"Rosalyn!" Olivia hissed in a stage whisper. But Mr. Forrester turned to her in interest—or was it merely relief?

"How do you mean, Miss Archer?"

"He ought to have said, 'All men *and women* are created equal.' For if, as you say, it was meant as a political statement, then he should have recognized that women, given the proper education, might rule as well as men."

"You amaze me, ma'am. Do you, then, consider yourself a democrat?"

Gordon laughed again, this time uneasily. "I forgot to warn you, Forrester, that one of my sisters is quite the bluestocking."

She was glad of his interference, which allowed her to escape Mr. Forrester's question. "Our own history proves it, Gordon. When has our nation shown more greatness than during Elizabeth's lengthy rule?"

"She had many advisers—all of them men," Gordon pointed out.

"You would have her a mere puppet, then? No, indeed, she was a skilled diplomat, and did not always comply with their advice. Besides, Mary Wollstonecraft has pointed out—"

"Really, Rosalyn, how can you quote that dreadful woman?" Olivia broke in.

Rosalyn looked from her sister to Lord Clifton, who was watching her with the born debater's gleam in his eye. Since Gordon's absence, it had been Rosalyn who read the newspapers and discussed issues with him. And though he persisted in considering her a "mere female," she knew he was always gleeful when confronted by an argument, no matter who initiated it.

Assuming his support, therefore, she continued, "All she says is quite true, Olivia, as you would know if you actually read her. Women are not supposed to use their native intelligence. We are considered so simple we need male protection, but are not allowed the education that would make us wise. We are exalted as virtuous, yet guarded night and day as though we could not be trusted to keep to that virtue. How illogical it all is!"

"And what would you have us do to change the situation?" Mr. Forrester asked with an amused twist to one corner of his mouth.

"You ought to give us our freedom, Mr. Forrester, as Great Britain gave America her freedom. You ought to give us room to learn and grow and—perhaps—become as wise and great as you men believe *you* are."

The amusement became a wide smile. "Miss Archer, I'd say some women don't need men to give them freedom. They've already claimed it."

She thought he was laughing at her and blushed furiously. What had possessed her to be so outspoken? She had never expressed such views to anyone before save, a time or two, to Olivia, who patently disapproved of them, and to Grandfather, who disregarded them.

Fortunately (for she was left with no logical response) Lord Clifton had recovered enough to reenter the fray. "If the United States is so devoted to freedom, I wonder you people have not united with us against Bonaparte. Now *there's* a tyrant . . ."

And so Rosalyn's brief foray into the conversation was forgotten.

Once the ladies had retired to the parlor, Worth Forrester was somewhat nonplussed by the new direction the conversation took. The baron called for the port and brandy, hospitably proffered his snuffbox to Worth, who declined it, settled back in his upholstered armchair at the head of the table, and asked his guest what he thought of his granddaughters.

Taken aback, Worth mumbled something about their being lovely young ladies.

"Lovely?" Lord Clifton took up with pleased surprise. "Well, I wouldn't go quite that far. Evelyn, maybe, is passing pretty, but too young, too vain, too silly. Mayhap she'll outgrow that. As for Olivia, she's out of bounds, you understand. Married, though no one's seen hide nor hair of that husband of hers for nigh onto three years. Makes her a bit waspish at times. Now, Rosalyn has a good head on her shoulders for a female. Of course, she's always mooning over her music—not good for her constitution, but what can a person do when she's sickly to start with? Still, I always considered Rosalyn—"

"Grandfather, Mr. Forrester is not interested in the marriageable qualities of your granddaughters," Gordon interrupted, taking a pinch of snuff from his own ornate box and inserting it in his nostril with an elegantly curled finger.

"My wife died last winter," Worth explained. "I've not had the heart to look at another woman since. Even if I had, my situation is much too unsettled for me to consider marriage again."

"Of course, of course," Lord Clifton agreed quickly. "I must beg pardon if I appeared . . . uh . . . I suppose living on the frontier is hard on females."

"On a great many of them, yes," Worth agreed. "But in this case, the reason was different. My wife was Shawnee; she died of a white man's disease."

"Shawnee? What the devil's that?"

"I think it's an Indian tribe, Grandfather," Gordon suggested, looking at Worth in surprise. Lord Clifton hid his own startled glance with a long drink of port, after which he stared at Worth and snorted, "Indeed!" And then, "What sort of marriage ceremony got you that?"

Worth said coolly, "A legal one, sir, according to both civil and Shawnee law."

"Hmph. More'n you'd have needed to do, no doubt."

Worth withheld a retort with difficulty and returned to his own drink, awash in sudden memory. Gentle Fawn—the shy girl he had first seen on that tension-filled meeting in the Shawnee camp of Brown Eagle. Gentle Fawn, offered in exchange for his trader stepfather's copper pots and secondhand muskets, rather than the promised furs. Brown Eagle's wily narrowed eyes going from older to younger man as his stepfather protested he had no use for a young woman, he was married. Brown Eagle pressed him anyway. What about the young man? ("What could

29

I say?" he complained to Worth later. "I had to unload my stuff, and I couldn't give it away. His mangy blankets weren't worth a tinker's damn, and his traps had all been sprung.")

His stepfather had thought they were cheated, but by the time he took Gentle Fawn as his wife, Worth knew her to be priceless. Even now it was possible for her calm, velvety-brown eyes to dance before his mind's vision, obscuring the present.

Gordon, apparently thinking that after Worth's information Lord Clifton would look more kindly on a prospective wedding between two people who were, after all, both English, decided now was the time to present his own case. "Grandfather," he said, "speaking of wives . . ."

Worth was not surprised at the tenor of Lord Clifton's initial objections to the match with Miss Constantia Glynne. They sprang from the same basis as his little speech to Worth about breeding royalty and nobility. But he was surprised when Gordon, who had displayed certain signs in London of being both a dandy and a snob, stuck to his guns and insisted that Miss Glynne, having been to the best schools, had the *savoir faire* if not the ancestry of an aristocrat, and her father, even if his expensive establishment was not always in the best taste, was a kindly man who greatly favored the match. When Lord Clifton suggested that of course he did, his daughter would be marrying a nob, the goal of every *nouveau riche* tradesman in England, Gordon retorted that money had played a certain role in his own decision, but he was not ashamed of that— the tradeoff was a fair one. Besides, he liked Constantia, she had a sense of humor, and he had always disliked females who took themselves too seriously.

Unexpectedly Lord Clifton turned to Worth and asked what he thought of Miss Glynne. Though he had met her only once, Worth loyally managed to convey that he was on Gordon's side. This seemed to carry some weight with Gordon's grandfather, who, downing the last of his port,

returned to amiability and suggested they were long overdue in the drawing room. Rising, he advised Gordon to
say nothing of the engagement to Olivia for the present,
and Worth detected relief in Gordon's eyes. It was clear
that the match, though not a favored one, would not be
unalterably opposed.

Once they had rejoined the ladies in the formal drawing
room—a long room with two fireplaces, dressed in faded
velvets and brocades of green and ivory—Gordon presented everyone with gifts he'd brought them from London: French perfume for Evie, a brilliant-studded tor-
toiseshell comb for Olivia, a sheaf of music for Rosalyn,
a special brand of snuff for Lord Clifton.

Then Worth, a little uncertain of his reception, presented everyone with beaver pelts from Illinois Territory,
which, he had understood, were much prized in England.
Though the eldest daughter looked at hers as if it might
return to life and bite her, she managed a grudging thank-
you and a comment on its beauty. Lord Clifton said, yes,
indeed, beaver pelts were very dear in London; he would
have a hat made of his. Evie thought she would like
a muff for when she went to London, and Rosalyn
thought it would make a perfect collar for her winter
coat.

Then she added perceptively, "Perhaps these are pelts
from animals you trapped yourself." When Worth admitted as much, she said, "Then they will be the more treasured, Mr. Forrester. Thank you."

As she looked away from his appreciative glance to
stroke the lustrous brown fur, Worth had a brief, warm
sensation of coming home.

A fire had been lit, and the chairs closest to it were
taken by Lord Clifton and Olivia. Her cool, polite questions concerning Worth and Gordon's journey from London soon lapsed. Then the youngest sister positioned herself near Worth and asked questions about his life in
America, batting her pale lashes and smiling encouragingly
for answers he could not give—for how could he acquaint

31

this innocent young lady with the rigorous, savage life on the frontier? His mother, worn out from unhappy bondage to that life, had insisted on returning to Virginia as soon as his stepfather's death had released her from it. He had accompanied her with reluctance, unsure he could make the change from frontiersman to gentleman. Even now, after eight months in Virginia and one in England, the high coat collar, tight vest, and swaths of neckcloth of his gentleman's clothes seemed an infernal invention designed to stifle his breathing. He still longed for the loose-fitting, practical buckskins and boots he used to don without thought.

Eight months in Virginia had knocked the roughest edges off him, thanks to his mother's sometimes irritating insistence on manners and forms. It had also accustomed (but not reconciled) him to the long hours of comparative idleness of plantation life and had given him a passing acquaintance with all those public issues which the remoteness of Illinois Territory had hid from him.

But eight months in Virginia had also destroyed his mother's long-held hopes of retiring to her childhood home near Richmond. When Julia Worth had petitioned for her rightful share of the family estate, once deeded equally to herself and her now-deceased brother, her sister-in-law, as his widow, had successfully blocked the effort. It was then that, seizing on the memory of her first husband, she had developed a longing to go to England. She had told Worth, half playfully, that it was some ancestral longing, no less deep because she had never been there. She would dream of living in England and awake with tears in her eyes. But without funds, the likelihood of realizing her dream seemed remote.

Unexpectedly there had been help from the past. Senator Randolph, an old friend of the family, had learned of their plight and of Julia's desire to move to England, and had volunteered to finance the trip to search for her dead husband's family. At first she had planned to accompany Worth, but they finally decided that he might make better use of the generously given funds if he traveled alone.

He had been in England over a month, waiting on the empty promises of the harried American attaché to take him to Devonshire. He had been introduced to numerous people named Forrester—the lawyer from the City; the squire from Northumberland; the woolen merchant from Yorkshire; the sporting lord from Shropshire. But none knew of Daniel Forrester, born in 1759, who had emigrated to America from Devonshire in 1782.

It was, Worth decided, a near-futile search. The only way he would find his father's family was by some act of God. And then, quite by chance, he had met Gordon Archer. . . .

His mind full of memories, he answered the youngest and oldest sisters' questions as well as he could and wished the middle sister had not taken her gift of music and vanished upstairs. Watching her leave the room, his eyes had been drawn to the wealth of dark hair that flowed down her back. It reminded him, for no good reason, of Gentle Fawn's blacker, straighter hair.

Now he could dimly hear, from somewhere above them, the hesitant strains of a complicated musical passage, repeated over and over with increasing dexterity on a pianoforte. When his eyes inadvertently went to the ceiling, Evelyn said, "You mustn't mind Rosalyn. She often prefers solitude to people. And her music is the most important thing in the world to her."

Her tall sister added solicitously, "The day was very tiring for her. She doesn't often come down to supper."

Worth was about to ask why not, but Gordon interrupted and suggested the four of them partake of a few hands of whist, Lord Clifton having buried himself in yesterday's issue of the *Times*, which Gordon had brought with him.

By the time they had gathered around the gaming table and dealt the first hand, the music from the upper floor had ceased.

⌒∾ THREE ⌒∾

The following morning Worth heard the music again as
he awoke. Morning was half over by frontier standards—
it was nine-thirty by the clock on the polished old cherrywood dressing table that squatted before a gilt-framed
wall mirror. But then, he and Gordon had stayed up long
after Lord Clifton and the ladies had retired, amicably
airing their respective countries' charges and disputes over
brandy. "Why can't our diplomats be like you and me?"
Gordon had wondered at one point. "It would be so easy
to settle the whole mess." Now Worth wondered if it had
been the brandy that had enabled him to agree with Gordon that the impressment of American sailors into the
British navy was a highly overrated issue.

He arose with his usual alacrity, went, barefooted, to a
window, and opened the shutters. Both sweet and pungent, the odors of herb and hedge and flower wafted to
him on the cool morning air. The sun had turned yesterday's innumerable raindrops, still imprisoned on blades of
grass and flower petals, into transient jewels. He eagerly
recalled Gordon's invitation to ride around the estate with
him after breakfast.

But the music seduced his ear. Soon he found he was
giving it his full attention. Was the piece now being exe-
cuted so beautifully the same one she had been struggling
with last evening? Reaching for his clothes, he dressed
hurriedly in shirt, pantaloons, and boots, smoothed back

his hair with his hands, and followed the sound to its source, two intersecting hallways away.

The door stood ajar, showing him a cozy parlor over-looking Torview Hall's front portico. He stood in the door-way and saw Rosalyn Archer at the delicately carved and polished little pianoforte across the room. She had tossed her shawl aside in the passion of her playing, and it lay in a pale puddle on the floor behind her stool. She wore another high-necked black dress, even more severe for lacking the white collar of last evening's costume. Her luxuriant brown hair was pulled back into a bun enclosed in a white net. Her left hand flew, a ripple of broken chords, while her right brought forth a joyous melody which seemed to pour from her own being into the in-strument.

Suddenly, as the melody switched to bass octaves, she faltered, dropped the right-hand part to concentrate on the left, then stopped. Without warning she looked around and saw him.

"Oh! I . . . had a *feeling* someone . . ."

"Excuse me for bothering you. But you do a mighty fine job of playing."

"Oh, I'm only learning it. It ought to go much faster." She smiled and added, "It's Mr. Beethoven's latest sonata. Gordie just brought it. I have them all, but this one is different."

He had a feeling that if he kept the subject on music, he could say whatever he liked, so he asked, "Why is it different?"

"It's like a story. The first movement is *Das Lebewohl*—'The Goodbye.' The second, very mournful, is *Abwes-enheit*—'The Absence.' The last—this one—is *Das Wied-ersehen*—'The Return.' It's very joyful. One can imagine so many things while playing it."

The German words flowed off her tongue as though they were simple English. Not knowing how to respond, he apologized again for interfering with her imaginings and started to withdraw.

"Mr. Forrester."

He turned back, surprised by the suddenly purposeful tone of her voice. "Ma'am?"

"I feel I ought to be the one to apologize—for my grandfather, for the way he lectured you at supper last evening. He had no intention of being rude. It's just his way. He believes his age gives him the liberty to say what he likes."

Worth was surprised. "I wasn't offended, Miss Archer. I only hoped I hadn't offended him."

"Not at all. He adores controversy. Your visit will be most stimulating to him, I am sure. A genuine democrat in our midst."

Her friendliness encouraged him. Unconsciously he took a step into the room and said, "But if I understood you rightly, he's already acquainted with one democrat—you, ma'am."

She appeared to be taken aback. "Are you joking with me, sir? I thought you found my remarks simply amusing. Grandfather certainly considers them amusing. He doesn't take me seriously."

"Why not?"

She observed him coolly. "Why, because I am a woman, of course. I am humored because I am not expected to conform, but I am not taken seriously."

"It has been my experience—very limited, I'll admit—that most English ladies only aim to amuse."

"Of course," she said immediately. "That is my whole point. Most of us simply do what's expected of us. Fortunately, we country lasses have somewhat more freedom."

He nodded in agreement. "Oh, I could see that right away. You and your sisters are a far cry from the languid ladies of London."

The phrase had leaped into his mind unbidden. He was surprised when she broke into laughter. "How perfect. Mr. Forrester, you are nigh to becoming a poet!"

He smiled, glad of her appreciative response but unsure whether to remain in the doorway or retreat. Sobering, she leaned forward in a confiding gesture and said, "One more thing, if you don't mind. I'm quite curious. Gordon told me only very briefly how the two of you met, and it all seemed quite adventuresome and . . . Would you not give me your own version of the encounter?"

She remained seated at the piano but gestured him to come into the room, to be seated on one of those seemingly fragile brocaded chairs. He did so, though suddenly aware he was only half dressed according to Julia Worth's standards. ("A gentleman does not appear before a lady in the morning until he is shaved, combed and coated, and with his neckcloth properly tied.")

"Well, ah—there isn't that much to it."

"Surely you are overly modest."

"Well . . ." He pushed back a stray lock of his blond hair and grinned. "Not so much modest, Miss Archer, as embarrassed. My only excuse is I don't know a dang thing about big-city life. You can hardly compare either Williamsburg or Richmond to London, you know. And where I come from, back in Illinois Territory, I'd never met a real lady of the night before. So when this one gave me her tale of woe about her pa being taken ill out in an alley, I was all for going to help the poor man. Your brother must have been watching us talk, because he came up as we left the tavern and said it was a trick. The woman protested in such vile language I knew he was right. If I'd accompanied her, I'd have been set upon and robbed. Thanks to your brother I still have my money—and my wits."

"But then Gordon said *you* rescued *him*."

"Oh, that wasn't much. The woman rushed off in a fit of anger, and we thought there was an end to it, but once we'd started walking back to my rooms on the Strand, two fellows came at us out of a dark alley. I didn't really rescue him. We both gave a pretty good fight, although we did get battered about some." His fingers went involuntarily to the worst spot, though it had been completely healed for a week.

Her eyes followed the gesture, and he thought there was

a hint less amiability in them. "But then—forgive my asking, Mr. Forrester, but just what were you and my brother doing in a tavern where—where you'd meet such a person?"

"I can tell you what I was doing—just looking around and quenching my thirst. As for your brother, you'll have to ask him that."

He was surprised at the look of repugnance that briefly crossed her face and wondered what he had said. He had only, after all, answered her question.

"I find it most peculiar that Gordie would frequent such a place after having just gotten himself betrothed to Miss Glynne," she said somewhat sharply.

"Men tend to look for spirits—*and* women—even then, ma'am, as you know," Worth said, unthinking.

"As I *know*?" she repeated in surprise. "I beg your pardon, sir, but I *don't* know. And I find it exceedingly odd that you would suppose I do. However, I do know all too well that men aren't to be trusted. I . . . thank you for your information. Now you must excuse me."

She turned her back to him, her earlier cordiality gone, and flipped the pages of her music to the beginning. When she put her fingers to the keys again, Worth saw there was nothing for him to do but leave.

He didn't see her again until midafternoon, when the Musical Society met in that same room.

They all arrived together—Miss Melinda Molton, the pert and pretty vicar's daughter, clinging to the arm of her fiancé, Duncan Halbarton, and another man trailing behind them. Duncan's blue eyes were anxious as he greeted his friend, but Gordon carried it off well enough. He gave Miss Molton's hand no more than an appropriate pressure, and clapped Duncan jovially on the shoulder as he expressed his good wishes—but turned rather quickly, Worth thought, to the third person, whom he introduced as Bernell Mayhew, "cousin, musician, legal counsel, and habitual visitor at Torview."

Older than the others, Bernell was probably not so tall

as Gordon's sister Olivia. His brown sidewhiskers somehow emphasized the beginnings of a double chin, and his
plump body seemed literally poured into his clothes. The
feebleness of his handshake (which Worth had decided
was typical of English gentlemen in general) was more
than compensated for by the appraising stare of his candid
blue eyes, as though any newcomer to Torview Hall must
pass his inspection before being fully admitted into the
household. As a result, Worth's own greeting was reserved, but everyone else surrounded Bernell affection-
ately, and it soon became apparent he was the unofficial
leader of the musical group.

The singers gathered around a small table placed near
the pianoforte, and Worth sat near the bow window next
to Olivia, who had her embroidery with her. Lord Clifton,
unmusical as a donkey, refused to attend these weekly
sessions, reserving the honor of his presence for special
musical performances on Christmas or New Year's Day.

After passing out the music, which was kept in a stack
on top of the piano, Bernell started them off by apparently
plucking a note out of empty air. Taking their pitches from
him, the rest came in during subsequent phrases. They
sang "Gather Your Rosebuds While You May" and "Hark,
All Ye Lovely Saints" and "Hard by a Crystal Fountain."
The last tune seemed to go on forever but was, to Worth,
no less delightful. When they stopped at the end of each
number, Olivia put down her needlework and dutifully
clapped. Worth enthusiastically followed suit. He thought
their voices wonderfully light and airy, almost ethereal,
and didn't mind the halts and repeats to get phrases right.
He had always treasured music, and was hugely impressed
by these complex songs, which Bernell called madrigals.

Possibly he responded too enthusiastically, for when
Evie and Miss Molton declared their throats quite exhausted and Olivia rang for tea, Gordon turned to him
and said, "Your turn, Forrester. Sing us an American
song. I know you can, for I heard you in London."

Worth was surprised. Gordon had heard him only once,

in a hackney coach at two-thirty in the morning, on their way home from a series of routs. The recital had been prompted by pure joy at his release from the night's entertainment, where too-small rooms were open to such crowds of fashionable people that one could scarcely breathe, much less enjoy any meaningful conversation.

Seeking to be accommodating, though he had no great voice, he agreed, and sang the first song that came into his head. "The Ramblin' Boy," a complicated ballad set to a simple tune, told of a poor fellow condemned to die because he had turned thief to satisfy his young bride's love of finery. Worth, his hands placed somewhat awkwardly astride his long legs, sang in the direction of Evie, who appeared the most appreciative of his effort. His ears were attuned to the memory of an accompanying autoharp.

When it was over, a brief, dead silence ensued. Then Evie clapped in approval, and Worth silently blessed her. She was joined belatedly by Gordon, Miss Molton, and Halbarton. Olivia, trying to be polite, pronounced it a most singular song and asked where he had learned it.

From a Kentucky mountain man, Worth confessed. This sparked some interest from Bernell, who said both the theme and tune were like a West Country folk song he knew. He immediately went to the piano to work out the similarity. Worth glanced toward Rosalyn, but she had turned to watch Bernell's explorations and did not see him look at her.

Tea arrived, and Worth turned with his usual appetite to the sandwiches and scones the maid in gray serge and white mobcap passed among them. He was relieved that the others then turned their attention from him to Miss Molton and Mr. Halbarton, who were speaking of their good fortune in having Lady Harriet Whitbourne for a patroness. Lady Harriet was giving a ball to celebrate their betrothal.

"How kind!" Olivia enthused.

Miss Molton smoothed a fold in her flounced skirt and

glanced toward Gordon before replying. But, as Worth had noted several other times that afternoon, Gordon's attention seemed drawn to almost anyone or anything but Miss Molton. This time he was studiously buttering a scone and did not raise his eyes when she said, "Yes, indeed, Lady Harriet has always been exceedingly kind to our family, ever since offering my father the parish living some dozen years ago. I confess I am quite overcome by her generosity in giving a ball in Duncan's and my honor."

"It's not so surprising," Olivia put in. "We all know Lady Harriet enjoys doing things for others. Just yesterday, as we were returning from taking some small necessaries to Mrs. Beecham, she introduced to me a most marvelous plan. She hopes to found a charity hospital at Blackroy Village." ·

"A charity hospital?" Duncan Halbarton echoed. "Astonishing."

"And long overdue," Bernell Mayhew added. "I'm pleased Lady Harriet sees the need for it. I daresay she is driven to a number of her good works, however, simply to counter her brother's reputation."

"Aren't you being a bit hard on the marquess?" Gordon asked. "I know he's generally considered a bounder, but most people don't really know him."

"And why don't they know him?" Bernell took up. "Because he lives all by himself in Blackroy Manor and barely leaves it except for short business trips to London or Dartmouth and Torquay. Even his peers, like Lord Brisbane down Dartmouth way, think he's remote and cold. And it seems deuced odd, not to say unhealthy, for a man of his position to live all alone."

"Doesn't he hold a hunt every year on Dartmoor?" Duncan asked. "He's not entirely solitary."

"Even that's odd. Have you ever been invited to it?" Bernell shot back.

"No, but then I'm unimportant folk, Bernell. My father's only a squire."

"Even so, I'd say the number of local people who have

been to Blackroy Manor might be counted on the finger of one hand."

"Lady Harriet did say he would put in an appearance at our ball," Miss Molton added. "Perhaps he is at last emerging from his solitude. We must remember that he lost his young wife in very unhappy circumstances."

"Exactly," Evie put in. "I believe he still mourns for her."

"After some fifteen-odd years?" Bernell asked with dark skepticism. "Come now, Evie!"

"Some men never get over such a loss. I'm told she was very beautiful."

"It does make sense," Olivia said. "I would find it difficult to believe that the brother of Lady Harriet is not, at heart, a good man. I know his tenants are neglected, but Lady Harriet has said herself that it is because he so often is sunk in a deep melancholy."

"You see? That's exactly what I meant," Evie crowed triumphantly to Bernell.

"That, of course, is one reason why she does as much as she can to alleviate their suffering," Olivia continued. "And why she has proposed the charity hospital. Of course, Lord Whitbourne must agree to her plan."

"If that is the case, she will never have it," Bernell said grumpily.

"Oh, Bernell, don't be such a pessimist," Miss Molton cried out. "Rosalyn, what do you say?"

"I?" Rosalyn looked startled, as though surprised anyone would ask her opinion. "I have no idea as to Lord Whitbourne's character or whether he would approve a charity hospital, for I've never met him."

After a short, constrained silence Gordon said, *sotto voce*, "Bravo, Roz. That put the cap on it."

"I think, too," Rosalyn added, looking directly at Worth for the first time, "that such local gossip must assuredly bore our American guest."

Worth smiled a disclaimer, but her eyes slipped away from his almost immediately. However, her words had their effect, for everyone's attention turned again to Worth, and Gordon had to explain for the benefit of Bernell and the betrothed couple the purpose of his visit to Devonshire.

"And so," he finished, "if anyone knows someone named Forrester . . ."

"If you're serious about helping Mr. Forrester find his kin, why don't you start with parish records?" Bernell suggested. "Try Ashburton first. You'll find records of all the births, deaths, and marriages for hundreds of years back at the church, you know."

"What about Rosalyn's genealogy?" Evie asked. "Have you listed anyone named Forrester in your Dart River study, Rosalyn?"

"I don't recall the name," Rosalyn said. "But I'll check again, just in case."

"I'd be grateful," Worth said, attempting to meet her gaze.

"Oh, it's nothing," she returned. As before, her glance was aslant and he didn't know if her refusal to look directly at him was due to shyness or hostility. He feared the latter and wondered what he had done to earn it.

⤲ FOUR ⤲

Rosalyn had been in an unprecedented and highly disturbed state of mind all day, and had spent far too much time wondering at her own reaction. Worth Forrester was Gordon's guest, and her contact with him was, therefore, of little consequence. Why, then, was she allowing his presence to occupy her thoughts? Why did she continually think of retorts she ought to have made to him last night at supper? Why was she haunted by the way he sang a raw American ballad which told in such a matter-of-fact way of a love that drove a man to outlawry and death? Or the way he looked at her as he sang, "My true love cries in deep despair; With her dark brown eyes and long, long hair . . ." (Afterward she had been too disconcerted to do him the common courtesy of telling him she enjoyed the song. But then, she was not certain she had.)

She had warmed to his modesty and his outspokenness almost immediately. She treasured truthfulness and disdained the hypocrisies of polite society invented to protect "female delicacy." So why, when she had sought a truthful reply, had she reacted with Olivia's prudery, simply on being faced with his honest version of the encounter in Soho? "You'll have to ask Gordon that" had somehow intimated that Gordon, at least, was indulging in the same sin as his father before him, but that was no astounding discovery. Perhaps it had been the confiding way in which he had assumed she knew of (and condoned?) such pas-

45

times—for one of the things that often angered her was that sins accepted as normal for a man disgraced a woman forever.

Whatever her reasons, she had in that moment become uncomfortably aware of Mr. Forrester as a man. Her original self-consciousness on turning from the piano to see his tall figure filling the doorway, his blond hair sleep-rumpled and his shirt unbuttoned at the top, revealing the hollow of his strong bronze throat, had suddenly returned, compounded. She realized then that she had not seen even Gordon so informally dressed since their childhood!

There was, undoubtedly, something about his very person that disturbed her. It was more than his state of undress that morning, more than the display of strength she had witnessed on his arrival, even more than his obvious foreignness or his disarming smile. It was some vitality, some presence that both attracted and alarmed her. Alarmed her *because* it attracted her, possibly. But no—such a thought did not deserve dwelling upon. She turned from it swiftly, to find refuge in rationality. Her state of mind could be explained quite simply, after all. Mr. Forrester's presence had upset the comfortable routine of her days. Quite naturally, she did not welcome the intrusion and would be more than happy when he had gone.

The sooner he traced his family, the sooner that would be. Thus inspired, she looked through her genealogy as soon as she had a chance, but discovered no clue to connect him to anyone listed in it.

"I'm sorry," she told him at supper with genuine regret, "but I don't find your surname among the families in my study. I checked it quite carefully."

Worth thanked her for her effort. Gordon said that would have made it too easy, and he wanted Worth to stay for a month at least.

Privately hoping the opposite, Rosalyn said, "I'll give you a list of the parishes I contacted when I began my research. You could write each one and ask for their records. If you try to go to each village personally, it will take you forever."

"I think I'll do both," Worth decided, smiling. "Thank you."

"Even if you don't find your father's family, couldn't you bring your mother over and settle here anyway?" Evie asked.

"That's possible, of course," Worth agreed, "except I have no idea how I would earn my living. Where in England is there a demand for a man who can do little more than hunt and trap and speak six Indian languages?"

"Sounds as if you'd make an excellent huntsman or gamekeeper," Lord Clifton said, "but those are hardly the occupations of a gentleman."

"I suppose not, sir," Worth agreed after a moment.

Rosalyn, watching him, noticed a passing sadness darken his face, and wondered if it was because of her grandfather's thoughtless dismissal of his talents or because he missed the life he had left behind. Or, possibly, because it was important to him to discover who his father had been. But she dismissed it, and said nothing. She had certainly done her part to help Mr. Forrester's search. Now it was up to him and the others. She hoped it would take him from Torview Hall far and often, and that he would either succeed very soon or give up the attempt and go elsewhere, for only then, she suspected, would she be left in peace again. That evening, knowing they did not need her to fill a foursome at cards, she retired early to her room, pleading fatigue.

The next day Gordon took Worth to Ashburton to look through the parish records. They were gone all day. They visited the fourteenth-century granite church with its birth, marriage, and death records, but found no Forresters listed. They ate at the London Inn, chatted with Bernell Mayhew in his solicitor's chambers, and strolled through the marketplace. They looked in at the woolen mill where Devonshire's famous serge was manufactured, and Gordon persuaded Worth to order himself a hunting jacket of the cloth from a local tailor as a souvenir gift from his host and Devonshire. Returning to Torview Hall, they stopped to inspect the remains of the last tin mine in the area, now idle a score of years. When they returned to Torview Hall it was after dark and the rest of the family had eaten the evening meal.

The following morning and for a week thereafter, they were out of the house soon after breakfast, not only to visit the village churches, but, on one day, to fish for salmon and trout in the Dart, on another to watch the autumn pony-drift, when the shaggy Dartmoor ponies, left to run free most of the year, were rounded up and iden-tified and the unlucky ones cut out to be trained for work in mines or on farms.

For these expeditions Worth reverted to his comfortable western buckskins. Seeing his uncommon height clothed in the light brown fringed leggings and beaded jacket Gentle Fawn had made him, Gordon grinned and said it was quite enough to make every Devonian they met believe the local pixies had conjured up a giant just to vex them. But he added that they looked deuced comfortable, and he wished he knew a tailor who could make *him* such an outfit.

Neither the jesting nor the hint of envy bothered Worth. He freely stopped along the byways and back lanes to talk to wagoners, furze cutters, journeymen thatchers, ped-dlers, even the inarticulate boys driving their masters' sheep or cattle at day's end. Those country folk would have been the more surprised to know that the wearer of the exotic clothing (who often had difficulty understanding their rapid, unique English) was trying to learn all he could about Devonshire, to picture himself as a native here, to grasp some ancestral sense of who he was and who his father had been.

Had that shadowy father he could not recall been a shepherd who moved his flocks from grazing commons on Dartmoor to in-country farm according to weather and season? A farmer, harvesting potatoes or distilling cider from prized apple orchards? A young clergyman of the established church, or, perhaps, a dissenter? One of those peddlers trudging the ancient roads, their goods on donkeyback, or a wealthy merchant or squire riding splendidly in coach-and-four to Plymouth or Dartmouth or Exeter on business?

No feeling such as his mother had experienced about England led him, that first week, to the truth.

Olivia had learned of Gordon's betrothal and spoke disdainfully to her sisters of the "ill-suited match." Rosalyn hadn't heard the exchange between them, but she could imagine it had been heated. She guessed Gordon was spending so little time at home in part because he either wanted to stay out of Olivia's way or was having his own second thoughts about the attachment.

Whatever the reason, Rosalyn believed herself relieved by their absence, and she returned with near-normal equanimity to her routine. She spent half her mornings at the piano, practicing pieces by Mozart, Couperin, and Scarlatti as well as the new Beethoven sonata. She wrote in her journal and read the newspapers and discussed them with Lord Clifton. She answered correspondence concerning her Dart River genealogical study, which she had started three years before. It had begun as a way to fill her time, and at first she was only concerned with her own family connections. But she became fascinated by the multiple relationships between the families of the area, and had expanded it to include all the gentry and aristocracy with property along the Dart River.

In the evening, when the others began to eat at a later time to accommodate Worth and Gordon and hear of their day's adventures, she reverted to her usual habit of having her supper brought upstairs, and no one suggested it was odd.

If she saw Worth Forrester at all, it was only to say good day to him in the upstairs hall as he went down to breakfast. Mostly, he seemed in good spirits, but even when the gray eyes were darkly solemn, his whole being exuded an alarming robustness and vitality, so foreign to her own state of health. The loose-fitting buckskins he wore, open at the neck, bestowed on him a certain savage splendor. It always shocked her a little to see him in them, although they suited him admirably. If she thought he seemed ready to linger and talk more to her, she discouraged him by inventing some duty to which she must hurry. She was not, she told herself, being inhospitable. It was only that they had little in common, and he didn't need her help to make his visit a success.

Whenever they were together, the three sisters spoke of the ball to be given by Lady Harriet Whitbourne for Melinda and Duncan. Evie was determined to have a new gown. She declared her old gowns no longer fit properly, for she had grown taller and fuller in the bust.

"We can alter the dress Rosalyn wore to my wedding," Olivia said sensibly. "You almost never wore it, did you, Rosalyn? And the two of you are much of a size now."

"We will not!" Evie cried in outrage. "It is no longer stylish. Besides, the color is not right for me."

"She ought to have a new gown, Olivia," Rosalyn interposed. "You should have one, too. I'm sure Grandfather will approve. Since I won't be going, it need only be two."

"I haven't time to make even one gown. I'd planned to alter one of my old ones, anyway. One can do wonders with new trimmings and gloves."

"If you haven't time you might ask Mrs. Beecham to come and help you, if she is well enough," Rosalyn suggested.

"Oh, yes, I daresay she is well again. The good Lord must watch over her. I saw her in town only yesterday with her big basket and that ancient threadbare shawl she persists in wearing."

"I shall be exactly like Mrs. Beecham in a few years if I am not to be allowed new clothes," Evie broke in, so decidedly that they all laughed and Olivia was cajoled into better humor and agreed to the project.

"I wonder," Evie speculated at another time, "if Mr. Forrester knows how to dance. If not, I'll volunteer to teach him. That would be proper, would it not, Olivia? Since he is a guest in our home?"

"I suppose so," Olivia conceded. "Provided there are others present."

"I'll play for you if you like," Rosalyn said, suppressing a sudden aching nostalgia for the days when she, too, might have danced.

Something in her voice must have suggested such feelings, for Evie said, "Poor Roz! Will you mind very much not going?"

"Not at all," Rosalyn replied briskly. "You know I dislike crowds anyway. I'll be perfectly content here with Grandfather. We have planned a game of chess, and we'll go to bed early, and feel much the better for it the day after."

Evie put her question to the American during their mid-afternoon Sunday dinner, following matins, which they had all attended in Ashburton. It turned out that Worth Forrester had only the most rudimentary knowledge of how to dance a jig or reel, and he confessed that minuets were a complete mystery to him. "But perhaps, as a stranger, I'm not invited," he suggested.

"Of course you're invited," Evie assured him. "The invitation listed all our names, and Mr. Worth Forrester especially, because Melinda and Duncan told Lady Harriet about you. I'll show it to you." And she jumped up from the table and went to the hall to fetch the invitation.

"Does Lord Clifton go, too?" Worth asked, after duly noting his name on the scallop-edged vellum, written in Lady Harriet's own hand.

"No, no, I never go to balls anymore," Lord Clifton said decidedly. "Frankly, I can't abide 'em. Silly chitter-chatter with the ladies, no spirits, and I never could jig worth a damn. I'm better off at home with Rosalyn. We'll have our own entertainment at the game table, eh, my dear?"

"Indeed we will, Grandfather," Rosalyn agreed with a little smile. "I have long promised to beat you at chess, and this time I shall. I've been working out a new strategy."

"Oho, secrets, is it? That won't fadge, y'know. You're up against a wily and seasoned opponent."

"I beg your pardon, but why won't Miss Archer be attending the ball with the rest of us?" Worth Forrester asked.

Rosalyn glanced toward him in surprise. Surely, by now, having seen her come and go, he knew the answer to that. "I am not well, sir," she said. "I never go to balls. I have not danced for seven years."

"How are you not well?" he persisted, with a perplexed frown.

Here they were, the dreaded questions, late in coming but inevitable. Rosalyn looked down at her plate, not responding.

"She suffered a terrible illness some years ago and nearly died," Olivia put in. "Ever since then she has been frail and must be extremely careful."

"She tires very easily," Evie added. "Even going to church, as we did today, is a trial for her."

"Her legs were paralyzed, you see," Gordon concluded. "We feared for some time that she would never walk again."

Worth's gaze had gone to each one of them in turn as they provided excuses for their sister. Then it returned to Rosalyn. "But you walk now."

"Yes, thank God, but not very well. I have a weakness in my right foot."

"Walking up and down stairs is especially hard on her," Olivia said. "That is why she often takes supper in her room."

"I see," Worth said at last, and Rosalyn felt a great relief that it was all said and they could go on to some other topic. But then he added, "It seems a great shame to me. Could you not attend just for the sociability of the event, and not dance?"

"No," Rosalyn returned, more curtly than she intended. "It is quite, quite out of the question."

Evie was right—church was always very tiring. Not only because of the jolting of the carriage during the five-mile journey to and from Ashburton, or the frequent changes of position during the service—from pew to kneeling pad and back again, straining her weak ankle—but because afterward they would walk through the churchyard to the resting places of their father and mother and Lord Clifton's wife. Rosalyn, treading the uneven stone path among the gravestones on Grandfather's arm, would feel her whole body tense with the fear of falling. So now she excused herself from the table ahead of the others, eager to rest. Because she knew Mr. Forrester watched her exit, she limped more noticeably than usual, to prove her case.

All but Lord Clifton, who considered anything involving music useless frivolity, assembled later in the upstairs parlor for Worth's dancing lesson. The servants had rolled up the Turkey carpet, and Rosalyn settled herself at the piano. Olivia unbent enough to dance a jig with Gordon to show their guest how it was done. Then Evie took Worth's hand and led him to the middle of the floor, explaining the steps.

Since the music was undemanding, Rosalyn watched them out of the corner of her eye as she played. Mr. Forrester looked as awkward as a young giraffe when he first tried to follow his partner, but amid much good-natured banter from Gordon on the sidelines, he soon picked up the steps, then the rhythm, and grew increasingly sure and agile. Olivia then suggested he learn the minuet, for one or two would surely be danced "for the older people." This was more intricate, but Worth finally mastered that form as well. As she played, Rosalyn found herself tapping her good left foot against the floor in time to the music, as if her hands alone could not adequately express the rhythm within her.

They stopped for tea. While sandwiches were being passed around and Olivia was busy asking everyone's preference for milk and sugar, Mr. Forrester rose from Evie's side and pulled up a chair next to Rosalyn.

"Tell me about this illness you had, Miss Archer."

"I don't usually speak of it, Mr. Forrester."

"Why don't you?"

"For one thing, most people are not really interested. Besides, I prefer not to think of it anymore. I'm grateful for the extent of recovery that has been allowed me, but I must be content with that."

"But it seems to me you'd think of it constantly when it limits you so much."

Taken aback by his words, she reached silently for a sandwich.

"I once knew a man who was temporarily paralyzed because of an accident," Worth continued. "But he was determined to regain use of his legs, and he did so after months of pain and trial. He forced himself, with the help of others, of course, to move his limbs, then to walk, then to ride horseback. Eventually he recovered entirely. Do you believe you might recover entirely, Miss Archer?"

"I can't say for certain. I have been in much the same state for several years now. Once the paralysis left me, I naturally worked hard to walk normally again. It was frightening at first even to try it. But my right foot doesn't respond as it should. And Dr. Ransom has warned me not to push myself too greatly and, especially, not to get too tired. That's why I don't intend to go to the ball."

"I think you'd enjoy dancing though, wouldn't you?"

"Of course I'd enjoy it, Mr. Forrester," she said, uncomfortable now with the surprising extent of his concern.

"But it isn't possible, so I put it out of my mind. And I hope you'll do the same," she added pointedly.

If she had thought that would end the topic, she was wrong. The very next morning, as she began her usual practicing, she again experienced the sensation that she was not alone. She turned on the stool and saw Mr. Forrester in the doorway. This time, she noted with a modicum of relief, he was properly dressed, wheaten hair brushed back tidily, buff-colored pantaloons tucked into tasseled high-lows, a loosely tied neckcloth and green coat covering his lean, tall frame.

Again he begged her pardon for intruding and complimented her on her performance, though she had just started the piece. She was certain he had a further purpose in besieging her.

"You . . . don't go out with Gordon today?" she asked.

"No. At least, not this morning. I have some correspondence to attend to. I received a letter from my mother yesterday, forwarded from London."

"Oh." She had not expected this turn in the conversation and let down her guard. "How does your mother fare?"

"She took sick after I left Virginia, but she is well again— She is staying with friends in Richmond, but she dislikes living on their charity."

"Are all of her resources used up, then?" Rosalyn asked in surprise.

"My stepfather was never well off. We lived month to month, and he never owned property. Then he was accidentally killed . . . you see, the Indians mistook him for a government agent. There was much unrest last year among the tribes in the Ohio River Valley."

His matter-of-fact phrases hinted at hardships totally alien to her, hardships he seemed to take for granted. She was flooded with unexpected compassion for him and said,

"Mr. Forrester, please come in and sit down. I feel quite foolish keeping you standing in the doorway."

He smiled and entered, sitting on the most substantial chair he could find. "Are you sure this is all right? I've noticed that English girls generally aren't allowed alone in a room with a man who isn't a relative."

"If I subscribed to that ridiculous convention, which seems to suppose all men are ravening wolves and all women perfectly helpless, I would certainly *not* invite you in. But I don't. Besides, the door is open and Donald and the carpenter are only a room away, mending a shutter."

Worth was not certain she relied on her own independence or the nearby presence of a trusted servant for her security. But before he could respond she continued, "Now about your mother's situation . . ."

"Simply that it's true she has no money. My stepfather left her nothing, and I was barely supporting myself."

"Doing what, Mr. Forrester?"

"Trapping, trading, sometimes acting as an interpreter between the government and the Indian tribes. I'm afraid they're quite right not to trust the white man, by the way." He smiled again, ruefully. "I get off the track pretty easy, Miss Archer, if you let me. What I meant to say was, I probably would have gone on living in the wilderness forever, but Mother was determined to return to Virginia, once my stepfather had died. She asked me to escort her, and since I was completely out of spirits at the time because of my wife's death, I allowed her to convince me my life had been wasted in the wilderness, that I should try civilization."

"I . . . didn't know about your wife," Rosalyn said. His mention of a second recent family death shocked her. She felt she understood, now, the source of his occasional air of melancholy. "I'm so sorry," she added.

"And I sure didn't intend to burden you with my sad history. Actually, coming to England, and your kind hospitality, have done a lot to cure my spirits." He smiled, and she could not help smiling back, her sympathy engaged

56

in a way she would never have anticipated a few minutes ago.

"Well, then," she continued finally, feeling herself floundering. "Granted your mother preferred a 'civilized' kind of life, as you put it, why could she not settle in another part of the United States? Why England?"

"It was a dream she had, a dream connected with my father and her memory of him. It may be only a dream, but I've committed myself to finding out if it's possible or not."

"I think," Rosalyn was moved to say, "she is fortunate to have a son so dedicated to her welfare."

He looked a trifle uncomfortable at her commendation. "Well, maybe. But dedication isn't enough. I need some luck—or the brains to think of another way to support her. She's an independent sort of woman, not unlike you, Miss Archer. She would consider herself disgraced to have to depend very long on friends for her support."

"Oh, *I'm* not independent, except in my thoughts. I can't be very well, when—" She stopped short, realizing what she had led herself into.

"But you are, ma'am. You have an independent spirit. That's why it surprises me that you've given in to a physical weakness."

She hardly knew whether to laugh or frown at the way he had cornered her—again. Indignation triumphed, but she suppressed it. "Mr. Forrester, if you want to write your letter now . . . the morning is fast waning and I have only begun my practicing."

He did not take the cue. "Are you afraid of being completely well again? Don't you want to live a normal life?"

"My life is entirely satisfactory to me. We cannot all possess your vast energy, sir. Besides, a 'normal' life for a woman seems to mean marriage—to some man who will tell her what to do and how to think, who will expect her to wear out her body to give him children, so *he* can carry on his family name. Why should I desire such a life?"

"You don't want to marry?"

57

"No, I don't. Does that surprise you so much, Mr. Forrester? I have yet to meet any man with whom I'd share my life. My father, my brother-in-law, even my own brother, much as I love him, are marvelous examples of the deficiencies of the male sex. I find that, in general, most men are selfish, undependable creatures, given to overindulgence and vainglory, with a sad tendency to feel sorry for themselves if their every wish is not gratified by the women they say they love. To survive such thralldom, women have had to become far stronger than they are given credit for. I hope I shall never need to lean on the uncertain support of any man."

If she had thought her little speech would divert him from his subject, she was disappointed. He came right back with, "Then you ought to do everything in your power to become stronger. If you would exercise more, you'd eat better. I can't see why you must spend your life cooped up in a few rooms. If you'd go out—"

"You sound disgustingly like a coachman who is anxious because his horses are off their feed." In spite of herself, her tone had become quite heated. "My appetite is no concern of yours, sir. Besides, my doctor has specifically instructed me that to become overly tired—"

"I'm not suggesting you become overly tired," he broke in. "Just that you become more active each day. If you'd exercise the leg muscles—"

"Last year," Rosalyn interrupted, in deliberate, icy tones, "after Mother died following a long illness, I was determined to attend the funeral, for we had always been very close. Olivia warned me against it, but I went anyway. It was a chill day and it rained during the graveside service. I became feverish the next day and developed dreadful pains in my legs and back. The doctor feared the original disease had returned and would paralyze me again. Fortunately—a true instance, I feel, of God answering prayer—I recovered after three weeks. But ever since then I have been especially cautious. And if you had ever experienced the horror of paralysis, you'd understand why."

"Yes . . . I see." That stopped him, but only for a moment. Then he said, "I suppose . . . it's a matter of whether you wish to live a shadow life now, for fear of something that may never happen again, or try to live a whole life for as long as you can."

She stared back defiantly, but her lips trembled. He continued, "Did it occur to you that since you survived that one severe illness with no return of the paralysis, there might be no danger of its returning?"

"It seems more prudent to follow the advice of a learned doctor than to guess—"

"Prudent! Is prudence all you want from life? Isn't it possible your Dr. Ransom isn't as learned in some illnesses as he is in others?"

She stared back at him in amazed anger. "You really are remarkably insensitive, Mr. Forrester. I can see why your mother thought you ought to return to civilization. Unfortunately, you have far to go before you learn simple manners."

"I don't believe it unmannerly to express concern for your problem—"

"I have no problem!"

"Or to offer a possible solution, so that you could attend balls, ride horseback—"

"I have no particular wish to do those things, Mr. Forrester. And it is rude of you to insist on your views when you know next to nothing about the situation—or about me." She rose heavily and walked to the door. "I have delayed your letter writing quite long enough, sir. I pray you, be kind enough to leave now."

He rose and acknowledged her dismissal with a bow, but she did not see it. She could not, in fact, look at him anymore, for she was perilously close to tears.

When he reached her he stopped again. "I must confess, Miss Archer, I find you as difficult to understand as I do the country folk hereabout. But not because of your accent. It's your motives that puzzle me."

She jerked the door open farther and silently stared past him into the corridor.

"At least you might try sitting in a warm-water bath each day, then have your maid massage your leg, and then exercise . . ."

In the midst of his sentence she returned to the piano and began, from memory, Mozart's third *Fantasia*. She poured her agitation into the sweeping runs that ran the full length of the keyboard, until the music possessed her and the tears obediently receded. When she finished the piece, she glanced cautiously toward the door. By then, of course, Worth Forrester had vanished.

❦ FIVE ❦

Rosalyn forced herself to go down to supper that evening, even knowing Gordon and Mr. Forrester were back from whatever afternoon expedition they had made. She had fought a cowardly inclination to remain in her room and avoid him, then decided she must not allow Mr. Forrester to dictate her actions. Besides, he might have reconsidered his remarks and be ready to apologize.

But it became obvious almost immediately that Worth Forrester felt not at all rebuffed by her morning's pointed observations concerning his lack of manners. He was not even being subtle when he said, addressing Olivia, "Ma'am, I was trying to encourage Miss Rosalyn to exercise more, in order to gain strength. Don't you think it would be a good idea for her to attend this ball we're all going to next week? Couldn't she dance just a little?"

Olivia looked properly horrified. "Oh, Rosalyn can't dance, Mr. Forrester. I thought you understood that. She has a lame foot, and . . . surely you have noticed her limp."

"As a matter of fact," Mr. Forrester said, "I never paid it any notice until it was called to my attention."

"Are you joking with me?" Rosalyn spoke in involuntary amazement, hardly aware she had done so.

"No, I mean it," he returned. "Your limp is not so obvious as you think. And if you would exercise more and massage—"

61

"We have been over that, Mr. Forrester," Rosalyn cut in. "And if you persist in this topic, I shall be forced to leave the table."

Worth looked around at the rest of them, but no one seemed ready to support his position. "Very well," he said finally. Then, more particularly to Rosalyn, he added, "I beg your pardon, ma'am."

If that was his apology, it was not a very satisfactory one.

The next day, when the Musical Society rehearsed again, Bernell brought Mrs. Beecham as Olivia had requested, and the seamstress was shown into the sewing room at the back of the ground floor, where Olivia had laid out newly purchased lengths of silver-spangled white muslin and peacock-blue messaline, as well as a quantity of ribbons and laces, to be made into a ball gown for Evie.

Rosalyn thought the rehearsal that afternoon was most unsatisfactory. Evie, impatient for her first fitting, couldn't keep her mind on the music, Bernell was out of humor for some undisclosed reason, Duncan naively appeared hurt to learn Gordon had taken off somewhere with Mr. Forrester and wouldn't be present, and Olivia, pleading other duties, didn't stay to listen. Rosalyn herself found it more tedious than usual to play repeated passages especially for Sir Harry Havisham, the squire who had taken Gordon's place in the Musical Society. Sir Harry had a pleasant enough voice but little skill in sight reading.

And so they broke up earlier than usual, each participant having an excuse not to stay for tea, and Evie persuaded Rosalyn to accompany her down to the sewing room, where Mrs. Beecham waited to take her measurements. The seamstress had agreed to stay at Torview Hall until the gown was completed.

For once Olivia and Evie were in accord, delighted both with the delicate fabrics and with the style Evie had chosen from *The Lady's Magazine*. As Mrs. Beecham placed the measuring tape about her bodice and waist, Evie stood quietly, her eyes fixed in pained resignation on the far wall, trying not to breathe. Rosalyn watched in sympathy. One didn't have to stand too closely to Mrs. Beecham to realize that she didn't believe in weekly baths, although her hands and face seemed clean enough.

Rosalyn felt a passing wonder that Lady Harriet, much less her fastidious sister Olivia, should have taken an interest in such a person, who was rumored among the country folk to be not only queer, but a witch. Mrs. Beecham's dress, a startling red calico peeking out from under a black sarsenet overskirt, was ragged at the hem and coated with the dust of the road. Greasy stains decorated the bodice, which fit her squat, rather lumpy frame indifferently. A multitude of little wrinkles lined her gaunt face, deep-set eyes, and humorless mouth. Her white-streaked hair, cut and primped in a parody of current style and unconfined by a bonnet, had been left to the vagaries of the wind and stood out around her face in peculiar wiry corkscrews.

Yet Mrs. Beecham obviously knew her business. Unrolling the delicate fabrics, she held each one in turn up to Evie, then began draping, pinning, cutting, all the time nodding her head and muttering to herself, apparently deaf to Olivia's anxious questions.

Fingering a fold of the shimmering messaline, its blue-green color so nicely complimenting Evie's delicate skin and sunny hair, Rosalyn felt an unexpected stab of longing. Such lovely, bright material! How would it feel to wear such a gown, made expressly for something as frivolous as a ball? How would it feel, wearing it, to take the arm of some young gentleman and walk (without limping) to a line of dancers awaiting the music, to float upon a wave of sound, light of step, without the sense of heaviness bordering on pain she so frequently experienced when climbing stairs? To be able to walk and run—to dance— without thought, without her right leg developing that tired ache, without the ever-present possibility that her ankle might turn . . .

Mr. Forrester had accused her of surrendering to her

physical weakness. It was not so! Surely she had tried. The fact that she could walk at all was proof she had tried. Besides, how dare he, a stranger and a foreigner, presume to tell her how to live her life? And she *was* content. She had forced herself to be content. . . .

But, stroking the cool silk of the fabric, she realized she was not content, after all. "A shadow life . . . or a whole life?" Did he really think she lived a shadow life?

"Olivia," she said hesitantly.

Olivia, helping Mrs. Beecham by holding a length of material at Evie's shoulder, said absently, "Hmm?"

"Olivia, I wonder if it would be too terribly tiring for me to just—just *watch* the ball Friday night."

Olivia glanced at her. "Oh, my dear, I don't think that would be wise! It's not just the ball, you know. It's going there and coming back in our drafty old coach. And the autumn nights can turn very chilly."

"I thought you were to stay overnight with Bernell."

"We are, but it's still over a mile to drive, and after all the excitement, how well could you sleep in a strange bed? And if you caught a cold, after such a fatiguing evening—"

Olivia's words suddenly smothered her. "I can dress warmly," she cut in impatiently.

"And what would you wear?" Evie asked her.

Rosalyn smiled at her for changing the topic. "Probably my rose dress—the one you would not have. I wore it only once and it's like new. Perhaps I could lower the waist, if it's as out of style as you say, and find a fichu to fill in the neckline."

"The color does vastly become you," Evie agreed. "I should think she could go, just this once, don't you, Olivia?"

"Of course she *can*," Olivia conceded. "I was only pointing out the probable consequences of such folly. At times, Rosalyn, you seem to forget you *must* be careful. But it is up to you, after all, if you want to risk another illness."

"Yes," Rosalyn said thoughtfully. "It *is* up to me, isn't it."

The rose dress, Rosalyn found to her surprise, was actually a little big on her. She had lost weight since Olivia's wedding three years ago. Calling Anna to her room, she had the maid pin the seams of the bodice for a better fit. Then she turned before the cheval glass critically.

It really was a lovely color, of the deepest, almost fuchsia, rose, with a subtle sheen in the silk moiré fabric. Embroidered flowers in white and pale pink embellished the neck and waistline, which was just under the bosom, and two lace-edged flounces finished off the skirt just at the ankle. The sleeves puffed, leaving her arms and neck bare. She began to consider what jewelry would be appropriate, and remembered the pearls she had inherited from her mother. She had never worn them.

"I declare, mum, it near puts roses in your cheeks," Anna said admiringly.

Rosalyn turned full face to the mirror but could not see that particular transformation. "Does it, Anna? Oh, it *is* nice to wear something besides black. Do you suppose all my old dresses are equally large? We must try them and see."

Putting on the bright gown had given her an inexplicable sensation of freedom. All Olivia's warnings, which she had become used to accepting as if they were the Word of God, now seemed like bars of a cage, designed to imprison rather than protect her. She remembered how she had argued so passionately to Mr. Forrester that women should be allowed their freedom. But it wasn't only silly customs that could imprison; it was the limitations one accepted for oneself. . . .

She felt somehow released into the world again, and that world suddenly glowed with new possibilities, infinitely desirable. She must experience more of it, much more. She would go to the ball, despite (or perhaps in defiance of) Olivia's warnings. Not because Mr. Forrester had suggested it—not at all. But because *she* chose to. It would mark not only the end of her year of mourning for her mother, but her own reentry into life.

"We'll try all my dresses, Anna, and see what needs alteration. Besides that, I've been thinking of asking you to massage my leg once a day. I have it in mind the muscles might be strengthened that way. Then they wouldn't tire so easily."

Maybe it was the weather—crisp, golden days with the only hint of coming winter the turning of the oaks and beeches and the sudden chill at night. Or maybe it was the prospect of a real outing, with all the excitement of dressing in her best and spending a whole evening away from home, seeing and chatting with friends and neighbors, of being even a peripheral part of the music and movement. Whatever the reason, Rosalyn found herself with energy to spare during the following days. When she walked, when she climbed the stairs, she tried not to give in to that weak foot, tried not to limp—and thought she succeeded, just a little.

Anna began to massage both her legs for fifteen minutes each afternoon, after Rosalyn had soaked them in warm water, paying particular attention to the right leg. She kneaded the muscles of calf and thigh with gentle firm fingers while Rosalyn lay, stomach down, on her bed. After the maid had helped her into underclothes and dressing gown and left the room, Rosalyn devised her own exercises. Lying on her back, she raised one leg at a time, held it as straight and perpendicular as she could, then lowered it slowly. It was much more difficult to raise the right leg, because the foot muscles were nearly useless to help, and she could not raise it so far nor lower it with so much control as she could the left.

Sometimes, before putting on her stockings and shoes, she looked at her lame foot critically. It was smaller and thinner than its mate, the blue veins near the ankle more pronounced. She knew instinctively it would always be that way, and that was why the right leg muscles, forced to do all the work, so often ached when she walked. She was not convinced that her program would really help them become stronger, but she felt the better for trying.

Told of Rosalyn's final decision about the ball, Olivia had only frowned and pursed her lips. Rosalyn guessed her older sister would tell no one, hoping she would change her mind when the actual date arrived. She was surprised, therefore, when she met Worth Forrester at the top of the stairs one morning and he asked her if it was true she planned to attend the ball.

"It's true," Rosalyn admitted. She added quickly, "I shall not dance, of course, but it will be enjoyable to talk to people and watch the others. I only hope Grandfather won't think I'm deserting him."

"Why don't you persuade him he can go as well?"

"I doubt I could. He detests large affairs. He hasn't been to a ball since I can remember."

She started down the stairs, trying not to hold on to the banister as tightly as she wanted to. After a moment's surprised hesitation, Worth matched his steps to hers. "Are you going to breakfast, Miss Rosalyn? I thought you breakfasted in your room."

"Usually I do, but today I decided not to bother the maids to bring it up. Olivia has set them a number of extra tasks. She is going out this morning with Lady Harriet Whitbourne to speak to someone about planning the charity hospital and has invited her ladyship to dine with us afterward. So, of course, everything must be perfect to a shade."

She hoped he didn't realize that she had also begun to seek out stair-climbing experiences as part of her decision to test his theory. It was one thing to admit to herself the exercise might be worth trying, but after the way she had scorned his suggestion she had no intention of admitting it to him.

They met Mrs. Beecham in the back hall as they were about to enter the morning room, where breakfast was laid. Since her arrival, the seamstress had kept to the servants' hall and sewing room, and Rosalyn had nearly forgotten her presence. Mrs. Beecham didn't seem at all taken aback by the encounter. Instead of simply curtsying and passing on, she stopped, nodded at Rosalyn's good morning, and looked more particularly at Mr. Forrester.

"Good maarnin' to 'ee," she said. "And who might this fine gentleman be?"

"This is our guest, Mr. Forrester," Rosalyn said indulgently. Olivia had told her of Mrs. Beecham's habit of speaking to her betters as though she were their equal. Taking her cue from Lady Harriet, Olivia had decided it was all right to humor her.

Mrs. Beecham raised her untidy head to look directly into Worth's quizzical gray eyes. "Mr. Forrester? Been a considerable time since Forresters been in these parts. Related to his lordship, are 'ee?"

"Oh, no, Mrs. Beecham, he's not related to Lord Clifton, he's from America," Rosalyn explained.

"I wan't talking of Lord Clifton, young lady. I wast talking of his lordship the Marquess of Whitbourne." Her eyes drifted briefly to Rosalyn, then back to Worth. "Proper high on t' trunk there, ain't you? Not much like, except t' eyes. Ess, definitely, t' eyes."

"Whatever do you mean?" Rosalyn asked, thinking this time the old woman had definitely overstepped her bounds. She had not been addressed as "young lady" in that tone since her mother had used it years ago when she had committed some childish infraction.

"I mean young Forrester 'as Whitbourne eyes. Gray eyes. An' Lord Whitbourne's grandmother, Lydia, wast born a Forrester."

"Oh, I'm sure that can't be," Rosalyn said. "I have charted the Whitbourne family tree, and . . ."

But Mrs. Beecham, having had her say, saw no reason to linger. She simply wandered away in the middle of Rosalyn's sentence, muttering something about spools of thread and scissors.

Rosalyn turned back to Worth with a slight smile and a shrug.

"Who is that?" Worth asked. "I don't think I've seen her before."

Rosalyn explained Mrs. Beecham's presence in the household as they took seats opposite each other at the round table in the morning room. After ringing for Donald she added, "She has a reputation for being odd, and I certainly see why."

He leaned toward her with both elbows on the table, hands clasped over his plate. "But who was she talking about? Who does she think I look like?"

"The Marquess of Whitbourne. We spoke of him the day after you arrived, remember? But she must be mistaken, because I don't recall—"

"The man who is a recluse?"

"That's Bernell's idea of him. It's true no one really seems to *know* him." She turned to order her breakfast from Donald, who had just appeared. After Worth had added his own request and turned his attention back to her, she said, "Whether he is a recluse or no, he's one of the two or three most powerful men in Devonshire. Certainly the most powerful in the Dart Valley. He owns extensive lands and enterprises from here to Torbay."

"What sort of enterprises?"

"I'm not sure of all of them. The woolen mill in Ashburton, for one, and a fleet of ships. Things like that."

"But you've never met him?"

"No, even though Lady Harriet is his sister. She's a good-hearted soul and not at all toplofty, even though she'd have a perfect right to be so."

"So this Mrs. Beecham thinks I look like the mysterious marquess," Worth mused, fingering a breadknife. "How would she know?"

"Oh, Mrs. Beecham used to live in Blackroy Village," Rosalyn explained. "Years ago, before he died, her husband was one of Lord Whitbourne's shepherds."

"I see." Worth sat in silence for some minutes, absently

stroking the knife, staring into space or, perhaps, out the unshuttered window to where Olivia, sunshade on her head and basket on her arm, was searching the rosebushes for likely blossoms for a bouquet.

Rosalyn thought how strange it was that she and Mr. Forrester should be sitting thus, perfectly amiable for once, nearly at ease, preparing to share the first meal of the day, when all her encounters with him up until now had ended by setting her back up. Strange and, somehow, pleasurable.

"I will check my research again, Mr. Forrester," she said. "In case I have overlooked something."

His eyes returned to her. "That's mighty nice of you, Miss Rosalyn." Somehow his drawl was always more pronounced in the morning—a warm, golden intonation, like the bar of sunshine that fell across the white cloth on the table. Right now she didn't even mind his calling her Miss Rosalyn, although when he had asked her permission (in order to keep her and "Miss Evie" separate) she had been uncomfortable with the idea.

Then Evie came into the room, still sleepy and slightly cross because she hadn't slept well, yet managing to look adorable in an old morning dress of yellow. Donald brought the cart with steaming hot tea, muffins and eggs, kippers and sausage. The talk turned general and finally settled between Evie and Mr. Forrester alone. When Rosalyn slipped away to look in her genealogy, the two of them hardly seemed to notice she had left.

Her research filled a fat folder which she kept on a shelf in her sitting room. It was difficult to keep the loose sheets in order, and she had long intended to alphabetize the material but kept putting it off. The Whitbourne family information lay on top, since the marquess represented the foremost aristocracy in the Dart River Valley. Rosalyn began tracing backward from the present marquess,

As with too much of her research, some information was missing. Lord Whitbourne had been one of five children, but only he and Lady Harriet still lived. The other three children, all boys, had apparently died in infancy, but their names and the dates of their deaths had not been sent to her. Apparently the parish priest in Totnes had not thought information about short-lived infants would be important to her.

The present marquess's father, Harold Whitbourne, had married Lady Amy Armistead in 1758. Lady Amy's father, Neville Armistead, Earl of Pym, had married a Lydia . . . and then Rosalyn saw, with a thrill of discovery, that she had listed no maiden name for Lydia, nor was there any information on Lydia's parentage.

Lord Whitbourne's grandmother Lydia was a Forrester. Mrs. Beecham *had* said Lydia, hadn't she? Yes, she was quite sure of the name.

Exclaiming in delight, she arose immediately to rush down to the morning room with the news. On the way, forced by her lagging foot to go slower than she wanted to, she reminded herself that even if Lord Whitbourne's grandmother had been named Forrester, it didn't prove a connection to Worth Forrester. But it was a start, an exciting possibility. . . .

There was no one in the morning room. She looked out the window and saw that Evie and Mr. Forrester were in the rose garden, talking to Olivia. Both blond heads shone like burnished gold in the sunlight. Suddenly shy of interrupting them, she decided instead to seek out Mrs. Beecham, to ask her what else she might know about Lydia Forrester.

Lady Harriet Whitbourne had not been to Torview Hall for a meal before, and Olivia wanted it to be an Occasion. Fortunately, Lord Clifton was in the mood to humor her, and even Gordon and his guest were present when they sat down to a five-course dinner in the early afternoon.

Lady Harriet was a large, handsome, hearty sort of woman who uttered nearly every sentence as though it were a pronouncement from Olympus. Nevertheless, she was noted for her compassion and good nature. She had even been known to poke a little fun at her own station in life, though no one else would have dared to do so in her presence. Once she had decided on a person's character or on a course of action, mere words could not change her mind.

Seeing them together, it appeared to Rosalyn that Lady Harriet and Olivia had become bosom friends in the past few months. Rosalyn sometimes wondered if Olivia herself wasn't one of Lady Harriet's "charities." It was perfectly possible the good woman had enlisted Olivia into her causes primarily to help Olivia recover from the shameful way her husband had abandoned her.

Lady Harriet was extremely pleased to meet a man from the United States of America, and immediately quizzed him on his reactions to England and, especially, to Devonshire. Worth, unaware he ought to feel especially flattered by her attention, answered her questions in his usual straightforward, frank manner. Lady Harriet was highly amused that he had expected Dartmoor "Forest" to be covered with the same heavy spread of trees that meant a forest in America. When he confessed that it had taken him a week to realize "withies" were willow trees, and asked if it was true Devonians had invented their own brand of English, Lady Harriet acknowledged good-naturedly that it was probably true. When she heard that Worth was looking for his father's kin she immediately offered to put whatever resources she had at his service. Worth, showing no great sense of humility at this generosity, said that was mighty good of her.

Rosalyn had never approached Lady Harriet for information about her family, thinking the marquess's sister might think her presumptuous, and she was not sure how to approach the subject now. Still, she could not let the opportunity pass. Finally she said, "Lady Harriet, Mrs. Beecham is here now, sewing a dress for Evelyn, and she told us a most curious thing this morning—that your grandmother's maiden name was Forrester. Is that possible?"

"Forrester?" Lady Harriet repeated, her eyes suddenly going blank. "Oh, no, my dear, my grandmother was a

Forsythe, of the Plymouth Forsythes. Her father was the Earl of Avon."

"Your other grandmother, then?" Rosalyn suggested.

"My other grandmother? Oh, of course, my mother's mother." Lady Harriet looked puzzled. "Do you know, I don't believe I recall her maiden name. You see, she died when my mother was born. I never asked about her, and no one ever said . . . How curious. . . ." Her voice trailed off uncertainly.

"Is it possible she was Lydia Forrester, a commoner's daughter?" Rosalyn pursued. "Mrs. Beecham told me later—I don't know whether to credit it or not—that Lydia Forrester's father was a moorman and the family, being ashamed of her origins, let her memory die. They never even had a portrait done of her."

Lady Harriet met this information with a nonplussed silence, her eyes averted from Rosalyn's intense gaze. Finally she shook her head. "Possible? Yes, I suppose so. I simply don't know. I shall ask my brother about it. He has access to all the family records."

"That might be the best thing you could do for me, Lady Harriet," Mr. Forrester drawled. "Wouldn't it be interesting if we were distantly related by marriage?"

"Intriguing, to be sure, my good man," Lady Harriet remarked. Then she turned to Newton, who hovered behind her chair, and asked if she might have some more of that delicious creamed squab.

Thus dismissed, Rosalyn dared not pursue the subject further. She sent a look of sympathy across the table to Mr. Forrester. He answered with a shrug and a smile, seemingly unaware that being called "my good man" placed him squarely in the servant class. Suddenly there seemed something so intimate in the exchange of their glances that she had to look down quickly at her plate. She was glad when Gordon, in response to Worth's question, began a complicated explanation of what a moorman was.

However, Lady Harriet brought up the topic of Worth's origins again just before she left. Touching Worth's hand with her fingertips as a goodbye gesture, she said, "So your father never hinted to you what part of Devonshire he came from?"

"My father died when I was very small," Worth returned. "And I understand he severed all connection with his family when he left."

"Then, young man, you must consider the possibility that he changed his surname. The people you're looking for may very well not be named Forrester at all."

SIX

His lordship the Marquess of Whitbourne arrived at Lady Harriet's ball when it was more than half over.

Rosalyn saw him enter from her vantage point on a settee which she was then sharing with her hostess. Much of the evening the couch had been occupied by friends who had not seen her for a long time. Everyone seemed delighted by her presence, by the fact that she and Olivia had come out of mourning for this occasion, and particularly by her apparent health. They seemed surprised to see her so "stout," as if they thought she was newly arisen from a sickbed. They enthused over her gown, her hair, her complexion. Rosalyn laughingly admonished them for flattering her overmuch, then sent them off to dance to the six-piece orchestra Lady Harriet had engaged all the way from Dartmouth.

But even Grandfather had said she looked "damned handsome," and she knew it was true. She had, after some argument with Anna, allowed the maid to curl her hair and arrange it in a different fashion. It now waved softly about her temples and burst into a cascade of shoulder-length ringlets just behind her ears where it was held back by pearl-studded combs. As for her complexion, all the ladies' embraces and the men's handclasps could not help but give her eyes a new sparkle and her cheeks a new bloom. Enveloped in the glow of renewed friendships, she watched the dancing with a smile, tapping her good foot in time to the music, making comments to the person nearest her.

She was learning things as she watched. When a couple joined hands to dance, certain emotions which they might successfully mask in other situations somehow revealed themselves. Melinda and Duncan danced with their eyes glued to each other, lips parted in smiles. Melinda and Gordon danced tensely, she avoiding his glance, he seeking hers. Bernell's obvious care and tenderness toward Olivia amazed Rosalyn. For the first time it occurred to her that her bachelor cousin might entertain more than cousinly feelings for her unattainable sister.

As for Mr. Forrester, partnering Evie he seemed almost boyish in his enjoyment of the dance. His dark blue coat, pearl-gray vest and pantaloons, and unfrilled but snowy shirtfront stood out among the more formal breeches and hose of most of the men. Yet his costume suited him exactly, and he himself seemed totally unconscious of any lack in his dress. All signs of melancholy vanished as he laughed and joked with Evie and watched with unabashed admiration her graceful dips and turns, while the candlelight shimmered on her peacock-blue gown.

They made a handsome couple. The sight of them brought an unexpected catch to Rosalyn's throat. Suddenly she guessed at another reason Gordon had for bringing Mr. Forrester home to meet his family: He meant him for Evie. And perhaps he was right, it would be a good match, Evie vanquishing Mr. Forrester's sorrow over his wife's death, and he in turn helping Evie take the inevitable step from child to woman.

By the time she came to this conclusion her throat felt so tight she could not trust herself to speak. About that time Lady Harriet, beside her, said, "Aha! There's Edward, at last! I had about given him up. Will you excuse me, my dear?" And she walked toward her brother, who had just entered the hall.

Lord Whitbourne wore black coat, breeches, and hose, their severity relieved only by a snowy mound of neckcloth and white satin waistcoat. Rosalyn could not see his expression from where she sat, but guessed it remained grave, even when the music stopped in deference to his arrival, and dancers moved back to allow him passage through the crowd. Squire Halbarton and Vicar Molton and their wives bowed and beamed their pleasure as Lady Harriet introduced them as the parents of the prospective bride and groom. Lord Whitbourne shook Duncan's hand and kissed Melinda's, then graciously signaled the musicians to continue. Rosalyn was momentarily panicked to see that Lady Harriet was leading her brother straight toward her.

"And this is Miss Rosalyn Archer, Lord Clifton's granddaughter."

They were before her almost before Rosalyn had a chance to rise and make her curtsy. The marquess's face seemed etched in stone, the bones prominent, the nose large and hooked, like an eagle's beak. As he bowed over her hand, she had the impression of a covetous alertness behind the gravity. When he straightened she noticed his gray eyes. Whitbourne eyes, Mrs. Beecham had said. Lady Harriet's were blue. Of course, it didn't prove a thing.

"A lovely lady like yourself is not dancing?" Lord Whitbourne asked.

"I . . . prefer to watch," Rosalyn said, flushing unexpectedly. She surely did not want to go into all that business about her lameness.

"A sensible choice. I have often wondered what people see in all this jigging about. It lacks dignity." He cast a disdainful glance toward the throng of dancers before seating himself in a chair, which he pulled up beside the settee.

When Lady Harriet excused herself and left them alone, Rosalyn had no idea what to say to him. His very presence was, in some indefinable way, more disturbing than even Mr. Forrester's. There was something enigmatic, almost sinister in his solemnity, in the glances of his opaque eyes. And yet he was not entirely unattractive.

"It was most gracious of you to come, if you do not care for dancing," she said at last.

"Oh, Lady Harriet informed me that my presence was absolutely required to put a cap on the affair, and I might well restore my shaky reputation in the bargain. Since I cannot resist a bargain, and since I was informed gaming would also be allowed . . ." He shrugged, leaving the sentence unfinished.

His eyes—a darker, more obscure gray than Mr. Forrester's—scrutinized her as she laughed. "Surely you are not under Lady Harriet's thumb, my lord."

"My sister and I understand each other, Miss Archer. I find that if I humor her in some things, she will allow me to go my own way in others without a murmur. However, it is fortunate we do not have to share the same living quarters."

"And are you humoring her in the matter of the charity hospital?"

"Indeed I am, although I have insisted on being consulted on each step of its establishment."

Rosalyn thought that must show a greater concern for the success of the project than Bernell would have given him credit for. She was about to say something to that effect when she became aware the music and dancing had stopped, and Evie and Mr. Forrester were approaching them.

The marquess stood purposefully, and she did the same, realizing introductions would be in order. But Lord Whitbourne bypassed them, saying to Worth, "And you must be the young American my sister spoke of."

"I am, sir," Worth acknowledged. He seemed uncertain whether he ought to bow to the marquess, but then Lord Whitbourne extended his hand. "I am Edward Whitbourne. I hope you are enjoying Devonshire, Mr. Forrester."

"I am certainly enjoying the kind hospitality of Lord Clifton's household," Worth returned, taking the marquess's hand in his iron grip. "As for the dancing, it is nearly as good an exercise as a ten-mile footrace."

Lord Whitbourne's lips parted slightly as he studied the American, but he did not quite deign to smile. Though both were tall and lean, Worth was the taller by several inches. Lord Whitbourne's heavy dark hair was white-streaked at the temples; his eyebrows were black peaks above his hooded, impenetrable eyes, his expression guarded and rapacious. Worth Forrester's eyes were clear and trusting, like the strong, clean planes of his face. It was a face that welcomed any opportunity, any new acquaintance, secure in its owner's power to deal with the unexpected.

Evie, who had been eagerly expecting to be introduced to the marquess, could wait no longer. Smiling in her most charming manner, she broke into the conversation, endeavoring to lead the marquess into an invitation to dance. Lord Whitbourne confessed that he was no dancer. Worth turned to Rosalyn.

"Are you enjoying yourself?"

"I am, immensely," Rosalyn admitted with a smile. Somehow it was easy to admit to this man that he had been right, since his satisfaction had no selfishness in it.

"So am I. But I would enjoy it even more if I could persuade you to try to dance, just one time."

"I am quite certain the jigs and reels are much too quick."

"But I'm told a minuet is next. That is hardly more than a walk in rhythm. If you know the steps, couldn't you try the minuet with me?"

"Well, I . . ."

"And whisper what to do next in case I forget?" he added with a smile.

"Evie can do that," Rosalyn pointed out.

"Evie will surely not lack for a partner."

And Rosalyn realized two young men were already at her sister's shoulder, seeking the privilege. The marquess gratefully surrendered her to one of them, and announced his intention to go to the game room.

"Do you play cards?" he asked Worth.

"A little. Gordon Archer introduced me to English gaming at his London club." He smiled his open smile for the closed-faced, craggy marquess.

"I should like to become better acquainted with you, Mr. Forrester. Perhaps you would care to join me?"

"I'd be honored, sir," Worth replied, not batting an eye, "after I have danced the minuet with Miss Archer."

He had trapped her into it so neatly she couldn't really object. And as he led her onto the floor she thought, This is what I dreamed of doing. Had she imagined her partner to be this selfsame Worth Forrester? Perhaps, but only because he had put the idea into her head in the first place.

"Your gown is mighty becoming to you, Miss Rosalyn," he said as they took their place in the line of dancers and awaited the music.

"After black, any gown would look good," she said, smiling. "But thank you."

The gown felt good on her, too. It was not so elegant or stylish as Evie's, but it suited her. She had put fresh lace on the skirt flounces but had decided against adding material to the low-cut bodice, which revealed the swell of her firm, high breasts. Olivia, appraising her, had frowned but said nothing. By then the carriage had been waiting for them, and Rosalyn had sent Molly for a cashmere shawl, which she promised to keep about her shoulders to mitigate drafts.

Except when I dance, she thought now as she took her place in line opposite Worth. Neither Olivia nor I ever dreamed I would dance. I hope I remember the steps.

Some of her diffidence must have shown in her face, for he smiled reassuringly at her. The weak foot tingled, but she resolutely ignored the warning—if it was a warning and not merely anticipation. Tonight, she told it, you will do as I say. She had not been conscious of limping as she walked onto the floor. She had been too absorbed in the moment, in that tall masculine presence by her side. Another wave of heat possessed her as she recalled the sensation.

The music began. She curtsied to Worth's bow, and as they advanced toward each other and he took her hand, she was more aware of his masculinity than she had ever been. His strength, his confidence in himself, the vitality that had at first alarmed her, now buoyed her up, gave her a new daring and assurance. And something else she could not explain—a tingle that coursed through her body, astonishing and exciting her, as their gloved hands met.

She was breathless as the dance ended, and proud that her leg had withstood the test. She tried to ignore a sensation of faintness as he returned her to her seat, even though it was more alarming than the slight ache in her right leg.

"Thank you for your help, Miss Rosalyn."

"Thank you for yours, Mr. Forrester." She had hardly been aware of guiding him, though she had murmured directions once or twice: "Promenade now," or "Turn me." But he had given her so much more.

"Won't you call me Worth now? Gordon does."

She took a seat and looked up at him. The faintness seemed to come and go in waves. She smiled slightly, as much as she was capable of at the moment. "I . . . will consider it."

"Good." He bowed. "I would stay longer, Miss Rosalyn, but I'm curious about this marquess. Do you suppose there is a relationship?"

"You had better go and talk to him. Maybe he will tell you."

They were interrupted by Olivia and Bernell. Olivia had seen Rosalyn on the dance floor and was anxious to discover how she had fared. Worth bowed again and left her in their hands.

Olivia sank into an adjoining chair, smiling, though her eyes retained their alarm. She looked younger, more gentle tonight. Maybe it was the green silk gown and the way

Anna had dressed her chestnut hair with a matching green bandeau holding her bun in place. Maybe she was simply finding pleasure in doing something frivolous for a change. Still, she could not forgo her omnipresent sense of responsibility.

"Rosalyn, you promised you wouldn't try to dance! And where's your shawl?"

"Somewhere about. I'm really quite warm, Olivia."

Olivia shot an anxious glance to Bernell, who said, "I'll find it for you, Roz. What does it look like?"

"White with silver and blue threads. I left it over on the settee near the far door."

He went to retrieve it, skirting the floor, where a Scottish jig had just begun. Rosalyn interrupted Olivia's attempt to scold her.

"I assure you I'm perfectly fine."

"You'll suffer for it tomorrow!"

"Shall I? Well, then it will have been worth it." She laughed a little to herself at the unintended pun on Mr. Forrester's name.

"You're light-headed. Shall I get you a fruit punch?"

Rosalyn smiled hazily. "Thank you, it's nothing. I'm sure it will pass." Her heart was beating heavily and her mind was quite devoid of thought. She was not at all sure the activity of dancing had been to blame.

Entering the room adjacent to the brilliantly lit ballroom was like taking shelter in a cavern after a walk in the sunshine. It took Worth's eyes several moments to adjust to its smaller size, its subdued, cooler atmosphere, and its muffled sounds. The windows were guarded with heavy velvet hangings, the floor was deep-carpeted. The light from an enormous fireplace at one end and a few three-tiered wall sconces cast flickering shadows everywhere. Additional candelabra lit the round tables at which about a dozen men sat. The candlelight glowed on the inlaid tile of the tables and the faces of the men alike.

The strains of the Scottish jig echoed behind him, and

Worth's mind was still with the dancing and the lovely woman he had just partnered. Rosalyn's transformation had been marvelous. It was as though her cool, self-possessed soul, freed of the black of mourning, had taken fire, and the resultant glow suffused her cheeks and created new lights in her eyes. It had even, he dared think, diminished the burden of a lame foot. He almost wished there were no family quest to distract him from her, at least not tonight. Having proved to her that she could dance, he was, all at once, eager to prove other things to her as well.

The marquess sat at the far table, near the fireplace. He saw Worth enter and stood to greet him. Reminding himself that his lordship did him a singular favor with such marked attention, Worth approached him with a smile. Mentally, he remained wary. The man reminded him of an Indian chief he had once dealt with, in whom apparent friendliness turned to treachery when one's back was turned. It was the eyes, he decided as they greeted one another, bowing. Lord Whitbourne's eyes never revealed anything.

"Won't you join us?" Lord Whitbourne asked, waving his hand toward two companions, who had also risen. "Mr. Forrester, may I present Sir Harry Havisham and Lord Buckleigh?"

Worth bowed again as Sir Harry, Gordon's successor in the Musical Society, reminded Worth they had met briefly at Torview Hall. Lord Buckleigh, who merely nodded to him, was older, stout, and somewhat untidy in his dress, with heavy sidewhiskers and a double chin.

"Thank you," Worth returned, "but I hesitate to interrupt your game."

"Not at all. We're only playing for pleasure. You're among friends, Mr. Forrester, and the wagers will be small."

"Very well, then." Worth sat in the vacant chair while Lord Whitbourne resumed his seat and collected the cards. But Worth glimpsed guineas and pound notes among the shillings and half-crowns the other two gathered up from the center of the table and realized he must be careful with his own limited resources.

"We'll make it five shillings, minimum," Lord Whitbourne said as he shuffled the deck. "Are you familiar with vingt-et-un, Forrester?"

"Somewhat."

"Good. We'll help if you have questions."

After Sir Harry had cut the deck, Lord Whitbourne showed them all the top card and replaced it on the bottom. Then he dealt them each a card with a long-fingered, graceful swiftness that approached sleight-of-hand. Worth, whose stepfather had introduced him to every game of skill current among the roving frontiersmen of half a dozen nationalities, recognized the touch of a confirmed gamester. When it was his turn to bet, he adopted the attitude of an amateur, fatalistically shrugging off the outcome as he declared the minimum wager.

The marquess, using his prerogative as dealer, doubled the bets after barely glancing at his own card, then dealt to Sir Harry, who overreached the desired number, twenty-one, on the fourth card, and was forced to pay Lord Whitbourne double his bet. Lord Buckleigh, though more cautious, fared no better.

As he waited for their hands to be played out, Worth studied Lord Whitbourne's profile. Even in victory, the craggy dark face showed no emotion. What would be his reaction to the news that a backwoods American was claiming relationship to him? Or did he already suspect it, alerted by information from his sister? Was this admittance to the game his lordship's acknowledgment that they possessed a common ancestor?

Diverted by this fascinating conjecture, Worth, too, lost double his bet to Lord Whitbourne. He resolved then to forget the possible relationship and concentrate on the game.

On the second round, the game and the dealership went to Worth on a lucky combination of cards, and when fortune remained with him on the third round, Lord Whitbourne conceded his defeat. "Not so new at this after all, are you, Forrester."

"Beginner's luck," Worth said with a disarming grin, collecting their coins and notes.

Sir Harry cleared his throat and said hesitantly, "Well—uh—if you g-gentlemen will excuse me, I'm for some dancing now."

Worth looked up, surprised, and caught Sir Harry's eyes leaving the marquess's face, which didn't move a muscle. Before he could respond, Lord Buckleigh made a similar excuse to leave the table. Once they had gone Worth raised an inquiring eyebrow toward the marquess. "Something I did—or said?"

"No," Lord Whitbourne replied. "They simply recognized that I wanted an opportunity to speak to you alone."

Worth waited expectantly for him to continue; even, perhaps, to claim some relationship. But the marquess only said, "You're a skillful player, Mr. Forrester, however much you try to conceal the fact. Where did you learn a French card game?"

"From French trappers and traders," Worth admitted. "A few still come up the Ohio River Valley from the Mississippi and St. Louis. We met and played at outposts, and over campfires."

"Interesting. And my sister tells me your father was originally from Devonshire. What else do you know of him?"

"Not much. I was three when he died. He married my mother when he had been in Virginia less than a year, so he must have left England sometime in 1782."

"And how did he die?"

"We were living in Lexington, Kentucky, and he had gone to Ohio on a hunting expedition. The hunting party was attacked by Indians, and everyone in it was killed. We—my mother—didn't learn of it until weeks later, when an Indian trader who came to Lexington told her. He had come upon the bodies. They had all been scalped."

"They really do that, then." The marquess's comment seemed more interested than horrified.

Worth nodded. "I've seen it done by white men, too."

"And what did your mother do then?"

"Eventually, when I was about five, she married that Indian trader, Jacob Stockton. Now he's dead, too."

"And your mother?"

"Back in Virginia, awaiting my becoming established in this country so that she can come here, too."

The marquess's face broke into a rare smile. "You realize you're reversing history? I find it uncommon for someone of your background to expect to settle in England. And doesn't the tension—animosity, I might even call it—between our two countries trouble you?"

"I was too far away from such affairs to be concerned with them. Back home, I worried about Indians and settlers and how abundant the game was. The way I see it, those Indians and settlers were probably pretty much like the United States and Great Britain—always at each other's throats, but neither one having the right all on his side."

Deciding he had talked too much without learning anything himself, Worth was about to ask Lord Whitbourne if he knew of a grandmother named Forrester when Lady Harriet entered the room and called for everyone's attention in her authoritative voice.

"Mr. Mayhew is preparing to play and sing his own composition, which he wrote especially for the betrothed couple. So you all must come and listen."

She stopped before their table. "Especially you, Edward. It is up to you to toast Miss Molton and Mr. Halbarton. So whatever devious tricks you and Mr. Forrester are considering for your next game, they must wait."

Wearing his good-natured acquiescence like a mask, Lord Whitbourne arose and bowed to his sister. "You have arrived at an opportune time, my dear. We had finished playing. However . . ." He turned to Worth. "I hope to recoup my losses from you at some future date."

Worth bowed. "It will be my pleasure, my lord."

⎯ SEVEN ⎯

Bernell's song, which he played and sang himself, was received with much applause and admiration. Lord Whitbourne's toast, though brief and only marginally complimentary to this couple he hardly knew, was equally well received. A midnight buffet was announced, and Olivia was distracted from her concern that Rosalyn was becoming overtired by her realization that Gordon was no longer at the ball.

"I thought he was with you in the game room," she said to Worth, who had rejoined her and Rosalyn to listen to Bernell's performance.

"No, he was never with me there," Worth said.

"Then where can he have gone? I've been looking for him since two dances past. He had been talking with Melinda again. I don't know what it was about, but the next I knew she was dancing the reel with someone else."

"There you have it, then," Rosalyn said. "I fear he's still too fond of Melinda."

"And so he scoured off to some tavern," Olivia took up in alarm. "That's exactly the sort of thing he might do!"

Rosalyn didn't respond immediately. She disliked saying it in front of Mr. Forrester, but she had to agree with Olivia—it was just the sort of thing Gordon did, go off to drink whenever there was something he could not quite face. As their father had done.

Mr. Forrester was watching her, awaiting her viewpoint.

"I'm afraid it's true," she said at last. "I had hoped, with his betrothal to Miss Glynne, he could consider Melinda only a friend, but . . ."

To his credit, Mr. Forrester didn't ask for further reasoning. He only said, "I'll look for him, if you like. If you're concerned about his welfare."

"You are very kind, Mr. Forrester," Olivia said haughtily, "but we can hardly expect a stranger to be knowledgeable about Ashburton and its taverns."

"I've been here with Gordon twice now," Worth said. "I have an excellent memory for directions and landmarks. There are not so many drinking establishments to search, as I recall."

"I think we ought to allow Mr. Forrester to help," Rosalyn said, smiling at him. "Else Gordon will forget we sleep at Bernell's tonight and come to grief trying to find his way home in the dark."

Reluctantly Olivia nodded assent. "I trust you can deliver him to us before he is *that* tosticated."

"I'll do my best," Worth assured her.

By the time they arrived at Bernell's big house a mile and a half from town, on the banks of the Dart River, it was two in the morning. Olivia expressed amazement that Rosalyn had not yet wilted. She had not only danced the minuet, she had eaten heartily of the buffet and continued to talk animatedly with a number of people throughout the evening. Bernell, to deflect continued admiration for his musical talents, had even persuaded her to take her turn at the pianoforte. To Olivia's surprise, Rosalyn played the Mozart *Fantasia* from memory. Everyone thought her quite marvelous, and Rosalyn, lifted by all the compliments into a heady euphoria, became more animated than ever.

But Olivia, predicting a relapse, had quite insisted they leave after that. Bernell had their carriage brought around, and, after expressing her thanks to Lady Harriet and her congratulations for the tenth time to the honored couple, Olivia gathered up her two sisters like a mother hen and departed.

Rosalyn's room that night faced a garden to the rear of the house. Long after Anna had helped her prepare for bed, she knelt by the low window, silk-clad arms on the sill, looking down on the dark moon-streaked shrubbery, unable to sleep. Even to lie comfortably still in the big canopied bed had been impossible. It had all been so extraordinary her head still spun. She had forgotten for huge chunks of time that she had any disability whatsoever.

Neither Gordon nor Worth had yet returned. Somehow Worth's departure from the ball had taken a certain spice from the evening, despite her own excitement, her (she considered the words with a certain wry irony) social success. She wished he had heard her on the pianoforte—a vain, self-centered wish, surely. She questioned his eagerness to be of service in finding Gordon, and realized her suspicion was colored by her disappointment that they had had no further opportunity for conversation. She recalled with particular poignancy the brief times he had held her hand or touched her arm or shoulder as they danced—and recognized the sensation as pure folly.

Now, the failure of Worth to return to the house with Gordon called up all the worst possibilities. Instead of rescuing Gordon from self-pity and drunkenness, he must have succumbed to drink himself. Or perhaps they were indulging in even more depraved sorts of behavior at the Golden Lion, where Olivia had learned the true measure of her husband. After all, it wouldn't be the first time they had frequented such places. There had been Soho, in London. Rosalyn suspected that neither Gordon nor Mr. Forrester had told her even half the truth about that episode.

What was it about men that made them indulge in such irresponsible activities? And why was she so desolate, considering it? It wasn't as though she hadn't known such things happened. Her father, charming when sober, had turned into a veritable devil with an excess of gin. Men, except for the very few like Bernell, were simply not to be trusted. The fact that a dance or glance or touch of a hand could stir her heart should not blind her to what men could be like. Surely Worth Forrester was no more immune to such indulgences than many another man.

When the big hall clock struck four, she slipped into bed, shivering. She thought of the Marquess of Whitbourne, whose relation Worth might be. When she had asked Worth about their encounter he had shaken his head and said the marquess was a difficult man to know. If they had explored the possibility of a relationship, he wasn't ready to tell her. She suspected they hadn't, but had become too absorbed in their gaming. Another disappointment—that Worth Forrester had been so easily deflected from his avowed purpose.

Of course, Lord Whitbourne was difficult to assess. A memorable man, yet an impenetrable enigma, to whom it might be easy to ascribe all manner of evil, as Bernell had done. Yet he *had* appeared at the ball at his sister's request; *had* given his good-natured if vague toast; *had* agreed to the charity hospital and professed interest in it.

And his very impenetrability was attractive. One could easily be led into a contest of wits with such a person and consider the activity as bracing as a tonic. His single word of admiration for her had stirred her in a strange way. She could guess how he might easily overwhelm a woman with such compliments, for they seemed out of character. Even a man might be in danger if he believed the flattery of the marquess. If Worth and he were, indeed, related . . . and if Lord Whitbourne did not take kindly to such a relationship . . .

She dozed, thinking in an inconclusive, irrational way (unconsciously contradicting her recent enumeration of his probable sins) that Worth Forrester was too nice a man to be trapped by Lord Whitbourne's flatteries.

When she awoke, night was lifting in an intangible way and she knew it was nearly dawn. She'd had precious little sleep. What had awakened her so suddenly and so completely?

The sound came again: stumbling footsteps, cautious voices, someone knocking against a wall, heavy breathing.

"Get the door, I'll hold him. . . ."

"We showed 'em, didn' we, Worth? All the shel-shelf-satisfied li'l ladies . . ."

"All right, Abbot, one more heave . . . good man. I'll stay with him while you get bandages. . . ."

Heat and cold chased themselves through Rosalyn's body. Perhaps Worth wasn't quite so intoxicated as Gordon; perhaps his voice was still clear enough to issue commands, his body strong enough to stand without aid. Still, the fact that he had stayed with her brother throughout the whole infamous night made him an accomplice to whatever forgetfulness Gordon had sought. How could he have failed them so, when they had depended on him to see that Gordon didn't come to grief?

Turning over, Rosalyn reminded herself to be grateful they were safely returned, whatever condition they were in. And how strange it was, when one thought about it . . . they had put their faith in this visitor, this American, only three weeks past a stranger, as if they had considered him a long-time, trusted friend.

"Is he quite comfortable?" Bernell asked anxiously. "Should I send for Dr. Ransom?"

"I think it's only a sprain," Worth said. "He's sleeping soundly now, but it will be painful when he wakes, and he may want a physician to see it."

They were on the stair landing. It had taken Worth a few minutes to realize that his host had not arisen merely as a result of the commotion in his hall, but because he had intended to rise.

"You'll need to rest, too, I'll warrant," Bernell said. "After being out all night."

"Right now, I don't feel tired," Worth said with a grin.

"Come have breakfast with me, then," Bernell suggested. "I'm used to rising early."

Light was filtering into the small east dining room as they sat at the table. Bernell ordered eggs, tea, and toast from his elderly housekeeper, and passed a bowl of purple grapes to Worth. As they munched on the fruit Worth told him how Gordon had come to grief, slipping on a dew-damp wooden step coming out of the tavern, falling with his arm turned under him and injuring his wrist.

"Of course he was drunk," Bernell said.

"I don't believe Gordon drinks too much, usually."

"No, only on occasion. This was one of the occasions. He's regretting having left Miss Molton to the tender consolation of his best friend. He's recalling that about nine months ago he could have been the fiancé of that lovely girl."

"Yes," Worth said. "He told me as much."

"Did he tell you why he threw her over?"

"He said a lot of things. He may very well retract them when he sobers up."

"Have you met Miss Glynne?"

"Only once." Worth efficiently stripped all the grapes off one side of a stem and popped them into his mouth. He wondered how to get the conversation away from Gordon, whose regrets he had no intention of discussing.

"About Lord Whitbourne," he said, as the housekeeper returned to set hot food before them. "I take it you haven't a very good opinion of him."

The lawyer seemed surprised at the turn the conversation had taken. Worth was impressed again at how Bernell's stout, unprepossessing appearance sheltered someone so undeniably talented in music. He was also impressed by the intensity with which Bernell spoke.

"You have put it too mildly, sir. I detest, fear, and loathe the man. I detest what he stands for, I fear his power, I loathe the way he uses and discards people."

Worth raised his eyebrows. "Ah, you're skeptical," Bernell noted. "Very well. I could tell you stories . . . but I'll tell you only one. This is not hearsay, Mr. Forrester."

"If you call me Worth, I promise to believe you," Worth said with a smile.

"Very well, Worth. And you are welcome to call me Bernell. Although it's a moot question whether it's preferable to Mayhew. I suspect we both suffer from being christened with our mothers' surnames."

Worth laughed acknowledgment. Bernell continued, "You've met Mrs. Beecham by now. What do you think of her?"

"She seemed . . . unusual."

"Yes, she is that. Some call her crazy. Some—especially the country folk—believe she's clairvoyant. There have been certain occasions . . . well, that's neither here nor there. This sad tale is about Mrs. Beecham. As a young couple, she and her husband worked for the former Lord Whitbourne, the present marquess's father. Mr. Beecham was one of his shepherds, and Mrs. Beecham was seamstress to the household. They had a daughter, Nellie— only child, apple of their eye, of course. She was nine or so when Lord Whitbourne died. The present marquess took the title, married a couple of years later, moved to Blackroy Manor, which his wife had inherited, and brought the Beecham family with him. And not too much later, he began to cast eyes on Nellie, who was, by all accounts, a very pretty child."

Bernell stopped to eat and drink a few mouthfuls. Suspecting what was coming, Worth waited without eagerness.

Having fortified himself, Bernell went on in short sarcastic sentences. "Lord Whitbourne got the girl with child. She was only fourteen. The parents were understandably upset, especially when Nellie swore Whitbourne was the man. Beecham confronted the marquess one fine day, on his return from the moor. He had been looking for some wild dogs that were terrorizing the flocks, and carried a gun. Whitbourne was just returned from hunting and also carried a gun. He denied touching Nellie. Beecham demanded some acknowledgment of his responsibility to at least provide a midwife, ease Nellie's milkmaid duties, give her additional wages. Whitbourne refused, and sneered something about the girl's back-alley habits. Beecham raised his gun in anger. Lord Whitbourne raised his—and shot and killed his shepherd."

"My God," said Worth.

"It happened at the same time that Lady Whitbourne, his wife of three years, was also with child and unwell. Mrs. Beecham often sat with her as she was sewing. She was an unlearned woman, but, to hear her tell it, the two of them had a certain spiritual kinship. Lady Whitbourne believed Mrs. Beecham had 'powers,' though she did not practice them. She claimed that the seamstress's presence soothed her, and her herbal teas helped her sleep. She was, by the way, already unhappy in her marriage, and afraid of Lord Whitbourne. Mrs. Beecham told me this, though she never said exactly why."

Another pause. Worth, finding he was less hungry than he had thought, guessed at exaggeration but reserved judgment. Bernell went on.

"About the time Nellie began to show, Lady Whitbourne got very ill. Mrs. Beecham had said little about her daughter's shame or her husband's death, which Lord Whitbourne claimed was an accident. She continued to minister to Lady Whitbourne because her mistress kept asking for her, and Lord Whitbourne, hoping for an heir, was choosing to indulge his wife. Then Nellie, whose work required her to carry heavy pails of milk, suffered a miscarriage and died. Mrs. Beecham's grief overwhelmed her better judgment. She went to the marquess and accused him of being directly responsible for the deaths of her loved ones. She cursed him to his face and declared he would never have a child of his own. Lord Whitbourne responded by forbidding Mrs. Beecham to see his wife again.

"Two weeks later Lady Whitbourne caught a severe

chill, contracted pneumonia, and died. A shock to everyone. Lord Whitbourne dismissed Mrs. Beecham from his
service, cut her off without a penny or any references that
would help get her a position with another family. He
spread the rumor that Mrs. Beecham was a witch who had
put a curse on his wife and caused her death. He forbade
anyone that he provided a living for—and many here-
abouts who might hire her are in that category—to employ
her. In effect, he turned her out to starve."

"But he did not succeed."

"He nearly succeeded. When I learned of her plight—
I was a novice lawyer and had just inherited this property—
she was wandering from village to village, begging and
telling her terrible tale of wrong at the hands of the marquess. Of course, people shunned her. They didn't want
to hear such things about their resident lord, so they claimed
she was mad or, as Lord Whitbourne said, a spiteful witch,
unhinged by grief. I had this unused cottage on the property and invited her to live in it. She has a little garden
and raises herbs and vegetables and sells them. Also, thanks
to Lady Harriet, she is beginnning to get sewing commis-
sions."

"She was fortunate to have someone like you," Worth
said. "Why did you believe her story, Bernell?"

Bernell turned away and cleared his throat. "Because
I've seen other evidence of what Whitbourne is like," he
said at last. "But I promised you only one tale, and I've
bored you long enough."

"You've bored me not at all," Worth assured him. "It's
a terrible story. But I hope you understand my interest in
the marquess."

"Yes, Olivia told me there might be a kinship."

"Mrs. Beecham seemed quite positive about it. Should
I believe her?"

Bernell shrugged. "I know it sounds like the merest
superstition, but she foresaw the disaster of Olivia's marriage. Not that it took a prophetess to foresee *that*. I fore-

saw it, too. But Olivia would heed none of us." His voice, more wistful than disgusted, faded off.

"What, exactly, is your relationship to the Archers?" Worth asked after a moment's silence. "If I'm not being too bold."

"My grandmother, Genevieve, was Lord Clifton's sister. Her husband, Richard Mayhew, was only a squire, however. No title."

"But it's not too close a relationship for marriage, then."

"Not at all. But Olivia cut off my hopes neatly by marrying that damned . . ."

"I'm sorry," Worth said after a while. And then, "She might receive word he's dead."

"I pray for it every night." Bernell shifted his feet decisively, with a small self-deprecating smile. "Among other things. Well, Worth, enough of that. You doubtless have been put near sleep by my ramblings, after your own nocturnal duties. If you wish to escort the girls home today, Gordon can sleep it off here as long as he likes, and I'll bring him back."

"You're indispensable to all of them, aren't you," Worth observed.

Bernell smiled wryly. "It seems I'm not alone in that. I think your services to the Archer family this past day and night have been incalculable."

"I only did what any friend would. Listened when he needed to talk."

"I'm thinking of Rosalyn, too. Olivia believes you put the idea of attending the ball in her head. That's been another of my prayers, you know—that Rosalyn stop behaving like a recluse. From the look of things last night, she's on her way."

◦◦ EIGHT ◦◦

But Rosalyn was experiencing some misgivings about last evening's carefree merriment. Even though she slept until nearly noon, she felt exhausted when she arose. She donned her dressing gown only to sink into a nearby chair to receive hot chocolate from Anna. Each individual muscle in the calves and thighs of both legs seemed to have its own peculiar ache. Her throat was raw, too, and she remembered how she had knelt compulsively on the floor by the open window with no more than the dressing gown protecting her, looking out at the moonlit garden, pondering. . . .

The three sisters and Mr. Forrester, joining them inside the carriage, returned to Torview Hall that afternoon. Gordon, just awakened, had truculently declined to accompany them, saying he would first consult Dr. Ransom about his injured wrist. Rosalyn, to avoid being scolded at by Olivia, had not mentioned her hoarse throat and sore muscles, even though silence gave Mr. Forrester the victory.

High hedgerow banks topped with yellowing beech trees lined the road along which they traveled. The dense barrier was alive with warblers and thrushes that called and chattered cheerfully above the scrunch and squeak of the carriage wheels. Mr. Forrester, to whom hedgerows were a notable phenomenon, said it was like traveling through a deep ravine.

Rosalyn found sitting across from him both a trial and a joy—an ambivalence that puzzled her. She wished to be part of the conversation but could not seem to speak freely. Worth had said next to nothing about the previous night's adventures, and Olivia, undoubtedly already guessing the worst, was too proud to ask. Rosalyn did not ask either, but for a different reason. Having come to what she felt must be the correct conclusion, she thought that either details of his night with Gordon or equivocation would only make her feel worse.

He and Evie were speaking of the countryside—the serene beauty of the Dart Valley through which they now traveled compared to the awesome barrenness of Dartmoor. "But the Dart can be cruel, too, Mr. Forrester," Evie said. "When it rains hard on the moor, the river can rise in a flash. People get caught and drowned in the fords downstream, just like that."

"From storms arising on the moor?" Worth asked, amazed.

Olivia nodded her head. "It's quite true, Mr. Forrester. Just last spring a farmer was crossing this side of Dartington at a ford usually as safe as this road. He saw a freshet coming, but by the time he'd turned his horse and wagon back, the river took him—and with such a force his body wasn't found for two weeks."

"We have an old rhyme," Rosalyn added. " 'River of Dart, River of Dart, Every year thou claimest a heart.' "

Then she wished she hadn't spoken, for Mr. Forrester's clear eyes were on her again for a long silent moment. "It's not only the river that can claim hearts around here," he said.

Rosalyn, feeling heat rise in her face, looked away.

"But don't you think the tors are interesting?" Evie asked. "Most people consider the tors on Dartmoor quite amazing. And the stone cairns, as well. They are so mysterious. No one knows how they came there. When Torview Hall was built, they say you could see five tors from the top floor of the house. But now, with new buildings and the way the pines have grown, we can see only two."

"You mean by 'tors' those granite outcroppings? Yes, they are unusual," Worth replied. "As a matter of fact, Gordon had suggested we ride out tomorrow after church to see . . . is it Hound Tor? The tor that looks like a succession of dogs' heads?"

"I should think Gordon would not be fit for such an expedition by tomorrow," Olivia cautioned.

"You may be right, Miss Olivia," Worth conceded. "I doubt he can guide a horse effectively with his injured wrist."

"Then I'll take you," Evie said. "I love to ride on the moor."

"You'll need good weather—and a chaperon, if you go so far," Olivia said quickly. "Neither of which is a certainty today."

"We shall take Donald," Evie declared.

"Perhaps Miss Rosalyn would care to accompany us," Worth put in, looking her way again.

"As chaperon?" Rosalyn asked wryly, but her words were drowned out by Olivia, who exclaimed, "On horseback? What a shocking idea, Mr. Forrester. Rosalyn cannot ride so far. Indeed, she does not ride at all. It is much too strenuous an activity for her."

Worth's eyes shifted from Rosalyn to Olivia and then back again. "Perhaps Miss Rosalyn should decide that for herself."

"In this case, Mr. Forrester, I quite agree with my sister," Rosalyn said. "I fear that even though I enjoyed the ball, it was rather taxing. And it's true I haven't been on a horse since before my illness. I scarce would know how to handle one."

As though that settled the matter, Rosalyn opened her reticule and made a pretense of searching for something within. Worth took a breath as if to reply, but all he said was, "One thing I'd like settled now. If it's not against your principles, I would like you all to call me Worth instead of Mr. Forrester."

He seemed to be addressing Olivia. She nodded, a little reserved but amenable. "If it would make you feel comfortable."

Evie said, "I think that is a most sensible idea, Worth."

Rosalyn didn't answer.

Evie, Worth, and Donald left on horseback early on Sunday afternoon, taking biscuits and cider with them. The weather cooperated. Rosalyn watched them mount from an upstairs hall window which gave a view of the stable yard. Evie had forsworn her childish habit of hitching up her skirt today. The green velvet of her best riding habit fell in smooth folds to the ground, and she appeared both grown-up and charming. Worth, dressed in pale buckskin breeches and the recently completed blue serge hunting jacket, gave her a boost onto the horse with the casual ease of uncommon strength. Sunlight set their hair and cheeks aglow. Rosalyn did not watch them ride away, but returned to the upstairs parlor and her piano. Somehow, resting was quite out of the question today.

But half an hour later even the piano had palled. She gave a sigh and returned to her sitting room to look over the pile of books that Bernell had brought her from the lending library at Exeter. Three she still hadn't read; yet they did not beckon. Instead of opening one, she sat down with her genealogy study and paged through it in desultory fashion. Suddenly, more purposefully, she returned to the first page.

"WHITBOURNE, Harold Albert George, Marquess of Whitbourne (1732–1792), married, in 1758, Lady Amy Harriet Armistead (1740–1789), daughter of Neville Armistead, Earl of Pym, and Lydia _____ (1720–1740)."

She stared at the blank space for a long time, then wrote, in pencil, "Forrester." Lydia Forrester (1720–1740) had been only twenty years old when she died—that much she knew. Amy had been the sole child of Lydia's union to Lord Armistead. There was no parentage for Lydia

Forrester, only for Neville Armistead, whose great-grand-father had been the first Earl of Pym in the days of Charles I. The incompleteness of her record irked her.

Perhaps Lydia had had a brother whose son had emigrated to America. If Worth was that son's son, that would make him the same relation to Lord Whitbourne as she was to Bernell—second cousin. It didn't confer any responsibility upon the marquess, but surely Lord Whitbourne, with all his vast wealth and holdings, could find a worthy niche in his empire for a relative in need of a position.

Her eye moved back to Harold and Amy's children. Boy, 1759 (he would have been the eldest); Harriet Elizabeth Ann, 1760; boy, 1761; boy, 1764. Then no more until Edward James Neville, 1770, the present marquess. Lord Whitbourne was ten years younger than his sister. Was that why he seemed so very different?

Their mother, Amy, had died when Edward was nineteen; their father, Harold, three years later. So Edward had inherited the title at age twenty-two, even though he had been the last of four sons born to the Marquess of Whitbourne. No dates on the deaths of those other sons. Rosalyn wondered if Lady Harriet had ever mentioned them to Olivia. But if they had died as infants, she could have been too small to remember them.

The puzzle of Worth Forrester's forebears was proving surprisingly engrossing. And why was there a certain charm in the very evocation of his name, in writing "Forrester" on the page? This would not have been true two days ago. When she tried to consider why it was true now, her thoughts became so confused with a multitude of unexpected emotions that she could not sort them out. The exhilaration of the ball had been followed by the dissatisfactions of the day after. Her disappointment that Worth had failed to rescue Gordon from his worse self, and had probably ended up himself participating in some sort of debauchery, lent a sharp-edged sadness to the memory of their dance together. The dance itself had been enchanted—Rosalyn the lame turned into Rosalyn the princess. Rather like Cinderella.

And the day after the day after? Surprisingly, her muscles were scarcely sore today, and the rawness in her throat had vanished. If she had known that would happen, would she have agreed to the horseback expedition? No, it would still have been foolish. She would need more than ten days of exercising to prepare for so strenuous an activity.

And yet . . . it seemed now that there was nothing she longed to do quite so much as ride horseback beside Worth Forrester to see the famous tors of Dartmoor. It seemed as if she had forever lost a special opportunity this afternoon, for after spending it in Evie's beguiling presence, Rosalyn had little doubt to whom Worth would lose his heart.

He could not have meant that about his heart, anyway. It was only a pretty speech. Even Americans could utter pretty speeches on occasion. And if he had reason to repeat it in earnest to Evie, Rosalyn chided herself, she ought have no reason to resent or envy her sister, she who had so long been firm in the belief that she would never marry.

Noises from the entry hall interrupted this unsettling reverie. Rosalyn arose and put the genealogy away and walked to the stairway. As usual, the weak foot lagged behind, like a dull child that must be prodded. Yet she *had* danced. . . .

Leaning over the balustrade, she saw Bernell and Gordon, in the hall below, greet Olivia, who had just appeared from the library. Gordon's left wrist was swathed in bandages.

"Gordon," she called down. "How are you?"

He looked up and waved with his good right hand. "Oh, I'll survive."

She moved down the stairs to greet them. "Did you see Dr. Ransom?"

"Yes, this morning. It seems our American friend was right—it's only a sprain. But I had a racking pain all night.

I can't ride a horse for a while, so Bernell was kind enough to bring me back in his gig."

"Always eager to find an excuse to visit Torview Hall," Bernell explained, his eyes on Olivia.

Did Olivia actually flush under his gaze, Rosalyn wondered, or had her own new and peculiar susceptibility made her suddenly suspicious of others? "You'll stay to tea, of course," Olivia invited.

"Of course," Bernell answered promptly.

Olivia smiled at him and turned to Gordon. "Grandfather is in a tweak about your escapade, Gordon. You must go see him. He's been trying to write a letter to the *Times* and couldn't even concentrate on the ministry's latest idiocies—because of you, he says. And you must allow me to inspect your wrist. Does it bother you terribly?" She guided Gordon away.

"Olivia seems happier, somehow," Bernell remarked.

"She is always at her best when someone needs tending," Rosalyn said. "Although I'm not sure her nursing instincts will be completely satisfied by a mere sprained wrist."

"And you, Rosalyn? I hope you suffered no ill effects from your arduous evening Friday," Bernell said.

"I'm quite well, thank you."

"And are stairs no longer a problem?"

"Well, they are, somewhat. But there's no real pain. It's just . . . a tiredness. Mr. Forrester thinks that, with exercise, that will improve. Do you think he's right?"

"I should think it's worth a try. Mr. Forrester seems to have a good deal of common sense about him."

"No doubt from living in the wilderness and having only himself to rely on. Well, then, I was about to take a turn in the garden, something I've not done for an age. Would you care to accompany me?"

Bernell bowed with a mock flourish. "My dear Roz, I would be delighted."

"And why have you not done this for an age?" Bernell asked as they descended from the flagstone courtyard into the rose garden. "Surely Dr. Ransom didn't tell you fresh air was bad for you."

"No, it's just . . . easier to be inside. I have rather used my infirmity as an excuse, you know, Bernell. So I could do the things I prefer doing, which are sedentary, anyway. And then, if the weather wasn't absolutely perfect, Olivia would discourage me. I'm beginning to suspect that if I had tried harder to do active things more often, I would be the better for it now."

"So long as you don't overdo."

"Now you're sounding like Olivia," Rosalyn protested with a laugh.

"She is only concerned for your welfare."

"I know that. But she has too often been more anxious than need be." She gave Bernell a sidelong glance. His eyes were on the gravel path that wound between rose-bushes and tall rose trees, his brow furrowed. Hoping she hadn't offended him, she said, "Bernell, your song for Melinda and Duncan was so lovely. You ought to find a publisher for it."

"I haven't time to go to London, and besides, I'm not satisfied with it. It needs more tinkering. I could use some help with the words, too," he added, with a meaningful glance at her.

"If I helped, would you try to publish it?"

He shrugged and met her glance with a half-belligerent, half-humorous grimace. "Don't push me, Roz. I'm a law-yer whose hobby happens to be music. I'm perfectly sat-isfied to write songs just for family and friends."

"I doubt anyone is *perfectly* satisfied with the ordinary if they can achieve better. And you are a true musician, Bernell."

They left the rose garden for a stretch of lawn, where tall orange and purple dahlias rioted above white amaranth and yellow coxcomb on the borders, and chaffinches and hedge sparrows argued loudly in the holly. The ground was given to little bumps and unexpected dips beneath its grassy surface, and Rosalyn's hand instinctively tightened on Bernell's arm as her weak ankle, jolted by an unseen rise, nearly buckled. She caught herself in time and remembered she must step more carefully.

"I think there's a family conspiracy going on," Bernell was saying. "Just before you left yesterday, Evie made a remark about 'when I become a famous songwriter like Tom Moore.' I told her I'm not likely to become a 'famous' anything. And she smiled this mysterious smile and said, 'Just you wait and see,' as though she had some kind of foresight."

Evie was the only other person who knew Rosalyn had sent Bernell's song to Mr. Braham. She set her lips in irritation as she recalled how Evie had wormed the secret out of her and sworn she would never breathe a word of it to Bernell. She ought to have known better than to confide in her sister.

"What do you make of her words?" Bernell asked. Rosalyn met his gaze with a shrug and smile.

"Oh, Bernell, how would I know? Evie always—*oh*!"

It was her lame foot, of course, settling in an unexpected hollow, wrenching her ankle. Upset by Bernell's remarks, she had forgotten to be careful. Without warning, without any volition on her part, she lost her balance and fell to the ground.

"Rosalyn!" Bernell called out in alarm. "A-are you quite all right?" He knelt beside her anxiously.

She was not all right. The sudden pain left her gasping. She could not even answer him, and tears gathered in her eyes.

"Might I . . . help you get up? Could you lean on me?"

She shook her head and bit her lip to avoid crying out again. Bernell looked at her helplessly. "Shouldn't you try . . . Should I . . . ?" He straightened and glanced around. "I'll call a servant."

"Just . . . wait," Rosalyn managed. "Wait until it . . ." She ended in a little moan as she tried to move the injured ankle. "Yes," she whispered. "Call someone. I doubt I can walk on it."

"But I shouldn't leave you here." He bent over her again but clearly did not know what sort of aid he could provide by himself. Rosalyn remembered that Donald, their only young, muscular footman, was gone with Worth and Evie, and Gordon had a sprained wrist. She could not imagine either Neville, the ancient butler, or Lord Clifton's seventy-year-old valet being of much use.

"Gordon's manservant, Abbot," she suggested. "If he's around . . ."

"Yes, of course." Still looking uncertain, Bernell turned away. "I'll hurry."

He left her. She felt dizzy, drowning in a pool of pain. Gradually she became aware of voices from the direction of the stable yard. Had Worth Forrester and Evie returned so soon? She tried to call Bernell, but she seemed to have no voice, and he was gone. . . .

The next thing she knew, a tall shadow was bending over. With no more than a moment's pause she was gathered up into a pair of strong arms. Instinctively she put her arms around her rescuer's neck and looked into the concerned face of Worth Forrester.

"Oh . . . oh, Mr. Forrest—" She broke off as the ankle, swinging free, was seized with another spasm of pain that took away her breath.

"I'm sorry—did I hurt you?" he asked anxiously.

Mutely she shook her head and averted her eyes. That one glance into his face, amazingly close to her own, had caused a strange sort of current to run through her whole being. All at once she was light-headed, almost breathless, and quite incapable of speaking.

Bernell, charging ahead of them, held the door open. Evie was somewhere about, too, making exclamations of pity. Worth asked, "Where shall I take you? To your bedchamber?"

"Y-yes, if that won't be too much trouble."

"No trouble at all," he assured her, and she had a vision of him lifting—oh, so easily—a heavy portmanteau down from the top of the post chaise.

This time, after looking at him with her answer, their gazes caught and could not seem to part. At last Worth turned his eyes away to say, "Miss Evie, you had better call your sister. And Miss Rosalyn's maid."

"The doctor . . ." Bernell suggested.

"Let's see how bad it is first," Worth said. "A storm is coming up. We saw the clouds moving this way across the moor. That's why we returned early."

They were through the hall now. Evie had run to the bell pull by the front hall table and pulled it, at the same time calling loudly, "Olivia! Gordon! Rosalyn's been hurt."

But somehow no one came immediately, and on the ascent up the big front staircase, Rosalyn and Worth Forrester were quite alone. And again their eyes met in a kind of wordless expectation, and an alien and alarming sensation of pleasure invaded her from head to toe, almost shutting out the pain. She did not fight the instinct to tighten her hold around his neck, and felt a slight answering pressure from his arms.

"Down this way," she managed when they reached the top. "The s-second door on the right." There seemed, suddenly, a kind of risk in his knowing where her bedchamber lay, a thought she would never have entertained before.

"Is it very painful?"

"Painful enough," she said with a forced laugh.

The door was slightly ajar. Inside, the curtains of the bed were closed. "The couch," she said when he stopped uncertainly. "I-I'll be fine."

He laid her carefully on the chaise longue, propped pillows under her head and another under her feet. She was amazed at his gentleness. At the same time she regretted the withdrawal of his arms around her.

Anna appeared in the doorway, followed by Olivia.

"Cold compresses for your mistress—as cold as you can get them," Worth said. The maid nodded and hurried away.

"You don't even know what's wrong," Rosalyn objected, amused.

"You turned your ankle. Bernell told me."

"Yes, my weak foot."

"Were you walking in the garden, on that treacherous lawn?" Olivia asked, approaching Rosalyn with a frown. She turned to Worth. "We appreciate your help, Mr. Forrester, but now, since we shall need to undress her foot . . ." It was clear she meant for him to leave.

Rosalyn said quickly, "Yes, thank you so much, Mr. Forrester." Her voice was not at all secure. It suddenly seemed outrageous that Olivia should exclude him from the room when he had been so helpful, and she gave him a sympathetic smile.

"Worth, ma'am," he said reproachfully. "If you would really thank me."

"Th-thank you, Worth."

He returned her smile then, his expressive eyes holding hers. She could not believe what she saw in them. Even Americans could make pretty speeches on occasion. But absence of speech, together with speaking looks, said even more.

Anna returned with a basin of cold fresh spring water and a pile of cloths. Worth had no further excuse to stay, once he had reiterated his orders to keep the injured ankle as cold as possible. Olivia, mouth pursed, thanked him again. In another moment he was gone, and Rosalyn, heat coursing through her at the realization, was bereft.

THE WHITECOMB LEGACY

that my actions? I told her how Worth had
....in the sky of the approaching storm—as

✥ NINE ✥

As though she had just been anointed queen, everyone, either severally or singly, came to Rosalyn's bedchamber, where she remained ensconced on the chaise longue, to see how she fared. Even Grandfather. His only comment, other than a "Tsk, tsk," as he stared at her now-bandaged ankle, was "Well, m'dear, I'll play you a game of chess after dinner to take your mind off it, if you like."

Rosalyn, remembering that she had deprived him of a confrontation on Friday, readily agreed.

Bernell reiterated his own thwarted desire to help her, but, of course, he was neither so tall nor so strong as Mr. Forrester. Rosalyn thought she detected some jealousy in his tone. When he expressed further frustration that he could not even go for a doctor, for wind and rain had struck in earnest about teatime, she assured him the injury was not so severe and she didn't want or need a scold from Dr. Ransom for her outdoor walk.

Gordon said Worth Forrester must think the Archers were peculiarly apt at spraining their limbs. Olivia, coming by herself, professed outrage at having discovered Mr. Forrester alone with Rosalyn in her very bedchamber, no matter how necessary his assistance.

"What were you worried about?" Rosalyn asked curiously, leaving Olivia mute.

Evie, after marveling that they had returned just in time to help Rosalyn ("Almost as though it had been planned,

Rosalyn, isn't that mysterious?") told her how Worth had seen the signs in the sky of the approaching storm—signs she would never have noticed—and had insisted they turn back before they reached Buckland-in-the-Moor. "He is really a most amazing man," she finished.

Rosalyn admitted that, yes, it was beginning to seem that Mr. Forrester had all sorts of unexpected skills. She was noticing that Evie had dropped "Mr. Forrester" in favor of "Worth." The name seemed to come from her lips most naturally.

Left alone, she could not help dwelling on those strange sensations she had experienced when Mr. Forrester ("Worth") had carried her up the stairs and deposited her with such care and gentleness on the chaise longue. Captain Fortescue also had been charming and helpful, *before* Olivia married him. And her mother had once told her Lionel Archer had captivated her to the point of witlessness with songs and merry ways before their wedding day. Rosalyn was determined not to be bamboozled by any man's flummery. She would not be made either a fool or a prisoner of her senses.

When, therefore, Worth Forrester returned at the same time the maid came to take away her supper tray, she viewed his continued concern for her injury with suspicion, and returned tartly, "If it had not been for your excessive notions about exercise, I would not be in such a state."

Worth looked momentarily as though she had hit him. Secretly dismayed by the sound of her own words, Rosalyn was on the verge of apologizing when he withdrew, saying he would visit her at another, more propitious time.

That time came later in the evening when Lord Clifton, chessboard under his arm, made good his promise. Worth arrived with him. "Can you imagine, this young man has never played chess?" Lord Clifton asked incredulously. "I told him he must watch us and get an idea of it, and then I shall teach him. That is, if you don't object to his looking on, m'dear."

Rosalyn, mindful of her recent lapse of good manners, said she had no objections, and the game began.

By now her ankle no longer throbbed if she kept it raised. When Anna had bandaged it she had been surprised that it was only a little swollen. Rosalyn suspected the initial pain had been out of all proportion to the injury, bur also that Worth's suggestion of cold compresses had been very helpful. She wanted to thank him again but couldn't find the right opening. Luckily, there was the game to concentrate on.

But even that didn't secure her wholehearted interest. Her thoughts wandered frequently to that tall, silent, exceedingly masculine presence seated on her right, as he observed the board with a concentration probably greater than hers. Sometimes she was saved from a foolish move only by Grandfather's explanations of the game to him. "Now it might look very inviting here for me to take her knight with this pawn. But then she could do away with this bishop and my queen would be exposed. . . ."

Life was not unlike a chess game. It might look very inviting to fall in love with a man like Worth Forrester (was that what all these alien sensations were—falling in love? Or were they something much more elementary?), but one must think ahead to what one would be exposed to in the future. Unfortunately, that was utterly unknowable.

Why was that so hard to bear in mind? Why, despite her warnings to herself, did she continue to be so exquisitely aware of the minute details of his presence—the strong bones and scattering of pale hairs on the back of his weathered, capable hands, the texture of his frieze coatsleeve, so close to her own shawl-covered arm, the white simplicity of his muslin neckcloth, the ever fascinating contrast of his tanned face and dark sideburns to his pale, burnished hair? She avoided his eyes, knowing that they, above all else, were her undoing.

Gordon joined them after a while, about the same time Rosalyn began to hear Bernell playing on her piano. Gordon restlessly complained he couldn't do a damned thing with his sprained wrist, not even shoot billiards.

"You can play the winner here in chess," Lord Clifton suggested. "I've nearly got your sister trounced."

"What a hum!" Rosalyn contradicted. "I've only lost three pieces to your six."

"Aye, but you're not concentrating," Lord Clifton observed with a gleam in his eye.

He proved it by checkmating her king three moves later. Gordon shook his head. "If you can do that to Roz, you'll make short work of me. Maybe I'll teach Worth instead—what say, Worth?"

At that moment Worth was looking at Rosalyn, who was carefully realigning her pieces. "Or would you rather Rosalyn teach you, Forrester?" Gordon pursued when he received no answer.

Rosalyn looked up, startled, and could not avoid Worth's gaze. Nor could she look away immediately, though she wanted to, for she felt as exposed to all three men by that one glance as if she had been stripped naked.

Worth, breaking his gaze, said, "I don't believe I'm of a mind for chess tonight, Gordon, thanks all the same. I have been thinking I should work harder to learn about my father's family. It would be easy to stay at Torview Hall indefinitely, but I must not impose."

"Nonsense, Worth!" Gordon broke in impatiently. "We all enjoy your company."

"Did Lord Whitbourne give any hint of a relationship between you and his grandmother?" Rosalyn asked.

"I actually had no opportunity to bring the subject up without making too much of the possibility," Worth admitted. "But I'm curious. Why were there no Whitbourne family records at Ashburton Church?"

"Because the old Whitbourne family home is near Totnes, so that is the parish where they were born, and where the births are recorded," Rosalyn said. "Didn't the priest from Totnes answer your letter?"

"I don't believe so. But of thirty inquiries, I've received only ten answers so far."

"My own information is so incomplete—he was not a very satisfactory correspondent, I recall. It might be worth the trip to inspect the parish records yourself."

"It's not far," Gordon put in. "We could ride down there whenever you like, Worth. Rather nice trip, actually, along the river. Of course, now I can't hold the blasted reins."

"Take the barouche if you wish," Lord Clifton suggested. "Donald can drive—or Mr. Forrester."

"I'd be most grateful," Worth acknowledged. "It's my first real clue, and I want to pursue it. But oughtn't Miss Rosalyn to come along? She has a particular interest in other families as well, and might get more information for her study."

Something—his tone of voice, or the mere fact of the suggestion—set Rosalyn's nerve ends atingle. An expedition to Totnes with Worth Forrester. Riding in the carriage—the close quarters, the opportunities for conversation, the inescapable assault on her senses, hard enough to resist at home . . .

She knew she ought to say no if she ever wished to restore her peace of mind, but only brought up the most obvious excuse. "I'm afraid I've no idea yet how soon I'll be able to walk."

"We'll wait until your ankle is healed," Worth said promptly. "Meanwhile, I'll investigate the connection in other ways."

He did not detail those other ways, and Rosalyn could not guess what they might be. She considered other objections, but even as she did so Grandfather and Gordon encouraged her, and before she knew it she had committed herself to the outing, possibly by the end of the week.

The next morning, as Rosalyn breakfasted from a tray in her room, Anna said Mr. Forrester had asked permission to visit her. A strange shyness came over her, and she responded with a quick no. He must excuse her today; she was not fit to see anyone. And so she spent the day, ankle on a pillow, working with Anna to alter her old gowns. She wished more than once she had taken advantage of the presence of Mrs. Beecham, now returned to her cottage, to have a new gown made. Her image in the mirror completely dissatisfied her. She even toyed with the idea of cutting and curling fringes on her forehead, a style she had before considered artificial and frivolous.

The following morning, chafing at too long a time away from the piano, she hobbled down the hall to the parlor, leaning heavily on Anna's arm. She played an old Beethoven sonata and then turned to concentrate on the new one Gordon had brought her. For the better part of an hour she became so absorbed in it that when she heard a slight sound behind her, she jumped.

And turned to see Worth Forrester seated in a chair near the door.

His confident smile was all she needed to set her off. "What a stir you gave me! Why did you not announce your presence?" A miserable flush started before she had finished the sentence. She doubted she had blushed as much in her whole life as in the past few days.

"I meant no harm, ma'am," he said. "I was just carried away by your music."

"No one interrupts me when I'm practicing," she fumed. "Someone should have told you. Besides, it—it isn't fitting that you be in here with me, alone."

"The door is ajar. And you told me once you didn't believe in such a convention."

"You were invited in the last time," she retorted acidly. "Do you think your assistance the other day gives you the right to harass me, sir?"

"Why, Miss Rosalyn, I'm not harassing you," he drawled, his voice at its most American. "I've only become very fond of your company."

"I cannot think why," she snapped, and whirled about

to face the piano again. "I still have considerable work on this piece, so if you'll excuse me . . ."

She turned the pages back to the beginning and began again. *Das Lebewohl*—three sorrowful chords . . .

Suddenly the music was lifted from the rack by a pair of powerful hands.

"Mr. Forrester!"

He held the music out of reach. "I thought you might teach me to play chess." His eyes were warm and teasing. "If you agree to it, I'll return your music."

"Gordon can teach you."

"Gordon is writing a long letter to Miss Glynne. He has sadly neglected his correspondence to her, and expected it would take most of the day."

"Then Grandfather—"

"He is busy with his steward. Miss Evie is out riding, and I doubt Miss Olivia would care for the task. I have only you, Rosalyn, to save me from utter tedium." The humorous excess in his words might have made her smile, but his eyes—deep gray pools of entreaty—reminded her this was no laughing matter.

"I'm practicing," she said crisply.

"I'll wait until you're done."

"Really, Mr. Forrester, I don't see—"

"Worth. And I think you see perfectly well."

"I told you, I—I'm not . . . eligible. I'm not like Evie. I am . . . quite determined to remain a spinster, and if you think otherwise you waste your time." She could not look at him as she said this, and instead studied the key board.

"What a demeaning title, 'spinster.' It could never apply to you, Rosalyn."

"It's demeaning only because society perceives it so. There is no good reason why women should be capable only of marriage and bearing children. We are not mindless animals. We have brains, ambitions—"

"I only ask that you teach me chess."

She blushed again at her own assumptions. Having produced that reaction, he added, "At least for now."

"I . . . cannot credit your good intentions," she said.

"If we are to go to Totnes together, we ought not be antagonists."

A reasonable request. She could think of no response that could reasonably reject it, even though his warm gaze warned her of the danger. "Very well," she conceded. "I'll teach you chess—later. After I have practiced."

"Thank you, ma'am." He smiled and replaced Herr Beethoven on the rack. His gaze responded alarmingly to her own reluctant smile. "One more question. Do you practice for some future performance?"

"Oh, no, simply for my own pleasure. Why do you ask?"

"It seems to me such dedication and talent should be heard by everyone. If you really believe women are fit for more than marriage and children."

He left her with a little bow. By then, intrigued by his statement, she would willingly have heard him challenge her opinions further.

When the piano had been at rest for half an hour, Olivia entered the upstairs parlor to find Rosalyn and Worth seated opposite each other at the gaming table, Rosalyn explaining in detail the ways in which the various chess pieces could move.

Olivia pursed her lips but only said, "Rosalyn, oughtn't you to have your ankle raised?"

"It's not paining me now, Olivia. If it does, I'll go to the sofa."

Olivia did not reply to this but went to the sewing cabinet and took out her embroidery. Then she seated herself firmly in the armchair by the bow window, to take advantage of the light. "Pray continue your game," she said. "I won't bother you."

Rosalyn was just as happy to have her there. It was much easier to concentrate on chess with a third party present. They broke up when Newton announced lunch, and afterward Gordon took Worth off for an afternoon of fishing. Rosalyn was left in peace until the members of the Musical Society assembled later that afternoon.

During their rehearsal Rosalyn noticed that Sir Harry was stammering more than usual and making sheep's eyes at Evie. Obviously flattered, Evie played up to him with fluttery laughs and smiles and side glances. Bernell, more concerned than usual with involving Olivia in the music, kept asking her opinion of each passage they sang. The only reasonable people present, Rosalyn thought, were Melinda and Duncan, who, for a change, did not ask why Gordon and Mr. Forrester were absent.

Once the Musical Society had dispersed, Olivia chided Evie for acting the flirt. Evie replied she had to practice sometime so she wouldn't be a perfect flat if and when she ever went to London. Olivia retorted that if her behavior grew much more outrageous she would lose all hope of going there. "I don't know which of you is worse," she scolded. "Evie playing up to that fop, Sir Harry, or Rosalyn allowing herself to be cornered by Mr. Forrester."

"I wasn't cornered, Olivia," Rosalyn protested, laughing. "We were playing chess."

"You were alone with him."

"Not for long. Besides, chess is as good as a chaperon. It takes such concentration."

"I declare, Rosalyn, you are no help whatever in setting your sister a good example."

"You set a good enough example for us both," Evie said impudently.

"Mother would have grieved to hear you talk so to me," Olivia returned with a sigh.

Rosalyn, to forestall further words between them, announced that she was going to Totnes with Gordon and Worth near the end of the week to learn more about the Forrester connection to the Whitbournes. "My ankle is so much better today, it should be well enough by then," she finished.

Olivia immediately forgot Evie's behavior to concentrate on Rosalyn's. When her concern for Rosalyn's health made no impression, she stressed the impropriety of the trip.

"If my own brother isn't security enough to guard against whatever evils Mr. Forrester has in mind for me, who is?" Rosalyn asked.

"You needn't be sarcastic, Rosalyn. I *have* had some experience with men, and I've also seen how Mr. Forrester looks at you."

Evie giggled. Retreating under her younger sister's quizzical gaze with heated cheeks, Rosalyn suggested they let Grandfather settle the issue at dinner, when she planned to join them for the first time since her injury. Olivia threw up her hands in defeat and left the room. Rosalyn refused to respond to the arch looks Evie threw at her, but she did feel some satisfaction in having stood up to Olivia's excessive protectiveness.

As she had expected, Lord Clifton backed her decision at the supper table. He even remarked he had noticed a new bloom in Rosalyn's cheeks. She had been cooped up too long, and unless Olivia wanted to go to Totnes herself as chaperon, she might as well consider Rosalyn perfectly safe accompanied by two stalwart young men and Donald to drive the horses. It was, Rosalyn realized with a queer flutter in her abdomen, an unprecedented show of trust for Grandfather to pair Worth, the newcomer, with his own grandson.

Olivia had no intention of chaperoning Rosalyn. She was expected at Lady Harriet's house in Ashburton for a series of meetings with an architect who had come all the way from London at Lady Harriet's expense to draw up plans for the charity hospital. She expected they would be at it for the better part of three days.

The next chess lesson turned into a foursome at whist which included Gordon and Evie. Rosalyn was relieved. She had decided she did not want to be alone with Worth, though the decision had nothing to do with Olivia's sense of propriety. She could not quite believe what was happening between them and, while she tried to sort it out in her mind, continued to wax hot and cold toward him. She, whose infirmity had made her an island of patience and stability between Evie's whims and Olivia's tempers, was now a veritable sea of unpredictability. She could not even anticipate her own reactions to him from one meeting to the next. Her every waking moment was now filled with speculation about him.

Hoping to hide her new sensations from everyone (especially after Olivia's remark about how Worth looked at her), she reverted to her old habit and the very next evening sent word with Molly that she would take her meal in her room as before.

She reckoned without Worth, who, on hearing the news, intercepted the maid with her tray and took it up himself. Not having expected him, Rosalyn was at a loss for words when, bearing the tray, he besieged her in her sitting room and immediately fired off a string of questions.

"What's the trouble, Rosalyn? Is your ankle worse? Is it some other disorder? Can I be of any help?"

Putting her hands to her temples, she shook her head. "It's nothing! I pray you, Worth, don't come at me like that! It is kind of you to bring me supper, but . . ."

He set the meal on the writing desk before her, beside a notebook bound in red leather—her journal. She had just written in it: "Am I excited about making the trip to Totnes because I have never been so far from home since I was twelve, or because Worth Forrester will be accompanying us?"

She closed the notebook quickly and laid it on the floor by her chair, suspecting that he had recognized his name upside down.

"Something you don't wish me to see?" he guessed. She wondered if he ever refrained from asking a question or making a statement merely because it would be uncomfortable for his listener.

"It's none of your business," she said coolly.

"I know that." He sat down on her small dressing-table stool. "But I'm beginning to feel responsible for the state of your health. Maybe you could regard me as your doctor."

She stared into his eyes. "I doubt I could do that."

"Perhaps it's just as well," he agreed. "My interest in you goes far beyond the medical."

"I . . . think you ought to go. They'll be awaiting you at supper."

"I suppose so." He stood, to her relief, then came nearer, to her anxiety. "What a pity we can't have supper alone together. Do you still plan on Totnes?"

"Oh, I . . . yes."

"Gordon will be with us," he reminded her.

"I know." She looked up at him, troubled by the surging, near-to-suffocating emotion his presence seemed to provoke. She noticed a sudden alteration of his expression too late. Before she could take alarm, he bent over and kissed her on the lips. It was a short kiss but very tender, very purposeful. It shocked her into immobility. Her lips trembled. She thought his did, too.

Before she could respond he backed away from her reluctantly, almost, it seemed, reverently, until he reached the doorway. Then, still not speaking, he turned and vanished.

~ TEN ~

"Mrs. Beecham was right!" Rosalyn exclaimed.

Her eye had been the first to catch the name on the brown-edged page of the old leather-bound folio. "Look!" She pointed to the middle of the page. "Neville Armistead married Mistress Lydia Forrester in 1739. She died in 1740, the same year their daughter, Amy, was born. Lady Amy married the Marquess of Whitbourne, as we know. Now why didn't Mr. Phipps write me Lydia Forrester's full name?"

There was no real answer to that except, as Gordon pointed out, Vicar Phipps himself. He had met them at the medieval Church of St. Mary and guided them to a room beyond the carved stone rood screen where the parish records were kept. Shrunk with age, he was given to repeating himself, nodding and smiling, frequently saying, "You might not credit this, but I recall . . ." Once he had shown them the books, he smiled and nodded his way out of the room and disappeared.

"Any more on Lydia Forrester?" Worth asked. "Any record of *her* family?"

They looked together. It was hard to concentrate on what she was looking for with Worth's head so close to hers. Indeed, it had been hard to concentrate on any rational thing in his presence, ever since that surprising kiss of two evenings ago.

"Lydia Forrester of Torcross," Worth read. "Where is Torcross? Very far?"

"It's down on the coast, south of Dartmouth," Gordon said. "So her family records would be in a different parish. Only half a day's journey at most."

Meanwhile Rosalyn had taken a pencil and a small vellum-bound notebook from her reticule. "I see they have the other names of the Whitbourne children here. You know, Lady Harriet's little brothers that died." She began writing them down. "Daniel, born in 1759, Harold in 1761, Randolph in 1764. It looks as if Harold died a few weeks after birth, and Randolph when he was two. Daniel—there is no death date for Daniel."

"My father's name was Daniel," Worth said. "Maybe he was named for some common ancestor of this Daniel."

"When was your father born?" Gordon asked.

"1759—huh! The same date."

The three of them stared at each other as the same idea hit them at once. Between Rosalyn and Worth myriads of dust particles danced down a shaft of light from the stained-glass window above them. The wood floor was scratched and dulled with the boots of untold pairs of feet, and the dim light cast everything—the dark, worn furniture, the blues and reds and golds of the stained glass—into some centuries-distant past. The old fortified town of Totnes, Gordon had told them on the way, had been founded in the mist-shrouded Roman days, maybe even earlier. Right now, the three-hundred-year-old church seemed equally ancient, equally mysterious. Rosalyn felt a little chill creep up her spine.

"What was his full name?" she asked.

"All I know is Daniel Forrester."

"The person listed here is Daniel Jeremiah Paul Whitbourne."

"Probably just a coincidence," Worth said, shrugging.

"But there is no death date. For the others, there is."

Again their eyes held in a shock of speculation.

"What do you think it means?" Worth asked at last.

"It means . . . this Daniel may have been your father. If he left England, there would be no record of his death here."

"It means," Gordon added, "that the Daniel listed here was the oldest child and would have inherited the title. He would have been Marquess of Whitbourne after his father's death."

"It means," Rosalyn resumed slowly, "that if this Daniel was your father, the title should have descended to you, as eldest son of eldest son."

Another little silence enveloped them. Worth broke it with a laugh. "But that's nonsense! Me—with a title? Besides, I'm an American."

"Who wants to settle in England," Gordon reminded him.

"We don't believe in titles. *I* don't believe in titles. My country fought a revolution to abolish privilege—begging your pardon, Gordon. Not that you haven't a right to *yours* . . ."

Gordon grinned. Worth flung out his big hands and walked away from them in a restless circle. "I-it's just so . . . absurd!"

"But isn't this what you were looking for?" Rosalyn asked, a little catch of excitement in her voice. "If you can prove this, you've a ready-made place here in England. You won't have to worry about how you'll support yourself *or* your mother."

"Unless my father forfeited his right to inherit the title when he emigrated."

"Bernell could tell us that, I should think," Gordon said. "But at the very least, you could be Lord Whitbourne's nephew. And if you are, you're his legal heir—his nearest male relative. He has no children, you know."

Worth looked a bit dazed. "B-but . . . isn't all this pure conjecture? My father's name was Forrester."

"Maybe Lady Harriet was right," Rosalyn guessed. "Your father changed his name. You said he left because of a family quarrel."

"Maybe he chose Forrester because it was his grandmother's name," Gordon put in.

"And she was not of the aristocracy," Rosalyn added. "He was renouncing his aristocratic ties. It all makes perfect sense."

"Does it?" Worth's smile was wry. "If so, it's an ironic sort of sense. I confess, I'm bowled over by the whole thing."

"A bit of food will set you right," Gordon suggested. "And I know an inn not far from here."

They decided, over a meal of veal cutlets, apricot tarts, and wine, that there was no point in pursuing Lydia Forrester's origins in Torcross before checking out the likelihood that Worth's father was the eldest Whitbourne. Little by little, Worth seemed to accept the possibility. Rosalyn remembered how Mrs. Beecham, on seeing him, immediately connected him to the Whitbournes.

"I don't see the resemblance, myself," Gordon said. "Maybe she *is* a witch."

"I think," Worth said, "I ought to write a letter to Lord Whitbourne. Tell him what we have discovered, and see what response he makes. Lady Harriet said he had access to the family records."

"I'd go easy about contacting the marquess too soon, old chap," Gordon broke in. "You may not realize it, but you'll be challenging his position."

"I've no intention of challenging his right to the title. What would I do with a title? My God!" Worth uttered a brief sarcastic laugh.

But the grandchildren of Lord Clifton, failing to see the humor, were arguing between themselves. "But he's the one who could help Worth," Rosalyn pointed out. "His own nephew. Surely he'd—"

"*Maybe* his nephew. But I'm not sure he'd help. You know what Bernell thinks of him."

Worth, remembering Bernell's story, said, "You're right, Gordon."

"Besides, you need proof that you are who you say you

are," Gordon went on. "Do you have any proof that Daniel Forrester—or Whitbourne—is your father?"

"I have a certificate of christening in Virginia. And a letter my father wrote my mother. His handwriting."

Gordon frowned. "Is that enough? I'm sure I don't know. We'll put Bernell on the case. But I advise you to move cautiously."

It seemed to Rosalyn strange advice, coming from her often heedless brother.

"We've plenty of time," Gordon noted as they resumed seats in the barouche for the journey home. "Why don't we make a little side trip and see Whitbourne Castle?"

Rosalyn thought it an irresistible idea. Worth said, "It depends on how Miss Rosalyn's ankle feels."

"It's fine," she assured them. "One would hardly know I'd hurt it."

"I don't think you really did," Gordon teased her. "I think you staged the whole thing just so Worth could carry you into the house in his big strong arms."

Rosalyn blushed. "What nonsense!" she said sharply. It was some time before she dared look at Worth again.

Past Totnes's north gate, the road began to rise steeply away from the town. When they had reached only halfway to the crest of the hill, Donald stopped the carriage to give the horses a rest. Gordon urged Worth and Rosalyn out to look at the view, which was truly magnificent. Beyond the ancient town they had just left, they could see the Dart winding through the gentle Devonshire hills, which were dotted with green pasture and gold corn stubble. The birches and alders along the river were tinged with orange and yellow, and the sky was a faultless blue overhead, with a white vapor haze streaking the horizon and gathering densely toward the Channel.

"Now look this way," Gordon advised, and they turned in the opposite direction to follow the forested road as it climbed the hill. At the crest, on a wide bluff overlooking the river, the top of a crenellated parapet and two square towers were visible above the trees.

"Whitbourne Castle," Gordon said. "Shall we continue?"

However, this ancestral seat of the Whitbourne family was far less imposing close at hand than Rosalyn had anticipated. An abandoned gatehouse of rugged gray moorstone, shadowed by massive oaks, guarded a road that overgrown weeds had reduced to a mere lane. The gate was ajar, its hinges rusted, its lock broken. The stone wall defining the boundaries of an old pleasure garden and promenade was crumbling. The vine-tangled orchard gave off a heavy tang of decay from the overripe apples, plums, and peaches that had fallen on the ground. When Donald drove the horses into the courtyard, the massive granite structure surrounding them appeared devoid of life, except for tenacious weeds that had struggled to light between cracks in the cobblestones. Windows and chimneys on the north were completely obscured with creeping green tendrils. Others, high on a tower above them, were ominously covered with iron bars.

"Gracious," said Rosalyn with a shiver. "It looks exactly like a setting for one of Mrs. Radcliffe's mysteries."

"It looks deserted to me," Worth said.

"It wasn't so, formerly," Gordon said. "A group of us came here about two years ago, and a caretaker came out and showed us around. There's a Norman keep which dates back to eleven-something. But most of the present castle was built in Tudor times."

"What does one do with such a place?" Worth asked in dismay. "I must say I hope you're wrong about my being the marquess's heir."

"An Englishman's home is his castle," Gordon noted with a grin. "But I'll admit this castle wants something to be a proper home. I suppose that's why Lord Whitbourne prefers to live in Blackroy Manor."

"It would cost considerable to fix it up," Worth said practically, his eye on rotting wooden casements and cracked stone corners. "I'm not used to stone, only wood."

"You simply can't please some people," Gordon said

with a mock sigh. "Here we offer you a castle and all you do is complain. Want to look around further?"

Worth declined. Pretending to be put out, Gordon called Donald to turn them around and start for home. Rosalyn was relieved. An unexplainable sense of oppression had seized her as she looked around at the deserted courtyard and the formidable battlements.

They arrived at Torview Hall in time for tea with Lord Clifton. He heard about their trip and their findings with much interest, accepting the possibility that Worth was related to English nobility with no more than a raising of his bushy eyebrows. Then he said, "A curious coincidence. Two letters with the Whitbourne crest arrived today, hand-delivered by a servant, addressed to each of you young blades."

At Gordon's insistence, Newton was immediately dispatched to Lord Clifton's study to fetch them. Gordon tore his letter open in eager curiosity. Worth opened his more slowly, a bemused expression on his face. It turned out the messages were the same. Lord Whitbourne requested the honor of their presence at Blackroy Manor for a fortnight of hunting on the moor.

"Well, well," Gordon said sarcastically. "It looks as though the Clifton-Archer family has at long last been admitted into the inner sanctum of the East Devon *ton*. I have never been invited to this before, nor have any of my friends."

"Nor I," Lord Clifton said, furrowing his brow. "Although I knew Lord Whitbourne's father-in-law, Lord Broughton, well."

"What sort of hunting would it be?" Worth wanted to know.

"Probably game birds," Gordon said. "You have to go farther north for good fox or deer hunting."

"I didn't bring a gun."

"I'll lend you a flintlock," Lord Clifton said. "And a mount, of course. You could try my elevating rib gun, if you like—for shooting on horseback. I never got the hang of it. Rather have my feet on the ground when I shoot."

Worth said the flintlock would be fine, thank you. Gordon asked, "What do you suppose Lord Whitbourne's after?"

"My guess is, he knows Worth is his nephew," Rosalyn said. "Lady Harriet surely informed him of your father's name and age, and he would know if his own brother emigrated to America, wouldn't he? This invitation is merely his first step in acknowledging the relationship."

Somehow the trip to Totnes had been not only a discovery but a release, a mutual experience that allowed a new familiarity between Rosalyn and Worth. She was losing some of her reserve in his presence. The realization that he sought her company, that he might even find her attractive, no longer seemed absurd or frightening. She was willing to allow his attentions—even welcome them—so long as he didn't push too far.

He seemed to understand her state of mind and made no effort to be alone with her, but for the next few days they were together a good deal, usually with Gordon and Evie. Olivia had sent back word she was staying longer than expected with Lady Harriet to confer with the visiting architect about the plans for the charity hospital.

Somehow, with Olivia away, they all felt a good deal freer to say what they liked, and there was much jesting and laughter at dinner, and lively political discussions between Gordon, Worth, and Lord Clifton during after-dinner smokes and drinks. Without Olivia to caution her, Rosalyn increased her schedule of exercises. Whenever Worth suggested it, even sometimes when he did not, she walked the grounds outside Torview Hall. The smooth pebbled path through the rose garden quickly grew humdrum. Using Grandfather's walking stick to prevent repetition of the previous week's accident, she sought the long, beech-lined lane to the gatehouse, the foot-paths between the hedgerows that separated pastures from beet and potato fields, the grassy slope that led down to the fish pond. When Worth was by her side, her energy seemed boundless and the lag in her step of little importance. Stimulated by the fresh, cool autumn air, by the scent of pine and brittle dying leaves, by birdsong and the calls of starling and magpie, she developed a hearty appetite and her cheeks bloomed.

Watching the change in approving silence, Worth made so bold as to suggest again that she try horseback riding. He told her he would enjoy the sights of Dartmoor even more if she showed them to him. She was, by then, ready for the idea, and was taken up in a nostalgia for her girl-hood, when she had loved to ride out on the moor with its broad, empty vistas. Cautiously she asked him if it was true one never really forgot how to ride. He assured her it was true. She nodded thoughtfully and said maybe, just maybe . . .

She was getting to know him better on their walks. She listened with fascination to his stories of his youth and young manhood, the trading and trapping expeditions with his stepfather, the visits to Indian camps. She and Evie even wrested from him, bit by bit, the story Gordon had alluded to the first night of his visit, of his heroic trek with the survivors of the Indian attack. In contrast to most men she knew, who needed little encouragement to boast of their deeds, he was reticent to the point of shyness about his abilities and achievements, and her esteem grew correspondingly.

She reached a familiarity where she dared to confess to him her favorite theory: Women should be allowed an education equal to men's, they should attend the universities, then there would be no reason why they might not be allowed positions of power. One time, when they trailed considerably behind Gordon and Evie on a cool hedgerow-shaded lane, she even argued against protecting women from physical hardship and moral ambiguities. "If Olivia had known about such things, she might have recognized Captain Fortescue's true nature before marrying him," she said.

Worth took issue with her. "Doubtless she would have married him anyway. Women in love are not rational." When she cast him a look of outrage he conceded, "Of course, had she recognized the prevalence of such male activities, she might have dealt with his sins differently and not driven him entirely away."

"You are taking his part!"

"Not at all. I was only pointing out—"

"That men can do such things and expect forgiveness, while women must forever be chaste and innocent, or woe betide them!" Rosalyn finished indignantly.

"Life is not fair," he pointed out with a good-natured smile.

"That doesn't mean we ought to accept the unfairness," she retorted. "Any more than we ought to accept cruelty and deceit."

Her anger was the deeper for a sharp hurt. His argument made it clear that he, like most men, was quite ready to allow anything to his fellow males while attacking females for the very ignorance they were not allowed to correct. She had no patience with such a viewpoint. The companionable walk ended abruptly as she turned and marched back to Torview Hall in silence.

The following day he brought up the ride to Dartmoor again, as though their tiff had not occurred. Having had a night to think about it, she surprised him by saying yes, she'd like to go. Then, with a gleam in her eye, she added, "We'll take a picnic and make an expedition to Wistman's Wood, on the West Dart. It's a lovely spot and I haven't been there for years. As long as the weather holds, we ought to take advantage of it. Bernell is bringing Olivia back tonight. And Gordon's wrist is much better, so he should be able to ride again. We can all go tomorrow, on horseback."

She was quite aware of—even amused by—his frustration.

⟨ ELEVEN ⟩

Miss Constantia Glynne, answering Gordon's letter, had invited Evie to come and visit her and her parents in London when Gordon himself returned. Evie was full of the prospect as they started for Wistman's Wood late the next morning. She wanted to know when Gordon was returning to London.

He reckoned the date of departure at least three weeks off, citing Lord Whitbourne's hunt, which would last a fortnight. Evie was surprisingly complacent about the delay, now that the long-dreamed-of journey seemed a reality. Some good weather would surely remain in November, and the theater and opera would be flourishing. She began to enumerate all the places she wanted to see: the Vauxhall Gardens, the Royal Opera on the Haymarket, Drury Lane Theater, St. James's Palace, Almack's, and many more.

"The Glynnes are not in society," Gordon cautioned. "Of course, you may choose from a great many sights other than Almack's and the Queen's Drawing Room."

All the more reason, Evie pointed out, for Olivia to give up her foolish fears and agree to the visit. Olivia said shortly she probably would, if only to get Evie out of her hair for a while. She was not in the best of moods, having made it clear the expedition was not to her particular liking. She had not ridden for several years, and had now committed herself to an hour and a half on horseback each way. Worth knew she had come only because she considered it her duty to keep an eye on him and Rosalyn.

Worth listened to the sisterly crossfire with a mixture of relief and irritation—relief because they had abandoned an earlier, equally vociferous argument about Rosalyn's fitness for the expedition; irritation because he would much rather be riding ahead with Rosalyn, who had somehow managed to pair off with Bernell instead.

His astonishing love for her continued to amaze him. It had originated in small things—the straight set of her back even when she limped, an escaped tendril of her heavy dark hair lying damply against a flushed cheek as they danced the minuet, the level gaze of her brown eyes as she put forth her frank opinions. It had blazed to life when he had seen her crumpled in pain on the lawn, then had borne her weight and sweetness in his arms. Her independent mind, such a contrast to the obedient compliance of Gentle Fawn, amused and fascinated him, even now when they were at odds and she had thwarted his attempt to be alone with her by inviting the whole family along.

But more important than his frustration was her triumph. He could only be proud of the way Rosalyn had deftly parried Olivia's objections to such a lengthy outing, and he had silently cheered her persistent efforts to hitch her right leg over the sidesaddle hump without anyone's aid until she succeeded. It seemed a measure of his devotion that he could dwell on that rather than his own desire to be with her, intense though it was.

It wasn't until they turned along the West Dart that Worth found himself riding beside Rosalyn, but by then talk had become impossible, for everyone save himself and Olivia was singing. Inspired by mention of Lord Whitbourne's forthcoming hunt, Gordon had started it off with:

> "Foresters sound the cheerful horn
> Hark to the woods away!

134

Diana with her nymphs this morn
Will hunt the stag to bay . . ."

After the seemingly interminable verses died a natural death, Bernell began a simple round and motioned Worth to join them. He caught on quickly, and the five of them sang the rest of the distance, silencing birds, startling cattle and sheep, sending small wild creatures for cover. Olivia, though not singing, looked less pained than before, and Worth's frustration gave way to pleasure at the joviality, the companionship and song, to which this English family had so freely admitted him.

Wistman's Wood turned out to be a stand of very old, stunted oak trees that had spread their tenacious roots deep among the rocky slope of Longaford Tor. From a distance the burnt-orange leaves against the green-gray of the Dartmoor hills startled the eye. Entering the woods, one saw vines and withered berries burrowing into the trees' crotches and decaying branches. Far below, at the foot of the slope, the West Dart rushed noisily and shallowly over stones and around rocks.

They followed a path through the wood until they reached a high windswept knoll on the wood's edge. Donald, who had followed them with a donkey laden with rugs and picnic baskets, began to set out the meal between two large oaks. Around them gorse and bell heather still spread scarves of yellow and pink blossoms.

Dismounting, Worth took in the broad panorama of boulder-strewn hillsides and granite-humped ridges that rose in the distance. Huddled clumps of oak and hawthorn and an occasional solitary mountain ash dotted a landscape that shimmered in the pale October sun. The vast, seemingly uninhabited distances were heart-stopping . . . and beautiful. His appreciation came with a sudden surge of recognition. His father's country—*his* country. Dare he believe it? Dare he claim some share in its future? Dare he make such a claim to the inscrutable, self-assured lord who might be his uncle?

He turned back to the others, seeking out Bernell. Last night he and Gordon had told the lawyer of their discovery at Totnes and the invitation to Blackroy Manor. Bernell had cautioned them to talk with Lady Harriet before discussing the find with Lord Whitbourne, for Lady Harriet would surely remember if a brother only a year her senior had emigrated to America after a family quarrel—and, more to the point, be apt to admit it. He had further cautioned them about Lord Whitbourne's response to any claim of kinship. "If Worth is indeed his nephew, he will have realized it by now, and I'd say, beware. Lord Whitbourne has nothing to gain and everything to lose by acknowledging it."

"But the invitation . . ." Rosalyn had put in.

"May be some sort of trap. If I were Worth, I'd be extremely cautious. It might even be judicious to think of an excuse not to accept."

Worth had smiled with polite incredulity. The recommendation was academic, for they had already accepted. They were to leave the next morning. Now, a chill invaded him as he thought of it.

He settled down on a rug beside Bernell and took a helping of chicken and biscuits from the platter Donald was passing around. "I didn't ask you this last night," he said, "but is it possible Daniel Whitbourne, if he was my father, forfeited his right to the title by emigrating?"

"Oh, the succession would still be valid," Bernell said, "unless he was deliberately cut out of it by the former Lord Whitbourne's will. Of course, if there was a family quarrel, I suppose that would be quite possible."

"I'm sure about the quarrel. So, supposing the present marquess is in no danger from me of losing his title, why should he not welcome a prospective heir? He has none now, has he?"

"No," Rosalyn answered from across the circle. "When the present marquess dies, the title will die with him—unless he produces an heir, which, of course, is still possible."

"Perhaps he will welcome you," Bernell said with a shrug. "Perhaps Rosalyn is right and the invitation is a genuine acknowledgment of kinship. Perhaps I'm being unnecessarily skeptical, but . . ."

"Even if I were really entitled to the marquisate or whatever you call it, I wouldn't take it. I've no use for titles. All I would ask of him is some sort of living for my mother and myself. Once I make that clear to him, he has no reason to be concerned for his position."

" 'The devil has his reasons that reason cannot know,' " Bernell misquoted darkly.

"Bernell, aren't you being overly pessimistic?" Rosalyn suggested.

"My dear cousin, I hope so." He turned to Olivia. "Has Lady Harriet ever told you that her father was once engaged in the slave trade?" he asked.

"Bernell, of course not!" returned Olivia. "Whatever makes you think he was?"

"It was common knowledge at one time—remember, I'm ten years your senior, my dear. Yes, he owned slavers—the ships that took Africans to America. He never investigated the horrendous conditions under which they were transported. Like most such men, he cared only about the margin of profit in his captains' ledgers."

"But the slave trade has been outlawed for several years," Rosalyn pointed out. "So what are you getting at, Bernell?"

"For many people, that was a black mark on the Whitbourne family name, even before the present marquess held the title. It's possible Worth's father was an idealistic young man at odds with his family over some principle. Could it not have been quarrels over profiting from such an abomination that led him to reject his family—and his title?"

"But that's it, Bernell!" Worth exclaimed. "My mother told me that the very reason they moved from Virginia to Kentucky was that my father detested living on a slave-labor plantation. What about the present marquess, then—did he continue to profit from the trade after gaining the title?"

"He did," Bernell acknowledged, his lips tight and stern. "I know because I was involved in legal matters for the Whitbourne family at one time. I wouldn't be at all surprised if he continues to do so, clandestinely, of course."

Worth's glance met Gordon's. The hunting party, once a pleasant diversion with an exciting opportunity to discover his origins, had become an adventure laced with vague menace. Gordon might have been equally uneasy, but he hid it by asking for another apple tart. The subject was dropped.

After they had completed the meal, Donald began packing up the remains for the return trip, and Olivia declared she must walk along the sunny ridge to warm herself. Bernell joined her with alacrity, and she accepted his arm, smiling. Jumping restlessly to her feet, Evie held her hand out to Worth and promised to show him a particularly spectacular view.

Worth looked back to Rosalyn and Gordon, but neither seemed inclined to move. Gordon lay on his back, arm shading his eyes, and Rosalyn leaned on one elbow beside him. She had removed her wide-brimmed hat, and strands of her dark hair had come loose from their bun and waved across her cheeks, now rosy from wind and sun. Her form-fitting, honey-colored velvet spencer outlined the high swell of her breast and narrow waist, and cascades of creamy lace adorned her throat. Worth longed, all of a sudden, to move it aside and place his lips there—and just managed, by looking away as he invited her to join them, not to move in her direction.

"I think not," Rosalyn replied to his somewhat incoherent invitation. "I feel lazy, and the sun seems warm enough to me here." She avoided his gaze as though well aware what it was saying to her. He was suddenly struck with concern that the lengthy ride had been too much for her strength after all, but felt powerless to ask if it was so.

"I'll keep her company," Gordon said. "You two go ahead. But don't get lost."

"Is it likely?" Worth asked.

"Indeed it is." Gordon sat up to show them he was serious. "The hills are so deceptive. You round one and suddenly everything looks the same, and when you try to go back, unless you're on a clear path, you might turn off in the wrong direction. One doesn't even see the cattle much; they hide in the clitters. Only the moormen really know their way across the moor. I don't know how. Instinct, I suppose."

"Detail," Worth said. "They look for small details—it's the same in the forest. You learn to recognize the difference between one tree and another."

"Oh, pooh!" Evie said, taking his arm. "I shan't get lost, even if you might. I know my way about. Come on, Worth."

It soon became apparent that Evie was intent on losing them from everyone else's view, and after a few minutes' walk, Worth felt obliged to concentrate his own powers of observation in case they did, indeed, round a hill and find everything looked the same.

"That tree," Evie said, stopping to clutch his arm and pointing. "That big old ash, standing all alone—isn't it magnificent? Now look straight behind it, way in the distance. Those are the Beardown Tors. And then beyond . . ."

While he looked and listened to her explanations of what was surely the most barren and inaccessible landscape yet, she bolted from his side to jump onto a low granite outcropping. Her sudden move alarmed him. "Evie!" he protested, following her. She turned and, from her new height, put her hands on his shoulders. Their heads were now on a level. She leaned forward and kissed him quickly on the lips, then moved back to look at him from under half-closed lids. "I've been wanting to do that for ever so long."

He shook his head, smiling. "I'm very flattered, but you shouldn't have."

"Why not? How did it make you feel? I suspect it was far too short a kiss to tell. You may kiss me longer, if you like. No one will see." She closed her eyes expectantly, then gave a surprised squeal when he gripped her shoulders, lifted her off her perch, and set her down beside him.

"I think we'll go back now, Evie."

"That's not very nice of you," Evie retorted, her blue eyes wide and outraged.

"You don't know what you're doing."

"I'm trying to learn some things. I'll be going to London shortly, and if some young gentleman . . ."

Worth could not suppress his sudden laughter. "Oho! So you were simply using me to practice on?"

"You have no right to laugh!" She marched ahead of him indignantly, shoulders set in anger. Worth thought of a number of things he might have said, but they all sounded like preaching, so he simply followed in silence.

Rosalyn had watched them go with a pang. All day she had been suppressing a constant wish to be alone with Worth, if only for a few minutes. It did no good to try to resurrect her two-day-old anger toward his attitudes, though she still would have defended her reason for it. His guileless good nature dispersed anger as the sun dispersed rain. Yet under all that good nature, she sensed something as rock-hard, as uncompromising, as his obvious strength. That toughness, both mental and physical, seemed more in evidence today, thanks to his apparel—those frontier buckskins with fringed arms and leggings that had alarmed her before. Though more loose-fitting than traditional riding clothes, they allowed his throat to be open to the sun and air and gave one glimpses of golden hairs lying against bronze skin. Her very physical reaction to his costume made her all the more wary. Watch out for the charming ones, her mother had told Olivia. She had spoken from experience, but Olivia had not heeded it. Rosalyn was beginning to appreciate the reasons for such heedlessness.

And so she stayed with Gordon, enjoying the bracing autumn air, the chill in the breeze that counteracted the sun's warmth, feeling, as she had told Worth, lazy—and, if the truth be told, also a bit sore. She had known all along the ride would be a test of her endurance, but so far she was satisfied she had not stretched it to the limit.

Gordon had decided to make one of his periodic confessions to her. "It's not that I don't want to see Constantia again," he was saying thoughtfully. "I admire her most awfully, and I'm sure I shall grow to love her. But it was probably a bad idea to come home, knowing I'd have to meet Melinda and face her betrothal to Duncan. I intended to be very casual and good-natured about it, but it was harder than I thought. All my old feelings came back. I thought what an infernal fool I'd been to turn away from her, and ended up with a proper fit of the dismals. At the ball, I thought if I could just get an admission from her that she had really loved *me* best, and Duncan was second choice, I could go away satisfied. But she refused me even that consolation, so I left in a blue funk and . . ."

"And proceeded to get yourself half sprung," Rosalyn supplied when he shrugged and stopped.

"Quite. It was Worth showed me what a sad rattle I was."

"Worth?" she asked, startled.

"Yes. He found me that night . . . well, you know that. We sat in the taproom at the Golden Lion all night, and he listened to my crotchets with enormous patience. I must have drunk a gallon of porter, but he just sat there and sipped on the same mug of cider, and finally told me what he thought of my carrying on so."

"What did he say?"

Gordon gave her a quick, shamefaced glance, then rolled

over on his stomach and busied himself pulling yellow blossoms off a spread of gorse just beyond his rug. "Pretty much what you would have said. Only coming from him it carried more weight, somehow. That it was obvious Melinda and Duncan were happy and I was behaving like a sapskull. That there was no point in my looking back; my life was ahead of me. That I ought to be grateful for Miss Glynne; not only was she an excellent young woman who would make me a devoted wife, but she'd bring me a more than comfortable living, and I could pay off my gambling debts."

"Are you in debt, Gordon? You never said."

"I knew it wouldn't be of any use to ask Grandfather to pay them. He'd just rant at me. But I'm hoping Mr. Glynne will agree to it—though the idea of asking him makes me feel like a coal."

"I should think so!"

"I suppose that's why I dislike returning to London. I'll either have to face the duns or Mr. Glynne when I do."

"I should think the best thing to do is go soon and get it over with."

"Exactly what Worth said."

"And then stop gaming."

He gave her a rueful smile. "There's that, too, of course." He flicked away a spider and sat up, squaring his shoulders. "Now I'll give you some advice, Roz."

"Me?"

"Yes, you—my sensible, self-sufficient sister." He smiled at her almost mischievously, then grew sober. "Marry Worth when he asks you—as I'm sure he will. He's an uncommon man, Whitbourne or no. I wish I had half his resourcefulness and integrity—maybe then I'd not be in such a mess."

"Really, Gordon? I thought . . . I was certain . . . the night of the ball . . ."

"And I've never seen him drunk," Gordon added. "If you were concerned about that."

She shook her head, disclaiming any such preoccupation, and looked out over the hills, frowning against the brightness of the day. "Oh, Gordie—thank you for telling me, but . . . it's really much more difficult than that!"

The wind had grown harsher and clouds were gathering across the moor by the time they all reassembled on the knoll, so they set a faster return pace. Olivia and Bernell led them along the ancient ridgeway toward the main road. Evie rode next, with Gordon, who was trying to find out why she was sulking, and Worth at last had his chance with Rosalyn. He kept her so busy with questions about the countryside and the people in it that she did not notice, until too late, that they dawdled and the others had left them behind.

Rosalyn answered his questions readily enough, but after what Gordon had said, her old reserve had returned and she could not look him in the eye. Dartmoor in winter was beautiful but dangerous, she said, with high winds and deep snowfall and, at times, the "ammil"—when the furze, tree branches, rocks, and rivers were all coated with an iron-hard glaze of ice, and the sound of the innumerable brooks and rivers was silenced.

"I'd like to see that," he said. "I find this countryside more intriguing the longer I stay." It surprised her he would react so to Dartmoor's most difficult times, but then she was beginning to accept that he did not always appreciate ease and comfort. And she was learning from him the need for challenges.

"And I had forgotten the—the freedom one feels, to be able to ride out here and view such distances," she admitted.

"You aren't overtired, are you?"

"I'm a little weary, and sore. But that's to be expected, isn't it?"

"Absolutely to be expected," he confirmed with a smile. "But more riding will surely cure it." When she smiled in return at his prescription, he added, "I'm happy you aren't angry with me anymore. I mean, about our conversation of the day before yesterday."

She hesitated. "In principle, I still am."

"Then I shall apologize."

"For saying what you did, or for believing it?" she asked.

"I think you misunderstood what I was trying to say."

"*I* don't think I did. You made it quite clear that—"

"Why do you distrust men so, Rosalyn?" he broke in.

Startled, she glanced at him sideways and tried to hedge. "I thought I told you once. Olivia's husband—"

"But you must realize not all husbands go philandering and desert their wives."

"Not just that. My father drank overmuch and—and abused my mother. So much so, we had to come to Torview Hall to live. And Gordon—"

"Gordon has his faults, but I would trust him with my life."

The conviction in his voice warmed her heart. "He . . . said as much about you," she admitted.

Encouraged by her thaw, he leaned forward in his saddle. "Rosalyn—"

She interrupted, looking away. "You're quite right, I ought not judge all men by two bad examples. It is quite as unfair as when men consider all women incompetent of thought. I—I have only used it as an excuse."

"Why did you?"

Another of his too candid questions, expecting a candid answer. But she knew, suddenly, that if she tried to tell him, she would break into weeping. Blinking away tears, she prodded her little mare into a canter, escaping his gaze.

He soon caught up to her, and because her newly sore muscles cried out against the jolts of a canter, she slowed to a walk again.

"Rosalyn . . ."

"Tell me about your wife," she said suddenly, gazing at him.

"My *wife*?"

"You never speak of her."

"I have had little occasion."

"Was she so different from English girls? What was she like, this American woman?"

He cocked an eyebrow at her. "That American woman was a Shawnee Indian, not much more than a child."

Rosalyn gasped. She knew next to nothing about "Red Indians," but she could not have been more shocked had he said he had married someone not quite human.

Suddenly her horse misstepped, jolting her harshly, and she winced. Worth, seeing the reaction, said, "Let's dismount and walk awhile. And I'll tell you how it came about."

"Very well." Her voice was faint, her energy suddenly drained. It seemed only a moment later that he was afoot and beside her, arms out to help her down. Her intense longing to feel those arms about her frightened her, and she didn't move.

"Come, I'll catch you," he urged, mistaking her hesitation.

She brought her right leg over the saddle hump with difficulty and let herself slide until his strong arms caught her, brought her gently to the ground, held her just a moment before releasing her. All at once her heart was beating heavily.

"What would Olivia say?" she murmured, trying to laugh. She was vividly aware that the road was entirely empty of passersby.

"That I've surely compromised you," he returned solemnly.

She flushed, took up her horse's reins, and moved ahead of him. Although hedgerows cast deep shadows across the path and wind nipped her cheeks, she was not conscious of cold. "What was your wife's name?" she asked at last.

"In English, her name meant Gentle Fawn."

"Did you speak her language?"

"Some. We understood one another well enough."

"And how did it all happen?" She stopped and turned, confronting him and the situation bravely.

"She was a—a gift to my stepfather from this Indian chief. She was an orphan girl of the tribe. To refuse to accept her would have been an insult to the chief, but to keep her for himself would not have set well with my mother." He spoke with his usual frankness, quite devoid of embarrassment.

"Understandably," she returned, with an admirable lack of embarrassment herself. But then, unable to meet his eyes, she turned and led her horse on ahead of him. "So you just—took her to wife, with no more thought than that?"

His voice resolutely pursued her. "Not at first. She traveled with us, acted as interpreter at times, as guide at others. She began serving us, doing the packing and cooking, whatever she could to please us. I came to depend on her, to care for her. And then I realized that she thought there was something wrong with her because I did not bed her. And so . . ."

His voice faded out on the obvious conclusion. "And so you did bed her," Rosalyn finished. "How very convenient it sounds. Doubtless the very thing Olivia's captain looked for when he took ship for South America."

"We were wed according to both white and Shawnee custom," Worth retorted, stung. "I loved her as I would have loved any white woman."

"Yet from interpreter and guide—roles of more equality—you made her into a mistress and a servant. She ended little better than your slave."

"She only behaved as her culture taught her to behave—to revere and serve men."

"Behavior not confined to Red Indian culture," Rosalyn pointed out. "Many English wives are little better than slaves, as well. And doubtless you'd expect the same from another woman."

She was aware that she was actively seeking another quarrel, and was put out of countenance by his laughter.

"Don't fear, Rosalyn, I would never mistake *you* for a slave!"

After an unsettling silence she managed coolly, "I was not aware I was implicated in this topic."

"You were not! Now wait a minute." Involuntarily, she stopped and faced him. "That's downright simple of you, ma'am," he said as he came abreast of her. Then, suddenly, he dropped his horse's reins and brought her, with dizzying swiftness, into the circle of his embrace.

His horse, left leaderless, moved on a few paces to investigate the edible properties of a clump of hare's-tail sedge, and her mare followed suit. Rosalyn did not notice. The hardness of his arms against her ribs had sent shock waves through her. His gaze seemed to take pleasure in the visible beating of her heart under the honey-velvet jacket. His lips stopped just short of claiming hers.

"When I kiss a lady, it means something," he murmured before he closed the distance.

The feel of his lips disturbed her even more this second time, for it was no gentleman's kiss he gave her. Determinedly possessive, it dazed and blinded her, as though a whirlwind had uprooted her from all that was familiar, spinning her into a void. Yet his arms supported her weakness, and after the first impulse, his lips gentled in their insistence, seeking a response. Meanwhile his hands caressed her back and shoulders, creating a cascade of sensation that sang from every nerve. Her response came, as irresistible as a tidal wave. Her arms answered his, her hands pressed hard against the solid lean muscles of his back, her lips gave back and sought that first harsh pressure of his—again. And all the time she marveled at the strength of this new desire and wondered where it might lead.

He released her slowly, surveyed her dazzled eyes, her parted lips, and said softly, "Yes, you *are* implicated, my Rosalyn."

She wrenched away from him in sudden distress, grasping for self-control. "Oh, you have complicated my life most unfairly," she cried out. She glanced about wildly for escape, and her heart sank. "The horses! Where are the horses? Now look what's happened!"

It turned out they had only wandered around a bend in the road, seeking forage. Worth laughed at her alarm and caught them easily, led hers back to her, and helped her mount. But the spell was broken. She rode a little ahead of him and barely spoke the rest of the way.

✔ TWELVE ✔

It had all happened as Rosalyn had dreamed and dreaded it might. And she must, somehow, quiet her pounding heart and consider everything rationally. She must not dwell on that possessive kiss and the astonishing sensations it had produced, though that was all she really wanted to dwell on.

Upon their return to Torview Hall, she had hoped to slip away to her room for a while to think, but in the front hall near the stairway she came upon Gordon, Evie, Olivia, and Bernell. Gordon was staring at a letter in his hand, and Olivia was saying severely, "Why didn't you tell us this at the beginning, Gordon? Here you've been home more than a month!"

"I thought he could put them off until I returned. I thought I need say nothing, and Grandfather wouldn't know." He looked up as Rosalyn appeared and addressed his next sentence to her. "Well, you said I ought to do it and be done with it. Roz. Now it seems I've no choice in the matter. This is from our solicitor in London. I must return immediately and find a way to repay my creditors to prevent the duns taking over my furniture and carriage."

Rosalyn was speechless and vaguely resentful that she must suddenly consider Gordon's problem just as she wished to consider her own. It was difficult to believe he had gone so far into debt in less than a year.

"I can still go with you, can't I, Gordie?" Evie was asking anxiously. "This won't cancel my trip to London with you, will it?"

Gordon looked annoyed, but only said, "If you can be ready by tomorrow morning."

"I'm sure . . . yes, I *will* be ready, even if I must stay up all night." Her eyes flew to Rosalyn's. "You'll help me get ready, won't you, Roz?"

"I've not yet made up my mind on this, Evie," Olivia warned.

"Oh, let her go," Bernell put in. "Surely there's no harm in it, since she's going with Gordon."

Maybe because it was Bernell who interceded, Olivia finally agreed. And it turned out Rosalyn had no time to mull things over, for she quickly found herself embroiled in Evie's preparations to depart. Evie needed her advice on selecting dresses, shoes, bags, hats, jewelry. Warned that she must be prepared for changes in the weather, she ordered muffs, scarves, and boots to be brought out of storage and added to the pile on her bed. A spot on her best dress must be worked out, torn lace repaired, stockings and undergarments searched for holes so that Molly could mend them, necessaries washed. The servants were sent scurrying for luggage and began the packing. Olivia helped little herself but spent the time debating whether Anna or Molly should accompany Evie as abigail, hairdresser, and chaperon. She finally decided that Molly, being older, would be the more responsible, and became increasingly cross as she pondered how they would get along without her.

Lord Clifton, who had grown used to leaving all decisions regarding his youngest granddaughter up to Olivia, had given his consent, but also took the opportunity to lecture Gordon at length on the virtue of staying financially solvent. He reluctantly agreed to pay for the post chaise himself (the idea of Evie or Gordon traveling by public mail coach was unthinkable) and dispatched servants to Ashburton to hire the chaise and pair from the London

Inn. Gordon, making his own hasty preparations in a far less sanguine frame of mind than his youngest sister, took out time to express regret that he must leave Worth behind, alone, to face Lord Whitbourne at Blackroy Manor. Lord Clifton, to dispel any awkwardnesses, assured the American that he was more than welcome to return to Torview Hall after the hunt and to stay as long as he wished.

They left within half an hour of each other the following morning. Evie and Gordon and their servants, in the largest post chaise to be had, with four horses and two postilions, took with them a mountain of luggage strapped to the top. Worth, on one of Lord Clifton's mounts, carried two changes of clothing and dress boots in saddlebags, strapped the flintlock to the saddle, and carried the directions to Blackroy Manor in his head.

Rosalyn wondered why his departure to a point less than five miles distant should seem to her like a voyage halfway around the world. Still, the memory of his words and his kiss remained, like a promise. When she recalled the moment she had confessed that her distrust of men was an excuse, she realized it was true—or, at least, it had become true since knowing Worth. Gradually, and without her quite realizing it, distrust of men had changed into a much more frightening distrust of her body to survive the natural consequences of marriage. Were her fears real? Could she have children, or would she be cheating any man she married (just supposing she changed her mind), either by insisting on remaining childless or by falling prey to the awful fate of permanent paralysis?

The muscles in her thighs and buttocks were sore from riding, but Olivia complained of the same discomfort. It was a normal reaction when one hadn't been on a horse for so long. How many other times had she and others taken alarm at what was only a normal reaction of her body? And if her advisers had been wrong in that, had they been wrong in other things as well? Did she truly not dare to have a child?

She spent sleepless nights remembering the details of that warning. Olivia had returned to Torview Hall after her husband's disappearance, red-eyed, keeping to her room, sullen when spoken to. "I'll never marry!" Rosalyn had cried in anguished sympathy to her mother.

"Perhaps it's best you don't," her mother had replied surprisingly. Then, haltingly, she had told Rosalyn about Dr. Ransom's speculations as she was recovering from the paralysis. Any severe strain might bring it back; any strain resulting in contraction of the muscles could, logically, paralyze those muscles again. A strain such as childbirth? her mother had asked him. Dr. Ransom had reluctantly agreed that childbirth might be just such a strain.

It was her mother's idea, then, agreed to by the doctor. Not a hard-and-fast rule. No one really knew. It was only "logical." But Dr. Ransom didn't know everything. Perhaps it only needed determination and the strengthening of her body to prove him wrong.

The peaceful days that followed Worth's departure only served to remind Rosalyn how much she had changed in the space of a few short weeks. Where she had once hoped for Worth Forrester's early departure so that her routine could return to normal, she now found her days empty of meaning without him. She could not concentrate on books nor on the music that usually absorbed her, and ended up wandering the paths of the garden or the byways of the estate in restless discontent. But even walking outdoors—which seemed less tiring the more she did it—held little charm without Worth's companionship.

Olivia noticed her lack of spirit and lost no time correctly guessing its cause. "Rosalyn, if I hadn't supposed you immune to men, I would say you have a *tendre* for a certain American visitor," she said one afternoon as they sewed together in the upstairs parlor.

Startled, Rosalyn looked up and blushed.

"I'm right, aren't I?" Olivia persisted.

Rosalyn pursed her lips and returned to her work.

"And you are even at a loss for words! Amazing."

"I understand such a thing may happen to the best of us," Rosalyn defended herself at last.

"Has he offered for you?"

"Would you object if he did?"

"It would be up to Grandfather, of course."

"But *you*, Olivia. What do you think of him?"

"I'll admit," Olivia said slowly, "that he seems a worthy enough gentleman, aside from his lack of style and his egalitarian ways. I suppose one could get used. . . . But Rosalyn," she broke off in amazement, "are you saying you'd consider an offer of marriage? You who were determined never to marry?"

Rosalyn met her sister's gaze with an unflustered candor. "With Worth Forrester, all my former objections seem . . . quite beside the point. I can scarce tell why. What do you think Grandfather would say?"

"If it turns out he is, indeed, Lord Whitbourne's nephew, implausible as it may seem, I don't see how he could possibly object to such a union. But Rosalyn . . ." Olivia hesitated, for once reluctant to throw cold water on her sister's quiet happiness. But her normal caution won. "Rosalyn, have you forgotten Dr. Ransom's warning? I thought that was the true reason you intended never to marry."

"I remember." Rosalyn grew very still and bit her lip. For a while she sewed in silence, looking intently at the stitches as though they demanded her full attention, yet aware Olivia awaited her response. Finally she said, "Suppose Dr. Ransom was wrong?"

"Why should he be wrong? He is a learned physician."

"But even so, there are some things he doesn't *know*."

"I'm sure that's true, but—"

"And he was wrong about refraining from exercise, wasn't he, Olivia? It hasn't hurt me one jot to dance, to ride, to take walks outdoors in the fresh air. Indeed, I feel better than I have for years. I have more appetite, and my right leg doesn't tire so quickly, so even if the foot remains the same, I walk better. The mishaps that occurred could have happened to anyone, couldn't they? I mean, you as well as I could turn an ankle on uneven ground. And when I became ill after Mama died, it did not mean a return of the paralysis."

"It might have."

"But it didn't! So I've concluded all that—that *fear* . . . has been imaginary. If I think I really am in health, and if I behave so, I will *be* so."

"I see Mr. Forrester has convinced you of it. But I must caution you—"

"No, Olivia, don't! You've cautioned me long enough, dear sister. From now on, I intend to be mistress of my own actions. I can't imagine why I didn't see before how . . . how *repressed* I was. Well, no more! You see before you a new woman. An independent woman. A woman who refuses to be frightened by gloomy prophecies."

Olivia frowned in amazement. "Well, all I can say is, I refuse to be responsible."

"And I refuse to allow you to be," Rosalyn said triumphantly. "So—we are agreed."

The Musical Society had not met that week, nor did they plan to meet the following week. With Evie in London, Bernell unusually occupied with a legal case, and Sir Harry away at Lord Whitbourne's hunt, there seemed little point in it. Rosalyn supposed she was the only one who regretted this, for the two lovebirds, Duncan and Melinda, did not need such stimulation for their happiness. But for her, the diversion would have helped pass the long dreary hours. Besides, she had, at long last, received a letter from Mr. Braham regarding Bernell's song.

After apologizing for the delay—he had been away in Europe—Mr. Braham expressed his delight with the music and his hope that he might sing it at a concert he was scheduled to give in Exeter for St. Nicholas's Day. Since he would be so near, he hoped to become personally acquainted with Mr. Mayhew then, and discuss with him the possibility of its being published.

It was fully as much as she had dreamed. Rosalyn hugged the letter to her with a little shiver of excitement and wondered how best to present the news to Bernell. She was still apprehensive of his reaction to her unauthorized use of his music, even though Braham's response had justified her faith in him.

Unexpectedly Bernell himself showed up that very afternoon, as Rosalyn, Olivia, and Lord Clifton lingered at the dinner table over fruit and wine. His rotund face was unusually serious, and he cut into Newton's introduction of him with, "I'm sorry to break into your meal like this, but I have important news. . . ."

Lord Clifton bade him be seated and motioned to Donald to bring him a glass of sherry. Bernell, facing Olivia, barely sipped it before coming to the point. "My dear, brace yourself. It seems your husband has been found."

Olivia's hand flew to her throat, and her wan complexion seemed to turn even paler. "Samuel? Wh-where? H-how . . . ?"

"He is alive," Bernell assured her, a frown furrowing his broad forehead. "And he is in England." He paused there and waited anxiously for her reaction, as though he must dole out the information bit by bit in case the whole story might overwhelm her.

"Go on, Bernell, go on," she said impatiently.

"Here, have some wine," Bernell recommended, pushing her goblet toward her. He took a large swallow of his own, but Olivia sat motionless, her mouth set in a grim line.

"He's in Plymouth, at the Horse and Groom. Not so far, you see. Unfortunately, he is wounded. There was a duel. The proprietor of the inn wrote me a letter, at Captain Fortescue's request. He believes he's dying and he wants to see you."

"D-dying?" Olivia's lips trembled. "But why were you notified instead of me?"

"He . . . wanted me to break the news gently."

"How kind of him." Olivia's voice was dry with sarcasm.

"So—I am to go to Plymouth to attend a dying man I've not seen these three years past." Her tone began a sharp, angry rise. "What does he want of me? My God, what does he expect? That I'll forgive him for abandoning me? Oh, I suppose that's it! He was ever inclined to plead for forgiveness, whether he warranted it or no."

"But Olivia," Rosalyn remonstrated gently, "if he's *dying* . . ."

"At least, m'dear, you'll know your true status at last," Lord Clifton put in. "As to whether you ought go to him— it's a hard thing, but I fear it's your wifely duty."

"I shall be most happy to accompany you," Bernell said in a low voice. "If you so decide."

They exchanged glances. Rosalyn could not fail to see the pity and love in his eyes. Olivia's gaze, frozen at first in resentment, finally softened, and she reached for his hands across the table. "Oh, Bernell, what would I do without you? Yes, I must go, mustn't I? And if you go with me, it will make the task much less difficult."

It was the closest she had ever come to admitting her dependence on him. Rosalyn, swallowing tears, did not tell Bernell of Mr. Braham's letter after all.

Bernell and Olivia left early the following day, in Bernell's chaise and accompanied by his manservant. As they said goodbye, Bernell asked Rosalyn, "Have you or Lord Clifton heard from Worth since he went to Blackroy Manor?" When she admitted they had not, he said, "I hope all goes well for him. Don't you think he'd send a message if he had learned anything positive about his parentage?"

Once they were gone, Rosalyn found herself dwelling on the uneasiness implicit in his questions. Bernell's old suspicions of Lord Whitbourne's character and motives, which she had once dismissed, now seemed to have possible truth. It also occurred to her that any English gentleman as smitten as Worth Forrester had appeared to be on their ride back from Wistman's Wood would have deluged his lady with love letters as soon as they were forced to part. Even Captain Fortescue, courting Olivia, had had occasion to write such missives. But, of course, Worth Forrester was no English gentleman in the usual sense, and she had little notion what to expect from him.

Still, the suspicion grew in her that Worth might not be enjoying a convivial English hunt after all, but be in some difficulty or even danger. This feeling was reinforced by the weather, which began to change for the worse about noon. Morning's pale sun gradually gave way to a leaden sky, which, like some great dense blanket, descended over the hills of Dartmoor. When Rosalyn took her morning walk to the stables, the wind stabbed through her woolen cloak and velvet bonnet and the stableman predicted snow on the moor by midafternoon.

Because the weather was so unpleasant, Rosalyn shortened her walk and was surprised, on returning to the house, to see Lady Harriet's landau at the front door. Lady Harriet was just descending from the conveyance, disdaining the help of her footman, who always stood by, just in case. She called out on seeing Rosalyn.

"My dear girl, I'm surprised to see you out on this blustery day!"

"And I to see you, Lady Harriet," Rosalyn returned with a laugh, hurrying to take her hand.

"Oh, I never let the weather stop me," Lady Harriet said with a shrug of her shoulders. "But I daresay we may be in for it soon. Is your sister at home?"

"Olivia? No, I'm sorry to say she's not. Pray come in and have some tea, and I'll tell you about it."

Lady Harriet's subsequent surprise at the resurrection of Captain Samuel Fortescue was almost, but not quite, equal to her disappointment that Olivia was not available to see the completed architectural plans for the charity hospital, which she had brought with her to take to Lord Whitbourne for his approval.

"I knew I could not get Edward into Ashburton for any reason whatsoever while his hunt is in progress, and I simply could not wait another week for the hunt to end. The architect is eager to return to London and wants to know if his plans are to be accepted before he leaves, of course. And so I decided to beard the lion in his den, myself." She gave a little laugh at her own metaphor, and Rosalyn, pouring tea, thought, how apt.

"I did want Olivia to see the plans, since she has contributed so much to the project. And I intended to invite her to come with me to Blackroy. She has often spoken of wanting to see the place. Indeed, it has a number of interesting features." She stopped for breath and a sip of tea.

"Olivia has told me so much of the charity hospital, I confess I am as interested as she is," Rosalyn ventured. "Do you suppose I might see the plans?"

Lady Harriet was delighted at the prospect of showing off her pet project and had her footman return to the carriage for the plans, which were then spread out on a large table in the library. Rosalyn's enthusiasm and intelligent questions delighted her even further. After expounding on the salient features of the hospital for half an hour—its receiving room, its examining room, its several wards, its kitchen, its supply cupboards, its offices for doctors and administrators—Lady Harriet, remarking on how unusually fit Rosalyn seemed to be these days, found it most natural to suggest she go with her to Blackroy Manor in Olivia's place.

Hiding her eagerness, Rosalyn agreed, if Lady Harriet would give her time to explain the situation to Lord Clifton, receive his permission, and ready herself for the trip.

Lady Harriet returned that she had all the time in the world but hoped Rosalyn might limit her share of it to half an hour or so. And she might be wise to plan an overnight stay in case the weather worsened as much as they expected.

Some forty-five minutes later they were on their way, with footwarmers and lap robes to ward off the cold, and the jointed top of the landau closed snugly over them to keep out the wind, though Lady Harriet's footman and maid, in the dickey, fared less warmly. Rosalyn wore her warmest pelisse, to which had recently been added a collar and front trim of beaver fur, made from Worth's gift.

Over an hour later they passed through Blackroy Village's narrow lanes. Rosalyn, remembering Bernell's accusations, noticed that the white cob cottages were indeed in poor repair, the thatched roofs needing replacement. Some windows were covered with nothing more than paper, and chimneys were crumbling. On the other hand, an occasional building of sandstone, home of some merchant or steward, looked prosperous and well kept. One such building, Lady Harriet pointed out, was formerly a school for laborers' children, established by Lord Whitbourne's father-in-law, Lord Broughton. It was closed now for want of a schoolmaster. Lord Whitbourne did not favor the education of the peasantry. "I have not been able to convince him otherwise," Lady Harriet said sadly. "Lord Broughton was a great one for charities, and I know he'd have favored the hospital. As for his daughter, Edward's poor wife, I always thought if anyone could turn Edward from selfish interests, it would have been dear Angelina. He doted on her. Unfortunately, it was not to be. One cannot understand why some people are taken so young when they might do great good in the world."

"It's a pity there were no children," Rosalyn said.

"It is indeed. I fear that early tragedy in his life is what has made my brother so cynical and stiff-necked. But I still insist he has some goodness at heart. It just takes a bit of prodding to get at it."

"Obviously, you have succeeded as well as anyone could, Lady Harriet," Rosalyn said, "for he has taken an interest in the hospital."

"Yes, I must give him credit for that," Lady Harriet admitted.

Then Rosalyn dared bring up what had been on her mind all along. "Lady Harriet, I had occasion recently to visit Totnes and look into the parish records of your family.

And I noticed there was no death date for the child who would have been your eldest brother, Daniel. What happened to him?"

Lady Harriet looked startled, then bemused. For a few seconds Rosalyn thought she was offended by her presumption, and would give no answer at all. Finally she said, "Ah, that strikes a sore spot in the family's history—and especially in my own heart, for Daniel and I were very close. There was only a year's difference in our ages, you know, and I loved him dearly. When he was in his early twenties, Daniel quarreled bitterly with our father—so bitterly he left home and none of us ever saw him again. To this day I don't know if he's dead or alive."

"And . . . where did he go? Do you know?" Rosalyn asked, her heart in her throat.

"He went to America, I do know that, for I received a letter a year or two later. It was the only letter I ever received from him."

"Lady Harriet . . ." Rosalyn tried to suppress her excitement. "Did it not occur to you that Mr. Forrester, who has been visiting us, might be that Daniel's son? For Mr. Forrester's father's name was Daniel, too. And Forrester was the maiden name of your grandmother, Lydia, who died when your mother was born. And the dates are right. Worth knows his father was born in 1759."

Lady Harriet turned guarded eyes on Rosalyn. "Yes," she said, "of course it occurred to me, almost immediately I saw him. There is even a certain . . . air about Mr. Forrester that reminds me of my dear lost brother. I am almost certain the young man is my nephew."

"Then why did you not say so?"

Lady Harriet's eyes went to her white ermine muff, then out the window, away from Rosalyn. "It was . . . because of Edward. I had no idea how he'd react." Her voice was tense and hesitant, so different from its usual authority that Rosalyn was startled. "You must know it is a very disturbing situation for him to confront the son of the brother who would once have been heir to his title. And he can be a violent man—not in ordinary circumstances, of course, but when aroused. And so I thought it better to say nothing until I knew how Edward would receive the news."

"Then Lord Whitbourne knows, too?"

"Yes, dear, he knows. I told him almost at once."

"And what was his reaction?"

"I have no idea. I only know he wished to get acquainted with Mr. Forrester before making any decision. He told me he would invite Mr. Forrester to the hunt."

"Yes, he did that. Mr. Forrester has been gone a week."

"Well, then." Lady Harriet relaxed her shoulders in a move like a shiver and smiled. "Doubtless it is all settled by now, and we will learn the results once we have arrived."

Beyond the village, a gatekeeper admitted them to a long avenue guarded on either side by rows of spruce trees. Between them Rosalyn caught occasional glimpses of a park adorned with open-air pavilions, Grecian statues, and artificially created springs and grottos. At the end of the avenue, a massive arch of pink granite framed their view of an immense, still-distant gray stone house. As they rode under the arch, Rosalyn saw the first snowflakes, driven by a harsh wind, light against the windows of the carriage.

❧ THIRTEEN ❧

Lord Whitbourne's butler, greeting them with unnecessary pomposity, Rosalyn thought, said his lordship and guests were still on the hunt and were not expected for another hour.

"Then you may serve us tea in the east drawing room, Jenkins," Lady Harriet said briskly, her manner more than a match for the supercilious butler, "and see that Miss Archer's and my valises are taken to appropriate rooms. We will doubtless stay the night, for the weather looks threatening."

"I was not informed your ladyship would be arriving. I regret there are no rooms ready."

"Well, see that they are made ready, my good man. We will make do with what you can provide."

The Palladian-style manor house had been impressive enough from the outside, its two-storied colonnaded portico reminding Rosalyn of a Greek temple. Inside she was further awed by an enormous central hall tiled in black and white squares, a vaulted ceiling with a profusion of mythic carvings, heraldic banners rioting over the door, priceless tapestries on the wall, and suits of armor standing about like gleaming guardians. From there Jenkins led them to a wood-paneled room with oriental carpeting in dark blues and scarlet, and furniture of gilt and red velvet. A roaring fire in the fireplace dominated the far wall.

Rosalyn, feeling chilled as much by the atmosphere as the cold ride, limped a little stiffly over to it to warm her hands, and wondered if coming here had been wise, after all. Jenkins told Lady Harriet the tea would arrive shortly, bowed, and withdrew. Lady Harriet went to a window, pulled open a velvet drape, and looked outside.

"It is indeed snowing. Well, all to the good. It may cut short their hunt for today."

"I hope we have not incommoded Lord Whitbourne," Rosalyn said. "By planning to stay the night, I mean."

"Not at all. What are two more people when he has a houseful of two dozen? As for rooms, I happen to know there are thirty bedchambers, so don't fret, my dear. And Edward has plenty of servants."

And what would happen, Rosalyn wondered, if Worth inherited all this? How would he deal with a house with thirty bedchambers and a park full of pagan statues, he who was used to sleeping under the forest roof or, at most, in log cabins and Indian teepees? All at once the idea of Worth Forrester as a future Marquess of Whitbourne was so richly comic she nearly laughed aloud.

Lady Harriet, ever inquisitive, might have asked what made her smile, but a servant entered with a tea cart, distracting her. The two visitors watched in silence as the uniformed maid, an uncommonly pretty girl, laid out a silver tray with a steaming pot and two cups, milk and sugar, and a plate of sandwiches on the low table before the fireplace. She looked neither to right nor left, nervously fumbled the napkins, rattled the teacups in their saucers, and nearly spilled the milk.

"You're new, aren't you, girl?" Lady Harriet observed.

"Yes, mum."

"What is your name?"

"Uh . . . Rebecca, mum."

"And where are you from, Rebecca?"

"From Staverton, mum."

"I am Lord Whitbourne's sister, so you may address me as 'my lady.' "

"Yes, mu—my lady." The girl cast a desperate glance toward the door, then stood before Lady Harriet, eyes lowered, and clutched at her apron, rolling and unrolling an edge of it between her fingers.

"Never mind. You may go. I shall do the pouring." The girl bolted in relief, leaving the door ajar. "My word!" Lady Harriet exclaimed. "What has happened to Edward's staff? I never knew him to have so untrained a girl. She didn't even give me a proper curtsy. Not that I give a hoot about curtsies, but one expects a certain standard."

"Perhaps he hired extra help for the duration of the hunt," Rosalyn suggested, reaching for a sandwich. She was suddenly hungry. Feeling sorry for the poor awkward maid (no matter how pretty) had taken her mind off her own uneasiness. Even the Marquess of Whitbourne had servant problems. She must remember to tell Olivia that.

"Lady Harriet, may I ask you a question?"

"Ask away, my dear."

"When your brother Daniel quarreled with his father . . . what was it about?"

Lady Harriet eyed her shrewdly. "I do believe, my dear, you are showing an uncommon amount of interest in young Forrester's past."

"For a man to come halfway around the world to seek his father's kin *is* uncommon, don't you think? I find it exciting to suppose he has a close connection to Lord Whitbourne—and to yourself."

"It is just as well you said 'suppose.' If Lord Whitbourne refuses to acknowledge the relationship, and Mr. Forrester cannot prove it exists . . ."

"Oh, but do you think he will be so indifferent? Wor— Mr. Forrester wouldn't dispute Lord Whitbourne's claim to the title."

"Wouldn't he? Well, then, that is all to the good. Don't

look so distressed, my dear. I'm sure it can be worked out to everyone's satisfaction. After all, we are reasonable people, are we not? I shall do my best to convince Edward to do his duty to his nephew."

"Thank you, ma'am. And about that old quarrel . . ."

"How can I tell what it was about? I was not present, and my father would never speak of it. Indeed, once Daniel had left for good, we were none of us to speak his name again in my father's presence."

"How difficult it must have been for you . . . and for your mother."

"Yes," Lady Harriet agreed, staring into the near distance over the rim of her teacup. "It was an unhappy situation. And all too common, I fear. My father had a way of putting people's backs up. Except for Edward. He doted on Edward, and indulged him in everything. I often thought it a ruinous policy, but I could say nothing."

By the time Lord Whitbourne's guests began to return from the hunt, large snowflakes had been falling for half an hour and were speedily covering the ground. Rosalyn and Lady Harriet heard the men's boisterous voices, cheerfully cursing the weather, calling for spirits and hot baths, but none of them entered the east parlor to encounter the two female visitors. More and more Rosalyn had the feeling that they were intruders in a male-only world and would not be welcomed by their host.

She was sure of it when, at last, Lord Whitbourne appeared in the doorway and exclaimed, "Good God, Harriet! Jenkins told me you were here and I couldn't believe my ears. What is it all about?" He strode into the room to confront her, ablaze with an angry energy, his color high, his hair awry. He carried his hunting hat in hand, and its curled brim and the shoulders of his hunting jacket were white with melting snow.

"Hush, Edward. Is that any way to speak to two ladies who have honored you with their presence?"

He ignored her playful tone and jerked a brief angry bow in Rosalyn's direction. "Madam," he acknowledged; then he returned his gaze to Lady Harriet. "So—what is it, then?"

"I have brought the architectural plans for the hospital for your approval. Mr. Landis couldn't wait another week before returning to London."

"You drove all the way here in this weather for that? You are a fool, Harriet. How do you expect to get home again?"

"Oh, we shall stay the night, of course. I have already so informed Jenkins."

"The devil!" He ran his hand through his thick, damp hair. "Well, we shall talk later. I must bathe and change. Make yourselves at home—but then, I see you already have."

With another short bow he turned and would have left them, but Rosalyn called out, "Lord Whitbourne!"

He halted and waited. "Yes, Miss Archer?"

"Mr. Forrester—has he returned with you?"

The marquess turned fully toward her. "I've no way of knowing yet who has returned and who hasn't. We don't hunt in packs, Miss Archer, like wolves. But we will all assemble at supper." He about-faced without waiting for her response and vanished.

Not long afterward, Rebecca returned to escort Rosalyn and Lady Harriet to their hastily prepared rooms. They turned out to be two small bedchambers on the third floor, reached after a bewildering number of turns and long corridors. The accommodations were plain but adequate, Rosalyn thought, and a cheerful blaze had already been set in the small fireplace to warm her room. Lady Harriet's "Hmph!" of disdain from across the hall proclaimed her less than satisfied with her portion, but she made no further complaint.

After changing into an emerald-green dinner dress with

long India silk sleeves, a dress Anna had helped her make over recently, Rosalyn's eyes went to the single window, hung with white muslin, which faced north. The moor surrounding Blackroy Manor now lay under a white mantle, but any sense of its distances was obscured by the rapidly falling snow. Indeed, the whole outdoors appeared one vast white void, with sky invisibly melding into horizon in the growing dusk. Soon it would be dark. Rosalyn could not help remembering Gordon's warning to Worth scarcely more than a week ago that one could easily get lost on the moor. With darkness and any familiar landmark made exotic by the new snowfall, even someone as perceptive as Worth might easily lose his way.

Her sense of disquiet was jolted further at supper when her eyes quickly sorted out the two dozen men present at the table. Worth was not here. Lord Whitbourne, having recovered his temper and his manners, bowed to her in solemn courtesy and offered her the place on his right. Lady Harriet was requested to act as hostess at the other end of the table, and they were seated amid many flattering comments about the unexpected pleasure of having two females to grace their table. Rosalyn suspected the compliments were false.

She recognized two of them—Sir Harry Havisham, who smiled at her from halfway down the table, and Lord Buckleigh, who had attended the ball in Ashburton. But the others, introduced as they awaited the first course, were strangers from all sorts of places: Lord Wynne from County Cork, Ireland, Sir Romney Wharton from the Isle of Guernsey, Lord MacLachlan of Inverness, Scotland. Lord Whitbourne's circle of acquaintances was amazingly broad. Rosalyn suspected they were business associates rather than personal friends.

"My lord," she said to her host as soon as a suitable pause occurred, "I do not see Mr. Forrester. Forgive my concern, but he is a guest here, is he not?"

"I am concerned as well," Lord Whitbourne admitted.

"He has not yet returned. Lord Buckleigh saw him last, only a few minutes before I gave the signal to give up the chase. We had had word of a sighting of roe deer come down from the north, and were on their track when the weather made it impractical."

"But are you doing nothing to find him?"

"I have just sent my head huntsman out with several others who know the country well. But Mr. Forrester was in company of my most trusted whipper-in. I should not worry too much."

"I'm surprised you hunted at all today, with the threat of snow."

The first appearance of a smile touched the marquess's lips. "Miss Archer, you do not understand men. They love such challenges. Actually, this weather is a most opportune time to hunt, for it drives the animals away from the more remote heights and toward us."

She turned back to her soup, but her recent good appetite had vanished and she could do no more than sip it. Trying to make conversation with her right-hand neighbor, she scarcely noticed that the servants waiting on the table were maids, not footmen, until Lady Harriet called out from her end of the table, "Lord Whitbourne, you seem to suffer from a want of menservants today."

"During the hunt, Lady Harriet, my footmen have other duties to perform. These young women were especially hired to take their place."

Lord Whitbourne's good-natured explanation seemed to provoke some veiled amusement among his guests. The serving maids were very young, Rosalyn observed, and all were uncommonly pretty, like Rebecca, who had brought their tea. They wore pert white caps and aprons over dark red dresses trimmed with pale blue collars and cuffs—the colors of Lord Whitbourne's livery. It might all be perfectly proper, but Rosalyn suspected uneasily that it was not, and the unusual pattern only added to her anxiety about Worth.

If Lady Harriet was skeptical of her brother's domestic

arrangements, she said nothing, but plunged into questions about the week's hunt to her neighbors. Grateful for the security of her presence, Rosalyn tried halfheartedly to do likewise. Conversation—or at least listening to it—was possible, but eating was not, not even this beautifully prepared procession of crab, truffled rice, stuffed pork, and woodcock and pheasant in cream sauce. Everything was washed down with an abundance of hock and sherry, readily supplied by the serving girls, and it was not long before the lord from Cork, on Rosalyn's right, was speaking less and less coherently, and she realized that he preferred to contemplate his glass rather than talk or listen to her.

Lord Whitbourne seemed to suffer no such impediment, but fielded conversation with various persons in earshot with the ease of an accomplished host. Watching him and observing at close hand the harsh, formidable angles of his face, which softened only slightly in conviviality, Rosalyn felt again the incomprehensible attraction of his self-assured power, even as it made her increasingly ill at ease.

After the dessert of fruit, cheese, and blancmange was brought, and wine glasses once more filled, Lord Whitbourne dismissed the serving girls. Soon afterward a footman entered, bent low, and murmured something into Lord Whitbourne's ear. Some flicker of the heavy eyelids and tightening of the lips warned Rosalyn of the import of the message before the marquess turned to her and said in a low voice, "I'm sorry, Miss Archer, it appears the search party was unable to locate Mr. Forrester and returned without him. The wind rendered further search impossible. Also, my whipper-in, Roth, just arrived and says he was somehow separated from Forrester near the start of the storm and hasn't seen him since."

Rosalyn stared at him in shock for a few moments. The sympathy in his voice did not extend to his hooded eyes, which seemed to mock her distress. With a little cry she pushed back her chair, rose, and hurried from the room without a backward glance. She had no idea where she was going or why, simply that her agitation was suddenly too great to bear in so public a place. Taking a wrong turn outside the door and blinded by sudden tears, she wandered down a corridor that turned into another, narrower one, where only a single candle sputtered in a wall sconce to show the way.

Finally realizing her mistake, she stopped and turned full circle. Wiping the blur from her eyes with her pocket handkerchief, she saw an open door ahead, from which pale light drifted into the corridor. She went forward again. If a servant was about, she could at least ask directions.

But the room—a large one with comfortable plush settees, chairs, and small incidental tables—was empty of people. She continued on with no sense of purpose, enveloped in a vague alarm, until she reached a large closed door. To her left a stairwell yawned, with stairs that led both up and down. She heard female laughter and voices below, and saw the flicker from oil lamps on the wall of the landing.

"Not yet," she heard one say. "We maun' wait t' be called tonight till the two lydies be safe asleep." The mocking sarcastic words were followed by a chorus of female laughter.

Her face suddenly hot and her heart pounding heavily, Rosalyn leaned against the wall and shut her eyes. For a moment she could not move; then, struggling to overcome an almost tangible sensation of decadence, she took several deep breaths and brushed new moisture from her eyes. Dare she descend those stairs, confront those laughing girls of dubious character, and demand to know what was going on?

She was further alarmed to hear footsteps climbing the stairs. In a moment, one of the serving maids, minus cap and apron, appeared on the landing and stopped stock-still to stare at her. At the same time the big door at the end of the corridor opened, admitting a blast of cold air, a wave of windswept snowflakes, and a snow-covered figure.

Both Rosalyn and the girl, diverted from confronting each other, turned to the door. Rosalyn stared hard as the snowman closed it behind him. With a joyful cry she threw herself into his arms.

"Rosalyn!" Worth's amazed cry was muffled against her lips. But the cold wetness of his buckskins through her thin dinner dress recalled her to self-conscious shyness, and she backed away from him.

"Would ye look at ter proper lydy!" came the girl's scornful voice, followed by a titter.

Rosalyn turned quickly in outrage. The girl stood with her arms akimbo, a derisive smile on her face. "Quick!" Rosalyn ordered. "Find someone to take hot water to Mr. Forrester's room at once, and bring him a good stout drink!"

The girl remained unmoving, her eyes stony. "What d'ye think I am, ma'am?"

"I know well enough what you are, but do it anyway— and before he catches his death!" As she spoke, Rosalyn had closed the distance between them. Angered by the girl's sullen immobility, she reached out, turned her by her shoulders, and gave her an impatient little shove.

"Don't be pushy, naow, I'm goin' all right!" The girl descended the stairs, hips swinging. Worth burst into hearty laughter.

"Rosalyn, you are a caution! Where did you drop from, the moon?"

She whirled back to face him. "Oh, Worth, I was so worried! What happened to you?"

"I got lost. It's a long story. Meanwhile . . ."

He shook the wet snow from his sleeves, peeled off his gloves, and blew on his fingers. His face was dark with cold and wind, and snowflakes still clung like hoarfrost to his eyelashes.

"Yes, you must warm yourself," Rosalyn said anxiously. "Oh, but I've so much to tell you!"

"And I, you." His glance indicated the stairway and the vanished girl. "You've entered a den of iniquity, Miss Archer," he said soberly.

"I'd suspected as much," Rosalyn returned.

∽✦ FOURTEEN ∽✦

"For my part, I believe young Forrester is our nephew, and you may as well admit it with good grace, Edward," Lady Harriet said in her usual decisive tone.

"My dear sister, as always your heart dominates your head. In my opinion, we have absolutely no proof of any relationship at this point," Lord Whitbourne returned. His tone was amiable enough but his eyes were hard. Rosalyn, sitting opposite them in one of the gilded Louis Quatorze chairs in Lord Whitbourne's private study, listened with a properly passive face and a sinking heart.

It was nearly two hours since Worth had returned from the moor, and they were waiting for him to join them in what Lord Whitbourne called "a civil discussion of the situation." It had been apparent to Rosalyn from the beginning that even with Lady Harriet as an ally, Worth's battle for recognition as a Whitbourne would not be an easy one.

"What have you shown me?" Lord Whitbourne continued. "That Forrester's father was named Daniel and he emigrated from Devonshire about the same time our brother of the same name left home, and that they were born in the same year. Coincidence, surely, but no proof. Daniel is not an uncommon name, and more than one Devonshire man may have emigrated to America in 1782."

"Ah, but you forget the resemblance, which to me is quite convincing."

"You are certain you recall the features, nay, the very mannerisms, of a brother you have not seen for nearly thirty years? You are an amazing woman, Harriet, but I must respectfully doubt such a memory."

"There is the letter Daniel wrote me from Virginia two years after he left us. Virginia is where Mr. Forrester was born."

"Have you reread it recently?"

"No," Lady Harriet admitted after a considerable pause. "I have looked for it, but I cannot seem to find it."

"I beg your pardon, my lord," Rosalyn put in, "but it may ease your mind to know that Mr. Forrester is not one jot interested in being Marquess of Whitbourne. He is only interested in acquiring a comfortable living for his mother and himself, since she has been rendered penniless. Surely you could do as much for your only nephew."

Lord Whitbourne turned his hard eyes upon her. "You have a personal interest in this young American, Miss Archer?"

Rosalyn blushed and wished she had not spoken. As she tried to frame a reply, Jenkins showed Worth into the room. He looked none the worse for his experience on the moor, the details of which Rosalyn had yet to learn. But looking closely into the countenance that, she now freely admitted to herself, she loved more than any other on earth, she detected a stern new resolve, and wondered what had caused it.

Worth bowed to everyone all around, took the seat Lord Whitbourne indicated, and replied to his host that, yes, his late meal had been more than adequate, and his limbs were now fully restored to warmth.

"I am most distressed," Lord Whitbourne said, "that you needed to face such an ordeal." Worth merely inclined his head in acknowledgment. "Roth informed me that a sudden blinding swirl of snow separated you when you were not more than twenty feet apart, and he never saw you again."

"That is odd, sir," Worth returned. "I could have sworn

Roth deliberately lagged behind me and then, when I paused at one point to allow him to catch up, he had disappeared. It was when I retraced my steps to find him that I got muddled."

"I shall certainly speak to him about this," Lord Whitbourne said severely.

"Will you, sir?" Worth's flat tone showed such unmistakable skepticism that Rosalyn, startled, glanced from one man to the other. The marquess's eyes narrowed briefly, but he ignored the insinuation.

"Now then," Lord Whitbourne said briskly, "we have gathered, as I told you, to discuss our supposed relationship. Forrester, when you asked me several days ago if you might be my nephew, I was dubious, and I'll confess I am not yet convinced of it. However, my sister here believes you are, indeed, our brother Daniel's son and heir."

Worth's glance went to Lady Harriet. "I am grateful, ma'am. Do you have proof, then?"

"I might have, if I can find it. A letter Daniel wrote from Virginia two years after he left home. In it he told of his marriage and the birth of a son. And I could guess that son was you, but to be perfectly honest, I don't recall any names."

"I have a letter my father wrote my mother, and a certificate of christening, signed by both parents," Worth said. "Are there other examples of Daniel's handwriting available here that could be compared to my samples?"

"All that may be completely unnecessary," Lord Whitbourne said. "According to Miss Archer, you have no interest in my title, only in a comfortable living for you and your mother. I'm sure I would be most happy to find something that would satisfy you in that respect."

Rosalyn was surprised that Worth didn't reply with his usual genial gratitude. Instead, after a lengthy pause, he said, "I'm sorry, sir, but I've decided that is no longer acceptable. Should I really be the son of Daniel Whitbourne, and should I still have the legal right as his heir to claim the title, I will do so."

Rosalyn gasped and held her breath. Lady Harriet frowned at her for misleading them, and Lord Whitbourne's brows contracted as he glanced at the floor before him. When he looked up, they had smoothed as though by force of will.

"Come now, Forrester, there is no use in your becoming antagonistic. I had hoped we might come to an amicable settlement without need for proofs, one way or another, simply as a gesture of goodwill."

"If I can't prove my case, I'll go away and not bother you further," Worth said firmly. "But if I'm legally Marquess of Whitbourne, I'll take steps to be so recognized."

With an almost imperceptible alteration of expression, the marquess changed his approach. "Then I must warn you that being an American citizen, you may not be eligible for the title. And even if you are, it is highly likely my father cut Daniel out of the inheritance, as a consequence of their quarrel."

"Then you know of the quarrel?" Worth countered. "Do you know the reason for it?"

"As a twelve-year-old, I was not privy to the event or the reason behind it," Lord Whitbourne returned. "As a matter of fact, I rarely saw Daniel in my youth, for I was at Eton when he left home, and had been since my sixth year. Our lives coincided only on holidays." His eyes narrowed. "All that aside, why are you so determined to take from me what has been mine for over twenty years? Or is such acquisitiveness a part of the New World character?"

His dry sarcasm heightened the tension in the room in an almost tangible way. Lady Harriet's face registered shock at the hostility in his words, and Rosalyn unconsciously put her hand to her lips. Worth's generous mouth became grim, and his gray eyes as relentless as those of the marquess. He stared back at Lord Whitbourne for a long moment before answering. Neither man's gaze wavered from the other.

Finally he said, "I only seek my birthright, as you might do in my place. The loss of your title will not mean that much to you. As I understand it, you have made your own acquisitions and are a rich man independent of your original inheritance."

"But what good is a title to an American?" Lord Whitbourne asked with a sneer. "Don't you believe in the great concept of equality for all men?"

Worth seemed to relax a little. He even shrugged. "It works well enough on the frontier, but the stakes are different here. I understand titles are an unfailing entree into English society. We'll need that—my mother and I—if we are to settle here."

His response seemed to mollify Lord Whitbourne, whose face, too, relaxed a little. "But you make it exceedingly difficult for me, my friend," he confessed. "What would you have me do?"

"I should think that is quite obvious, Edward," Lady Harriet interposed. "We must honor this young man's claim, if it's a true one."

Lord Whitbourne's eyes flashed anger, quickly masked. "Still, I won't move an inch without proof of Forrester's connection to us."

"I will find it," Worth said promptly. "Somehow."

"I will look again for that letter," Lady Harriet promised him.

"And I," Lord Whitbourne said, "will look into the contents of our father's will and consult my solicitor in Dartmouth. You might be interested to know, Forrester, just what you would be getting with that title. I'll have Bottersley draw up a list of what holdings go with the title, and we can meet again when that is accomplished."

"In a neutral place—such as Ashburton?" Worth asked.

"Very well, in Ashburton. I must insist that whatever proofs you come up with be subject to the scrutiny of an expert. And there will be all sorts of legalities to be got through."

Worth bowed acknowledgment. Lord Whitbourne, continuing to assume a genial mask, rose and poured them each a small glass of sherry from his liquor cabinet, and proposed a toast to Worth's prosperity. Worth replied tightly with a toast to the marquess's good fortune.

Lord Whitbourne then left, and Lady Harriet, recalling belatedly that the object of her visit had been to show her brother the hospital plans, hurried after him, leaving Rosalyn and Worth alone in the study.

It was several long moments before either of them moved or spoke. Rosalyn stared into Worth's eyes and saw them gradually soften, saw his body relax its rigid control. Finally he said, "All this was not exactly what I anticipated when I left Virginia."

They grinned at each other, then moved together on mutual impulse. As he grasped her hands she said, "Why did you do it? Why did you change your mind like that—about the title?"

"I was considering it for several days. But after today . . ." He dropped her hands to draw her into his arms. It seemed so natural a gesture, she hardly thought of her response as surrender. She simply put her own arms around his waist and hugged his big body to her as tightly as she could.

"Thank God you're safe," she murmured.

His lips were in her hair. "One would almost suspect you of loving me, after all."

She had never learned to play the coquette, so she said, in a voice muffled by his frockcoat, "Your suspicions might well be correct, sir . . . after all."

His hands tightened on her shoulders, then cupped her face so he could gaze into her eyes. She waited long, almost unbearable moments, but the kiss she expected never came. Instead he said, "We must talk, but not here. Come with me." He took her hand to lead her from the room.

"Where are we going?"

His swift glance was amused. "My bedchamber."

Olivia's predictable outrage echoed in Rosalyn's head. Young ladies who go to gentlemen's bedchambers do not maintain their virtue—or, at least, the outward appearance of virtue. In the same moment Rosalyn rejected the convention of appearances, realizing without further deliberation that she could trust Worth utterly, though she could not have said how she knew. She made no protest.

They hurried along the corridor, passed a drawing room where a few men were bent intently over gaming tables, climbed a wide staircase silenced by heavy dark carpeting, and took another wide corridor where gilded mirrors reflected their swift passage and candles flickered from weighty chandeliers. They met no one, but behind the closed doors they passed Rosalyn heard the dual tones of male and female voices. Movements, murmurs, laughter, other noises whose meaning she could only guess at. A chill of uneasiness crawled up her back. Worth had spent the whole week here, among these . . .

He was gripping her hand harder, walking faster, until her lame foot rebelled and she had to protest. "Wait, Worth, not so fast!"

Just then he stopped abruptly and plunged to the right, into a room whose only light came from a blazing hearth. He sat her down before the fire in a green damask elbow chair and pulled up a matching straight chair, until they sat almost knee to knee. The firelight burnished his profile, turned his hair to the palest gold, emphasized the hollows under his cheekbones, the cleft in his chin, the set line of his jaw. The smell of burning oak logs, pleasantly pungent, became one with the scene, so that ever after the odor of burning oak would remind her of this big, resolute man to whom she had lost her heart.

"Now," he said, leaning forward and taking her hands in his again. "You asked why I changed my mind. Isn't it obvious, if you only look about you?"

An unaccountable skepticism suddenly seized her. "You mean the 'den of iniquity' you spoke of, Worth?" she asked caustically. "I'm certainly not so naive I don't realize what is going on here. However, since the marquess is a widower and has no wife to turn to, you doubtless would consider it unjust of me if I expected him to be celibate, the way widows are expected—"

She broke off as a smile began to trouble the corner of Worth's mouth. It goaded her into saying, "What I can't help wondering is how you have fit yourself into all of this."

"You're jealous," he noted, a gleam in his eye.

"Not at all. I am only reaffirming my understanding of the way men are."

He laughed. She withdrew her hands and sat back in her chair, aloof but less offended than she ought to have been. "Rosalyn, you're wonderful!" he exclaimed at last. "You have just come into my bedchamber with utter trust, and now you turn around and accuse me of consorting with tarts."

"I am merely trying to understand your change of attitude about the title. How can you be so outraged by his lordship's behavior if you yourself have taken advantage of the—of this unsavory situation?"

"And what makes you believe I have taken advantage of it?"

"You have *not*? And yet, you've pointed out to me, more than once—"

"I may have overeaten, and drunk too much, and everyone, myself included, gambled excessively evenings, but . . . I slept alone. And when I did—when I could sleep at all—I dreamed of one Rosalyn Archer, whom I love very much."

She gazed into his eyes, which laughed at her and dared her, at the lips she found so surprisingly sweet, at that rugged honest face that had challenged her, from the moment they had met, to rediscover what life was all about. And finally she gave a short laugh, which was an admission of faith in him.

"Oh, I don't know why I should believe you, but I do— I do. And I'll believe your explanation . . . somehow . . ."

She stopped, because he was smiling back at her with

so much love in his eyes she restrained herself with difficulty from throwing herself into his arms.

"You know," he began, his face growing serious, "I don't remember my father, but if Mother's stories of him are true, he lived a noble life. I think of him now, and contrast him to his brother, and realize what a travesty the title 'Marquess of Whitbourne' has become. And I feel a real urge to restore some . . . some integrity to the name. Because I'm convinced this is my family, Rosalyn. The Whitbourne legacy is my legacy. I want it to be an honest legacy, a noble one. When I rode about the estate and Blackroy Village, I talked to some of the country folk who remember his father-in-law, Lord Broughton. It seems he was an enlightened landlord, and everyone admired and respected him. Lord Whitbourne is, I'm sorry to say, more distrusted and feared than respected. And I remembered what Bernell said about poor Mrs. Beecham, and I'm beginning to feel I owe it to a lot of people to fight for what belongs to me."

"What about Mrs. Beecham?" she asked, startled.

"You didn't know? That he turned her out after getting her daughter with child and shooting her husband—'accidentally'—when the poor man dared to protest?"

"No." Rosalyn stared at him, aghast. "I didn't know."

"It's all true—ask Bernell. And after a week here, I'm certain there are other stories, just as terrible, in which Lord Whitbourne is involved."

"Worth!" A sudden idea had just seized her. "When you were lost today, out on the moor . . ." She hesitated, almost afraid to continue.

"Yes, what about it?"

"The way he looked when he announced you must be lost and the servants would no longer search for you. His eyes . . . mocked me, as though . . ."

"You're wondering if they really searched? I doubt they did. And did Roth leave me accidentally, or deliberately, on his lordship's orders, expecting I could not find my way back again? We'll never know the truth, of course."

"But that would mean he wanted you to die!"

"Hush, darling. I suppose one can hardly blame him for wishing I didn't exist."

"Of course one must blame him! You yourself have just accused him. He is not fit to be a lord."

"You're right—that is exactly what I think." He rose suddenly, with a huge gesture that was half shrug, half dismay. "What a damnable situation! If I had suspected it, I think I never would have come. But now I have, now I *know* . . . I can't leave it alone." He turned and strode to the window as if seeking a way out.

Rosalyn rose impulsively, wanting to reassure him with a caress. Then, suddenly shy of touching him unbidden, she stopped and watched his tense, motionless back. Beyond the heavy window hangings, snow still pelted the panes. She sought to divert a sudden trembling that threatened her composure by saying, "It won't last."

"What?"

"The snow. It never lasts this early in the season. It will melt directly, in the sun. Oh, Worth . . . !"

He turned at her involuntary cry. With an effort she suppressed her agitation and managed to speak without a tremor, even ventured a little smile. "I—it just occurred to me that . . . if he would have you perish on the moor, he could very well arrange to have you murdered in your bed."

"A fearsome thought," he acknowledged solemnly. He took a step forward and embraced her without warning, held her head tightly against his chest, and stroked her hair. "Yet I doubt he would attempt such a thing while you're here," he murmured.

"Then I shall stay," she declared, finding reassurance, courage, all the things she needed, in the refuge of his arms.

"Here, in my room? All night?" He pulled away to gaze at her, and his eyes twinkled mischievously. "Would you really do that for me, Rosalyn—risk your reputation to protect my life?"

"Of course!"

The merriment left his eyes as he drew a gentle finger down her cheek, along her jawline, and under her chin. "I believe you would, at that," he said.

His voice had grown very soft, very tender, and her whole being suddenly responded to his touch and the sound of his voice with little premonitory ripples of fire. When his lips met hers, the ripples burst through her like the lightning displays she had sometimes glimpsed across Dartmoor on summer evenings. And when he drew her hard against him, one hand and arm crushing her ribs, the other ravaging the heavy hair at the back of her neck, she was no more nor less than her singing, surging desire, meeting him halfway, her lips and tongue and hands as eager as his to tease, search, caress, clasp imprudently in an astonishing, unexpected, all-consuming need. . . .

He pulled away too abruptly, so that her hands dropped ignominiously to her sides and her eyes opened in surprise. He held her shoulders at arm's length and waited for her to meet his gaze. She felt half-drunk with emotion, dizzy, hardly able to stand, and not quite sure what had happened to her—to them—until she dared meet his eyes and saw the light in them matching her own.

Then he blinked, extinguishing it, and his voice came, little more than a whisper. "My darling, Rosalyn. We must stop."

She only stared back until his eyes took fire again and his hands tightened convulsively on her shoulders. For a moment she thought he would pull her back into the delirium of his embrace. Instead he let her go entirely and said, "Come. I'm taking you back to your room."

"No, Worth, I can't let you—"

"It was a joke. I'm in no real danger," he reassured her.

"B-but I . . ."

His hand clasped hers urgently. She could move neither toward him nor away, still caught in the wonderful terror of her desire. "Rosalyn," he said in a low intense voice.

"My darling, don't you know that all this past week, when I knew what was going on all around me at night, I could only think of you, dream of you, long for *you* and now here you are, and far too willing. . . ."

Oh, yes, she knew. She understood all too well, thanks to her own beating heart and the longing that was a physical ache within her for the feel of him in her arms. But the only touch he would allow her now was the joining of their hands as he led her back to the room she had been given, across the corridor from Lady Harriet. She could not resist, could not protest his restraint and self-control any more than she could have resisted his passion, had he insisted on fulfilling it.

"At least," she whispered as they said goodnight at her door, "do be on guard. And return with us tomorrow."

"I will, of course," he agreed. "There is no further reason for me to stay."

⟨∼ FIFTEEN ⟨∼⟩

Rosalyn was particularly grateful, the next day, for Lady Harriet's influence with her brother. Having achieved her aim—for Lord Whitbourne approved the hospital plans almost absentmindedly—she was eager to return home. The morning was crisp, cold, and bright, and the snow-drifts across the road ran surprisingly deep, making carriage travel impossible. Therefore, Lady Harriet demanded the use of Lord Whitbourne's sleigh and an early start so that she could be home before the sun turned the roads into seas of mud. Lord Whitbourne, eager to see the last of her, agreed.

Neither he nor his sister seemed surprised when Worth met them at breakfast and asked if he might ride his horse along with Lady Harriet and Rosalyn and return earlier than planned to Torview Hall.

"You may even drive the sleigh," Lady Harriet suggested, "and we'll tie your horse on behind. Then I can leave Blandford behind to bring home the landau when the roads are decent again."

And so they departed soon after eight o'clock, while the marquess's guests still slept. Rosalyn's vast relief at leaving Blackroy Manor was leavened by uneasiness, even though Lord Whitbourne remained hospitable to the end, promising to send word to Worth as soon as his solicitor arrived from Dartmouth with the desired information. As he bid them goodbye, he told Worth, "Don't forget,

Forrester, you still owe me the game we would have played last night, had not our plans been altered by the ladies. You promised me an opportunity to recover those two hundred guineas."

Worth acknowledged the promise with a formal bow, then jumped up to take his place in the front seat of the open sleigh. He seemed not to recognize the menace beneath the surface joviality of Lord Whitbourne's invitation, but to Rosalyn it contained a threat as deadly as a challenge to a duel.

She leaned toward him from her rear seat. "You won two hundred guineas from the marquess?" she asked in a low voice. "I think he would prefer to duel you for it, rather than play cards with you."

Worth turned and shrugged. Any response he might have made was canceled when a servant, having been sent to locate a misplaced glove of Lady Harriet's, dashed out of the house, waving the missing item aloft.

Lady Harriet took it and settled back beside Rosalyn with a large sigh. "Well, then," she called to Worth, "we can be off!" She turned confidentially to Rosalyn. "The good Lord knows I shall be relieved to return to the comparative sanity of my own household." It was the closest she came to acknowledging her awareness of the situation at Blackroy Manor.

Lady Harriet dominated the conversation on the trip home, favoring them with her opinions on everything from the expectation of a severe winter to the efficacy of mineral magnets for the toothache. She asked Worth to tell her what he knew of his father's death and, after hearing of it, shuddered and said, "So sad! And he was so young. All the years between fall away when I think of him." Tears glimmered in her eyes unashamedly. As she dabbed them away with a handkerchief she said, "You know, Mr. Forrester, if the title cannot be yours, I could myself grant you a living, even without Lord Whitbourne's consent."

Worth, from his front seat, turned halfway around. "That

is mighty kind of you, ma'am. But if things don't work out, I'll probably go home, to America."

"To America!" Rosalyn echoed. "But why?"

"I didn't come here for charity," he said, turning to face the horses' rumps again. "Only to seek what is rightfully mine."

"B-but supposing your kin had been poor farmers or— or other people with no means," Rosalyn pursued. "Would you have returned then, as well?"

"Maybe—maybe not. But this is different."

Her eyes searched the back of his head, but she managed not to ask why it was different. She could not very well argue with him in Lady Harriet's presence, seated behind him as she was and forced to raise her voice. She wished she could see his eyes. All she could view was his pale hair poking out from under his dark beaver hat, waving down to the high collar of his blue serge hunting jacket. His broad shoulders were set and stiff, as though defying her to challenge his decision. For the first time it occurred to her that Worth Forrester might be as stubborn as Grandfather, once he had chosen a course of action, and she was seized with sudden apprehension.

Did Worth really intend to return to America—alone? Had their mutual declarations of love last night meant nothing to him, then? Had she been the only one to discover an overwhelming sense of belonging when he had taken her in his arms? Had she even understood wrongly his reasons for returning her so precipitately to her room, those passionate protests which had so devastatingly echoed her own desire?

By the time they arrived at Torview Hall she was too upset even to ask him what he had meant about going home. The beautiful rapport of the night before had vanished.

Worth had offered to drive Lady Harriet home to Ashburton, and when no servant came out of the house immediately he leaped down to hand Rosalyn out of the sleigh, then deposited her valise on the step and went to unhitch his horse from the rear of the vehicle. Rosalyn hesitated by the carriage, ostensibly to say a few last words to Lady Harriet, in reality hoping for a word or even a glance from him promising her an explanation. None was forthcoming.

When Newton finally opened the big front door and the stableboy came to lead Worth's horse away, Worth only waved to her before resuming his seat on the sleigh, and his glance told her nothing. He might have asked Donald to drive Lady Harriet home, but, having committed himself, he would not have thought to turn the task over to a servant. Rosalyn remembered then that it had not bothered him at all to be conspicuously servantless at Blackroy Manor, even amid that well-tended aristocratic company. If he returned to America, he would resume his former ways, doing everything for himself. The mere notion of such a life was foreign to her. Did he recognize that and suppose she would not be able to learn, to adjust to something so new? Did he not even intend to give her the choice?

She waved a last goodbye to them and climbed the steps to the stone portico. She was surprised when Lord Clifton met her at the door. Returning her quick hug, he confessed it had been damned lonely with all of his girls gone, and he had been concerned about the snow blocking the roads. He so seldom expressed any emotion, Rosalyn was unusually touched. She kissed his cheek and told him she would leave it to Worth to tell him what had happened at Blackroy Manor.

"I've a little news of my own," Lord Clifton returned. "We've a letter from Gordon."

Talking about it, he led her into the hall and handed her the letter. Pleading fatigue, she excused herself and took it to her room to read.

Gordon was riding high again, his future father-in-law having cheerfully paid off his debts. He must also have recovered from the brief resurgence of his love for Melinda, for he had agreed on a date for the wedding to Miss Glynn: December 30. Barely time for the banns to be published, Rosalyn thought, adding up the weeks on her fingers. She wondered if this had been the price Mr. Glynn had exacted for such a prompt erasure of debt, then put the thought aside as uncharitable, especially when she read Evie's postscript:

"Dear Constantia has invited me to be one of her bridesmaids, and I have accepted. Gordon was right—she has the most delightful sense of humor, and she and the whole family are so friendly and hospitable, I quite feel at home. They have made it clear I am to stay as long as I wish— at least until the wedding."

Well, that took care of Gordon and, apparently, Evie, too, for the present. And while it should have heartened Rosalyn, it didn't, simply because of her own uncertainty about Worth's intentions toward her. How easily love could dominate and color one's whole existence! How it magnified and made difficult the least exchange between them! She ought to have found it simple to approach him and ask him plainly what his intentions toward her were, but she could not.

She was, quite suddenly, exhausted. Her short-lived uneasy slumbers of the night before had been permeated with nightmarish dreams of Worth in danger. Now, after a light lunch, when she wanted to put her thoughts in order, she could only toss fretfully on her bed. Not even the hot bath and Anna's soothing massage helped. About midafternoon she fell into a profound sleep.

She awoke to a disturbance in the hall outside her room and realized, even as she came out of the too-deep and too-lengthy slumber, that Olivia must have returned. And not only Olivia, but Captain Samuel Fortescue, apparently still alive.

It was past Lord Clifton's supper hour, which she had missed, but a second supper was being prepared as quickly as possible for the newcomers. Captain Fortescue was put to bed in a hastily freshened room adjoining Olivia's bedchamber. Olivia, foregoing her own comfort, was anxiously supervising his meal—an herbal broth made from one of Mrs. Beecham's recipes, to the suppressed disgust of Mrs. Holbrook, who disliked anyone but herself holding forth in her kitchen.

"But how is he, and what happened?" Rosalyn asked Bernell as she joined him for warmed-over roast beef in the dining room. Lord Clifton and Worth kept them company with cheeses and wine.

"His wound was not fatal, and we believe he will recover after all, but he developed a fever," Bernell said dispassionately. "Olivia disliked nursing him in the inn and insisted on our returning as quickly as possible. We would have left this morning, but the roads were too treacherous."

"So he'll recover," Rosalyn murmured.

"So it seems," Bernell replied. His eyes were pained and weary, and lines she had never before noticed seemed to have etched themselves overnight around his heavy jowls and his high forehead. She read in his stolid expression the death of all his hopes of the morning before.

"My dear, I'm sorry," she said softly.

His smile faded almost as soon as it appeared. "Olivia is happy, in any event. I think it took about five minutes for her to revive all her feeling for him, to forget how he had wronged her."

"Because of his illness," Lord Clifton guessed. "Olivia can never resist anyone who needs nursing."

"But is there any hope he will mend his ways, once his health returns?" Rosalyn put in.

"We can only wait and see."

She shook her head in admiration for his stoicism. "Bernell, I fear we shall never properly appreciate you, but . . . I do have one thing. Wait a moment."

She rose from her chair, surprising everyone, and left the dining room. She was back shortly and, without speaking, put Braham's letter in Bernell's hands. "This came the day before you and Olivia left."

190

"It's addressed to you."

"Nevertheless, it concerns you." She resumed her seat as he gave her a wondering look, then turned his eyes to the page he had unfolded. Rosalyn watched anxiously, aware of Worth's and Lord Clifton's unasked questions.

Bernell raised his head and said accusingly, "You sent Braham my 'Song of the Night' without telling me?"

"Do finish it before you get in a pet," Rosalyn begged, but his eyes had already raced eagerly on. Before he finished, the expression of amazement and joy on his recently sorrow-deadened face was all the reward she needed.

"It's probably just as well," Bernell confessed to Worth much later, as they shared a bottle of Madeira before a blazing fire in the library. "I've been a bachelor for thirty-six years, and I doubt I'd make a satisfactory husband to anyone, especially anyone as set in her ways as Olivia. I'm much too used to my solitary life."

His tongue had been loosened by an excess of wine, but even before that his sorrow seemed to have been vastly mitigated by the letter Rosalyn had shown him.

"Will you, then, devote yourself to music?" Worth asked.

"It all remains to be seen, doesn't it?" Bernell said cautiously. "One singer's enthusiasm does not a career make. But it does give one pause."

"Before you abandon the law entirely, I'd like your help on a certain matter."

"Anything, old chap, anything at all," Bernell promised with winy enthusiasm.

"I didn't want to speak of it before Rosalyn because—well, things might not turn out after all. And if they don't, I can't have her influencing my decision."

"Got in a bit over your head there?"

"Lost it entirely." Worth flashed him a brief grin. "But if I can't offer her the life she's accustomed to, I will not ask her to marry me. I may have to return to America."

"You don't believe she'd go with you? I saw her eyes on you, Worth. She'd go in a moment."

"That's just the trouble—it wouldn't be fair to let her. She has no conception of the frontier, and if I returned, I can't see what I could do other than return to Illinois Territory. But I saw what that life did to my mother, and I'm damned if I'll let that happen to Rosalyn. It's not her lameness, God knows. It's not that she hasn't the spirit, the willingness. But she needs her friends, she needs her familiar Dart Valley. Above all, she needs her music— well, you know better than I do how gifted she is. What kind of man would I be to demand she give it up just for me?" He shook his head. "I've as much as challenged Lord Whitbourne to his title, and I've decided, if I'm to win Rosalyn, that I must succeed in the challenge. That's why I need your help."

Having gained Bernell's complete attention, Worth summarized his interview with the marquess. He did not go into any details about the rest of his week at Blackroy Manor. "In spite of his apparent goodwill, I don't trust him," he finished.

"You're quite right not to," Bernell agreed. "So, to begin with, we must be absolutely certain everything is legal as far as your claim is concerned. If we can enlist Lady Harriet, so much the better. I will have to check the precedents, but I believe there will be no problem if you apply to become a British subject."

Once his identity and intent to settle in England were established, everything hinged on the will, Bernell said. It was possible that Worth could be heir to the marquisate even if his father had been disinherited; it depended on how the will read. They must make sure whatever Lord Whitbourne presented to them was authentic, that he did not succeed in altering it in some way before they saw it.

"Lady Harriet, as eldest child, may have her own copy of the will. If she is amenable, perhaps we can see it before the meeting. Of course, you realize that even if we succeed in establishing your right to the title, not all Lord Whitbourne's properties will revert to you. For instance, Blackroy Manor is his as part of his wife's dowry."

"Then even if I do become Marquess of Whitbourne and inherit that decrepit castle near Totnes, he will remain master of Blackroy," Worth reflected.

"Afraid so."

"Damn. Then nothing I do will help the poor devils who live in Blackroy Village or work at the Manor."

"Not until his lordship kicks off," Bernell said cheerfully. "But when that times comes, you would be legal heir to that property as well."

Worth only frowned ferociously at the floor.

"You seem to have developed as strong an antipathy to his lordship as I have," Bernell noted.

"Rosalyn believed Lord Whitbourne wanted to challenge me to a duel. I'll confess, had he done so, I would have jumped at the chance."

"I think, one way or another, you already have," Bernell noted wryly.

❧ SIXTEEN ❧

Olivia had changed. Only a week after the return from Plymouth, her eyes had regained their youthful sparkle, there was an eager spring in her step, and the prettiness that had first engaged the roving eye of the captain bloomed once more in her face.

Fresh from her own overwhelming experience with Worth at Blackroy Manor, Rosalyn could only conclude that Olivia's love for her captain, now resurrected, was at last appreciated by him. Samuel Fortescue, black-haired and mustached, with a seaman's tough, wiry body, was rapidly mending. He was quick to credit his amazing recovery to Olivia's devoted care, and it was a joy to see the new tenderness and respect he showed her. When he was well enough to join the others at the dinner table, he even interested himself in the affairs of Torview Hall, spoke of giving up his ship's command and settling down, and hinted he might be of use to Lord Clifton in the management of his estate.

Only time would prove his sincerity, Rosalyn kept reminding herself. One could only hope for the best for Olivia's sake. For her, a side benefit was that Olivia was now so engrossed in her husband she had no time to worry about Rosalyn's health.

Despite the weather's settling in at its November worst, with cold winds and rain, Worth was away most of the time, conferring with Bernell in Ashburton, involved in mysterious activities no one but he knew about. It irked and distressed Rosalyn that he did not consult or confide in her concerning what must be his preparations to assault Lord Whitbourne's right to his title. Didn't he know that what they had said to each other at Blackroy Manor, not to mention the kisses they had exchanged, bound her irrevocably to him, and made her as much a party to the outcome as he? She was assailed again by doubts. He had changed his mind, or he had only been dallying, with no serious intentions. Perhaps he thought she would not accept him unless he had the title securely in his grasp. She was frightened by the possibility that he would return to America without explanation or, what would be even worse, without another word of love to her.

Amazing—this new emotion which interrupted sleep, made food unnecessary, and disordered her formerly rational mind. Right now, anger and love dwelt side by side, fighting each other, and she hardly knew which would win.

They were never alone. The ordinary pattern of the days did not seem to provide casual opportunities for *tête-à-têtes*. Worth was often gone by breakfast time, and on two occasions he was away overnight. When he was in the house he no longer stopped in the doorway of the upstairs parlor as she practiced, and if he chanced to return in the afternoon, it would be as the whole family, including the recuperating captain, assembled for tea.

Until one morning, earlier than usual. She was at the piano again—her most reliable method of shedding self-pity—and sensed, as she had before, the presence of someone in the doorway. She broke off and turned around hopefully.

After longing for it for so many days, the sight of him—thick, slightly tousled, blond hair, strong bronze face, and tall frame that nearly filled the doorway—rendered her speechless.

He smiled as though nothing had happened to halt the progress of a casual friendship between them. "Good morning, Rosalyn. Dare I interrupt?"

"You have always dared to before," she reminded him,

swallowing a sudden sensation of breathlessness. She rose and indicated a chair and wondered why they were now behaving like two strangers.

He declined to take it, saying, "I only wanted you to know that a letter has arrived from Lord Whitbourne. Bernell and I are to meet him and his solicitor this afternoon at the London Inn in Ashburton."

"Oh! And . . . are you prepared?"

"As much as possible. Lady Harriet still hasn't found that letter from my father. But we have found the record of his sailing from Dartmouth, and have secured the services of a handwriting expert from Exeter, one who will not be in the pay of Lord Whitbourne. And we've taken certain other precautions against fraud, as far as the will is concerned."

"Still, the proof of your identification . . ."

". . . is uncertain," he admitted. "But the evidence is strong enough, Bernell believes, to submit to his majesty's courts."

"How kind of you to tell me all this . . . at last, Mr. Forrester."

His eyebrows rose at the sarcasm in her voice. "What's got you riled now?"

Tears filled her eyes unexpectedly. She brushed them away. "Nothing. My misunderstanding, that's all. I'd thought our . . . relationship was sufficiently advanced for you to have confided your doings to me these past days. I—I have taken a certain interest . . ."

His eyes softened for a brief moment, but she, searching for a handkerchief in her skirt pocket, did not see that. When she did raise her head, blowing her nose as if a sudden cold had overtaken her, his face was politely blank. "I'm sorry, Rosalyn. It has been a complicated situation, and I thought it best to wait until everything was set." He smiled at her. "We'll know the best—or the worst—this afternoon."

She nodded her head shortly, made speechless by his imperviousness. He bowed slightly and turned to go.

"Wait," she said, almost under her breath. "W-what time do you meet him?"

"At noon." He faced her again. "Do you wish me luck?"

His eyes searched her face for more this time, but she would not give it. "Of course," she said stiffly. "Good luck, Mr. Forrester."

He frowned, but turned then and left her. The fact that he did not object to her formality left her desolate for several long minutes. At last she turned back to Herr Beethoven.

Das Wiedersehen. How well, she thought as she dove into the wavelike, ascending runs which announced the return to joy, did the composer capture all the ambiguity of a reunion with one's beloved. The glad greeting, the first early ecstasy, the quiet serenity at the prospect of an enduring love, then the plaintive theme that introduced doubts and forebodings. But the theme of serenity kept surfacing, ever hopeful, and, in the end, prevailed.

She and Worth had not achieved that serene ending, and she was, right now, drowning in doubts and forebodings. If only there were something *she* could do about the situation. . . .

When she went down to breakfast she was alone in the morning room, and Donald reported that Mr. Forrester had already left the house. She had no idea why or where he had gone if everything was, indeed, set. As she ate, she mulled over the whole state of affairs and considered the probable viewpoints of everyone concerned—Lord Whitbourne, Lady Harriet, herself, and Worth. She was suddenly seized by a disturbing thought. Pouring herself a second cup of tea from the pot Donald had left on the table, she stared into space a long while, thinking. The letter—the all-important letter. Why would Lady Harriet even remember it if she hadn't come across it recently?

Finally she arose, the second cup unfinished, and went to the bell pull to summon Donald. When he appeared she said crisply, "See that the barouche and pair are made

ready, Donald. I'm going into Ashburton this morning.
And I'll need you to drive me."

She could see the surprise in his usually well-trained
face. She had never before independently ordered one of
the carriages. "It's been raining and cold, mum," he ventured.

"I won't mind," she reassured him. "And I—I have
Lord Clifton's permission." Once he had bowed and left
her, she hastened to her grandfather's study to obtain it.

She often wondered later if things would have gone as
they did had she not seen Mrs. Beecham on the streets of
Ashburton, wandering from one shop to the next in her
self-possessed, absentminded way, her threadbare shawl
over her head, an old woven basket on her arm, her too-
long black skirt dusting the town's walkways and front
stoops. What if she hadn't stopped the carriage and called
out to the seamstress, asking if she would accompany her
to Lady Harriet's house? Or if, once Mrs. Beecham was
seated, uncomfortably close to her, she hadn't asked her
how she had been so sure of the relationship between Mr.
Worth Forrester and Lord Whitbourne from the first glance
she had given him in the back corridor at Torview Hall?

For several long minutes after that question, Mrs. Beecham was silent, her eyes closed, and the musky odor that
emanated from her drove Rosalyn to seek a cologne-scented
handkerchief from her reticule as antidote.

Finally the woman nodded her unkempt head and said,
" 'Twas because of a locket Lord Whitbourne's mother,
Lady Amy Armistead that was, had, wi' a picture of her
firstborn that none cud take fra' her, not e'en atter her
husband ordered all t'other pictures of Daniel out of t'
house. A picture of Daniel, about twenty-two year old,
just afore he quarreled wi' 'is father an' left 'ome an'
country for good. Many a time she showed it me, as I sat
sewin' wi' her in t' big house. An' how like Mr. Forrester
iss to that miniature."

"And what happened to the miniature?" Rosalyn asked,

but Mrs. Beecham only shook her head and mumbled something unintelligible.

"Lady Harriet must have known about the locket," Rosalyn said. "Perhaps she has it now herself, for she must have inherited her mother's possessions." Mrs. Beecham did not respond.

Lady Harriet seemed pleased to see Rosalyn, and showed only brief surprise that Mrs. Beecham accompanied her. She graciously admitted them to her upstairs sitting room, which looked out onto the street, and offered them tea. Her maid, bringing it in, looked askance at Mrs. Beecham in an elegant Hepplewhite chair, but, seeing an impatient gesture from her mistress, served her anyway. Mrs. Beecham sniffed her tea before sipping it, held it with a trembling hand, and muttered to herself, not heeding Rosalyn and Lady Harriet, who sat opposite each other across the teatable.

Rosalyn had explained that she chanced to meet the seamstress and had brought her along, hoping she, as well as Lady Harriet, could shed some light on an important matter. Now, with a dry mouth and constricted throat, she said, "Did you know Mr. Forrester is to meet today with Lord Whitbourne and will, we hope, prove his parentage?"

Something flickered in Lady Harriet's eyes, and Rosalyn decided it was annoyance rather than surprise. But she answered civilly enough, "I don't believe I did. Is that why you're in town?"

"In a way," Rosalyn admitted. "Worth said you hadn't found the letter his father wrote you from Virginia."

Lady Harriet was busy buttering a scone. "That's right, my dear."

Rosalyn took the plunge. "Of course, Lady Harriet, I can't imagine why you would offer it as evidence, even if you did find it. Why would you want to injure your own brother for the sake of a stranger—and an American, at that, someone you'd never met—even if he did claim to be your nephew?"

Lady Harriet's composure seemed strained and her voice took on a harsh edge. "What do you mean?"

"I was reviewing in my mind all that occurred at Blackroy Manor—and my memory of it was that you mentioned the letter before you knew Worth would try to claim the title. After I had, in fact, told you he didn't want the title. Probably it seemed safe enough, then, to mention it, to force his lordship to do something for Worth. But when it comes to his losing the title . . ."

"And why did you tell me that, if it wasn't true?" Lady Harriet interrupted.

"It's what he had told me. I had no idea he'd changed his mind."

"And why did he?"

"Because, he told me afterward, he wanted to restore the title, which would have been his father's legacy to him, to . . . to a proper regard, to . . . restore its integrity, its nobility, if you will. That's the way he put it."

Amazingly, Lady Harriet's frozen face crumpled. She turned away and groped for a handkerchief. Failing to find one, she put her napkin to her eyes, dabbed the corners, tried to speak and failed, then shook her head and rose from the table, only to meet the unblinking gaze of Mrs. Beecham across the room. To Rosalyn, that gaze seemed suddenly implacable.

With a sigh Lady Harriet fell back in her chair, fumbling again for a nonexistent handkerchief while she gradually regained control of her emotions. "My dear Rosalyn," she whispered finally. "If you knew. If you only knew . . ."

She sniffed hard and raised her head at last. "I have indeed been in a quandary, and you have put it exactly right. I was convinced early that young Forrester is Daniel's son, and I so wanted Edward to do the right thing for him, but I also knew Edward would not be one bit inclined to it, so I . . . I spoke of the letter to induce him to act. But I was afraid to tell him I had it in hand."

"Then you *do* have it?" Lady Harriet nodded. "Do you also have a—a locket from your mother, with a miniature of Daniel?"

Lady Harriet frowned. "How did you know? Oh. . . ." She glanced at Mrs. Beecham, then back to Rosalyn. "Yes, I have that, too, and in it Daniel looked so like Mr. Forrester it quite shook me. But you can see my position. If I bring forth the letter and the miniature, I'll be giving young Forrester the title, and earning my brother's everlasting hatred for the act."

"Are you sure that will happen? There's the question of the will," Rosalyn reminded her.

"I have a copy of that will myself," Lady Harriet said. "I looked it up, just as soon as I could. In spite of the way he behaved, shutting out all mention of Daniel from daily life, I'm convinced Father always hoped for a reconciliation, because in his will he even stipulated that every effort must be made to find Daniel, should Father himself die, so he might learn of his new responsibilities. But again, I—I thought it best to leave everything in Edward's hands."

"Has he *threatened* you if you spoke out?"

"No, nothing like that. He wouldn't need to. I know him well enough. My nephew is quite right. Edward has used his power as marquess wrongfully, too many times. That young Forrester should speak of *restoring nobility*, rather than simply gaining position from the title . . ." She fought tears again and looked down. "It cuts me to the quick." She buried her face in the napkin and was silent, but an occasional shudder wrenched her shoulders.

"Lady Harriet," Rosalyn said, after a long pause. "You're a good woman and you've done many things, over the years, to atone for your brother's deeds. Can't you see that if you present the letter and miniature you'll do more, by that one act, for all Lord Whitbourne's victims than you've done in the past? Including the woman who sits here in the room with us. As for his lordship's hating you, I doubt he cares much for anyone except himself. Surely that mustn't prevent you from doing the right thing."

There was no immediate response, but moments later Lady Harriet's shoulders were quiet. And when she finally raised her head to look at Rosalyn, the answer was in her wounded eyes.

⌘ SEVENTEEN ⌘

With the greatest reluctance the proprietor of the London Inn escorted Rosalyn, Mrs. Beecham, and Lady Harriet to the private back room Lord Whitbourne had reserved. Only Lady Harriet's imperious insistence had won over the orders of her brother that those closeted within were not to be disturbed. He refused, however, to knock or open the door for them. Lady Harriet did that herself, a stern purpose on her face.

Seven men looked up with varying degrees of amazement and pique. They were seated about a large round table which was cluttered with papers, portfolios, pens, and inkwells. A five-tiered candelabra in the center shed extra light into the shadowed room. Seeing the three women, the men felt obliged to stand, one by one. Rosalyn's eyes found Worth immediately. He was facing her, Bernell next to him, and she saw a wry amusement in his expression.

"Be seated, all of you," Lady Harriet announced before anyone could speak. "I have some information which is pertinent to your investigation. Who is the handwriting expert? Ah, there are two of you? Very well, put your heads together over this." She marched around the table and laid her age-yellowed letter before a short, bald individual. Going to Worth next, she laid before him a chain and locket, which she opened. "If you've never seen a likeness of him before, Mr. Forrester, there is your father—and my brother."

203

She straightened to face Lord Whitbourne, who, white-faced, was the only one of the seven who had not reseated himself at her command. "There you have it, my dear Edward. All the proof you or the others need of Mr. Forrester's identity. I'm sorry to do it to you, but for honesty's sake I had no choice."

To his credit, Lord Whitbourne took the bombshell they had leveled at him with the *sang-froid* of a true aristocrat. In the next half hour, as the two handwriting experts agreed that this letter and the one in Worth's possession were written by the same man (the fact that Daniel, in the letter, had named his wife and newborn son and explained his change of surname reinforcing their deductions), the Marquess of Whitbourne sat silent, with hooded eyes. The miniature was passed around, and all present commented on the resemblance to Worth. The two handwriting experts, one brought in by Lord Whitbourne, one by Bernell, affirmed their written conclusions over bold signatures, handed the papers to the marquess, rose and bowed, and left them. The city magistrate that Bernell had insisted be present shook hands with Worth, congratulating him and welcoming him to Devonshire. Then, bowing hastily to his lordship, he, too, took his leave.

Rosalyn sighed in relief. Surely the acknowledgment of Worth's inheritance had been too public for it to be denied now. Lady Harriet took one of the vacated chairs and indicated Rosalyn and Mrs. Beecham do the same. Rosalyn found herself next to Worth, while Mrs. Beecham took a chair directly opposite Lord Whitbourne and fixed on him her unblinking gaze.

Ignoring her, Lord Whitbourne turned at last to his solicitor from Dartmouth, a lean, stoop-shouldered man whose concave face, except for the appendage of his nose, reminded Rosalyn of a hollowed-out cucumber. "Well, Bottersley, it looks as if we are down to the business you've been sorting out these past two weeks—the disposition of lands and assets according to title."

"Quite so, my lord," Bottersley returned, and opened

the portfolio before him. In a dry monotone he began to read off holdings belonging to one Edward James Neville Whitbourne, Marquess of Whitbourne. After each asset he gave the date of its acquisition, how it was acquired, and which man would properly receive it, once the marquisate reverted to Worth. At the end Rosalyn was shocked to realize that all Worth would acquire as marquess were the buildings, grounds, and surrounding farms of the deserted Whitbourne Castle, and a nearly bankrupt tin mine near Princetown, the assets Lord Whitbourne had inherited from his father.

"I find such disposition of the property most singular," Bernell objected. "Almost as if it were planned. Surely your father, the former marquess, was not in such poor circumstances."

"No, indeed. The fault is partly mine. I chose to put money into Blackroy Manor rather than Whitbourne Castle, and sold some other properties to finance it. But the tin industry has long been dying. I'm not responsible for that, nor for the fact that the slavers my father made much of his fortune from are now outlawed."

Beside her, Worth's body stiffened, but he made no comment. Rosalyn glanced quickly at his face, wondering if he thought his whole future prospect had suddenly turned to dross. She could read nothing in it.

"How many acres are included in the property around the castle?" Worth asked Lord Whitbourne. "What is grown there, how many tenants have you, and what sort of income did they make for you last year?"

As Bottersley shuffled his papers to find the answers, Lord Whitbourne said abruptly, "I have a proposition to make you, Forrester. I owe it to my ever kind sister to have all of you present as witnesses to the integrity of my intentions." His harsh eyes went to each of them in turn, skimming only over those of Mrs. Beecham, who had not altered her relentless gaze. "You came here for fortune but succumbed to the desire for a title, once you saw it within your power to acquire one. I hardly need tell you that a title without a fortune to maintain it is worse than useless. It is a millstone about your neck. Much will be expected of you as Marquess of Whitbourne, especially if you follow through with your intention of bringing your mother over here. Especially if "—his eyes fell briefly on Rosalyn—"you marry. In order to respond to the requirements of your position, you will need money. Agreed?"

"Agreed," Worth echoed after a moment.

"I, on the other hand, have not done too badly in my various business pursuits, but I would feel as bereft as a hunter without his gun, as disadvantaged as the merest furze-cutter, without my title. I have grown accustomed to it; it suits me. Your right to the title may be legal as of today, but certain steps will need to be taken to confirm you in it. Therefore, before you agree to it irrevocably, I propose . . . a game."

"Wagers?" Lady Harriet asked, startled. Her brother looked in her direction.

"I've learned two things about Mr. Forrester, my *dear* sister," he said, the emphasis on "dear" only adding to the sarcasm of his address. "He is an expert at cards, and he is quite unassailably honest. Therefore—yes, a game. A game between the two of us, winner take all. If I win, I retain my title, and, as you promised before, Forrester, you will say no more about it and return to America. If you win, you will gain title and Whitbourne Castle, and, in addition, I will deed to you my ownership of the Ashburton Woolen Mills. It's a thriving industry and, with prudent management, should give you good returns, which you could put into renovating Whitbourne Castle."

"You . . . are quite serious about this?" Worth asked.

"I am, indeed. And as you surely recall, you do owe me a game."

"But you've not made the stakes worth my while, my lord. You can't expect me to take you seriously."

Lord Whitbourne's brows knit fiercely. "What sort of stakes would you take seriously?"

Worth stared back for a long moment while Rosalyn

looked at his profile, amazed he would even consider such a question. Worth's face grew set and determined. "Blackroy Manor," he said at last.

"I beg your pardon?" Lord Whitbourne sounded as if he genuinely had not heard. His expression was blank.

"I will agree to the wager only if you add Blackroy Manor and all its farms and cottage industries to the mills. Winner take *all*, didn't you say? Well, then, you, too, must agree to leave Devonshire if you lose."

Rosalyn could contain herself no longer. "Worth, you mustn't! You have the title now, and some property. You could work out loans to build it up, and . . ."

He turned to her, and her voice died. His eyes didn't really seem to see her. Instead she saw in them a faraway spark, responding to the challenge, reflecting his unalterable determination. "I'm sorry, Rosalyn, but I must decide this alone." His eyes swung back to his uncle. "What do you say, sir?"

Again a lengthy silence held them all in thrall as the two antagonists faced each other. "Agreed," Lord Whitbourne barked at last.

"But Edward, where would you go if you lost?" Lady Harriet asked anxiously.

He gave her a twisted smile. "I still have at my disposal a few resources which are not in the Dart Valley—*if* I lose. Shall we ask our solicitors to set forth the terms of the wager?"

Worth nodded assent. Bernell and Bottersley brought out fresh paper and quills, dipped them in the inkwells, and began scribbling. Rosalyn almost bit her tongue to keep from protesting a second time, and Worth became aware of her distress. His hand covered hers reassuringly under the table, where she was tensely clutching her reticule.

"I'm doing this for you, Rosalyn," he said in a low voice.

"But I don't want you to," she whispered.

"Would you rather we fought with pistols? A duel is

inevitable between us. Today, tomorrow, next year—it's inevitable. There is no point in putting it off."

"What is your pleasure?" Lord Whitbourne asked him from across the table.

Looking up, Worth hesitated only a moment. "A variation on the first game you and I played—quinze."

"Most appropriate," Lord Whitbourne said. "Shall we agree that the first person to win two consecutive deals is declared victor?" He drew a deck of cards out of his vest pocket as he spoke.

Worth smiled slightly but raised a hand in rejection. "I'll agree to that. But I must call for an unopened pack of cards. Perhaps the innkeeper can supply us."

Lord Whitbourne shrugged, pocketed his cards, and turned to the bell pull to summon a servant.

The game Worth had designated meant that the object of each round was to obtain cards totaling fifteen, instead of twenty-one. The deal alternated between Worth and Lord Whitbourne, as, for a while, did the winner of each round. It might have been over after the first two, Rosalyn thought impatiently. Instead, they played four, then five, then six, suspense building with each shift of dealership. And as the tension mounted, the minutes and seconds began to stretch out to an eternity.

The five people in the room might have been mummies for all the noise they made, and the silence grew unnerving. Rosalyn hardly dared breathe, and the very sound of her pulse seemed deafening. One would have thought the only movements allowed were the hands and long nimble fingers of the two players, alternately dealing out their destinies; the only noise, the shuffle and slap of the cards on the table.

She could almost feel Worth's intense concentration in her very veins, but after their brief exchange she did not again look at his face. It still seemed incredible that he was willing to stake their entire future on a game of cards. She knew him so little, after all. In spite of what he had said, she had not imagined Blackroy Manor was that important to him.

Lord Whitbourne's sharp-boned face was solid granite, unassailable. Even the slate-gray eyes seemed composed of a rocklike hardness. Yet, as she sought to plumb what lay behind those eyes, she was aware that they flickered occasionally in an odd way. One might almost say they flinched, as though withstanding an invisible attack.

And then she remembered Mrs. Beecham's silent presence, and looked at the woman seated opposite him. The person in the room Lord Whitbourne had most wronged sat immobile, elbows on the table, hands clasped under her chin, her clouded old eyes still fixed on the marquess. Rosalyn wondered if she had moved at all since taking the seat. Grief-crazed widow, madwoman, witch . . . the unblinking gaze of such a woman could rattle nerves of iron, and, as the moments passed, it became more apparent that Lord Whitbourne was not, after all, entirely impervious. As he dealt the sixth round, even though he never looked at Mrs. Beecham, Rosalyn was certain his hand holding the deck of cards trembled.

The score of rounds won stood at three to two. If the marquess won this round, it would be over for Worth. Rosalyn could have seen the card Worth held but refused to look at it in case her expression somehow gave it away. The second card, dealt face up, was a four of hearts; the third, a three. Worth frowned, glanced at Lord Whitbourne a suspicious moment, but only said, "Stand," the signal that he had enough cards.

"Look sharp," Mrs. Beecham said. " 'E's trapped 'ee, Mr. Forrester."

Her low hoarse West Country voice, unheard until now, only compounded the tense atmosphere of the room. His eyelids flickering at her words, Lord Whitbourne dealt himself a single card—a five—and glanced up at Worth to show his hand. Worth turned up a six, giving him a total of thirteen.

"I believe I've taken you, Forrester," Lord Whitbourne

said gravely, and showed his down card—the ten of spades, giving him a perfect fifteen.

"Trickster," Mrs. Beecham said loudly. For the first time Lord Whitbourne looked directly at his tormentor. "Murderer," she continued, "betrayer, libertine, whoremonger, defiler of children . . ."

Lord Whitbourne leaped to his feet. "Someone kindly remove that woman from the room. She has no business here."

"On the contrary," Bernell said, "I think she has as much at stake here as anyone, my lord."

"I have won the wager fairly." The marquess looked around at the four people watching him. "You all saw that. The woman is out of her mind, as she has ever been."

"What did you see, Mrs. Beecham?" Worth asked sharply.

" 'E slipt ye the second card, an' kept t' top one for hisself," she crowed, her gleaming eyes on the cards lying spread before them.

"The woman is queer in the attic," Lord Whitbourne insisted.

"I'd say, rather, that she has quick eyes," Worth contradicted. "For I thought I heard you slip that card myself." He rose with menacing abruptness.

"Nonsense." Lord Whitbourne's hand moved like lightning, scattering the remaining deck across the table. "It is simply your word against mine. You all weary me." He turned to Bottersley, who had risen when the marquess did.

"The game is over. You may record the result. I have retained my lands *and* my title. Mr. Forrester's challenge has been rebuffed. A pity, Forrester, but that's the luck of the draw. I bid you all good afternoon."

"But, my lord . . ." Bottersley began as Lord Whitbourne turned from the table and walked to the door. The marquess ignored him, opened the door, and disappeared. After a moment's shocked pause, the solicitor scrambled to gather his papers into the portfolio and ran after him.

The stunned silence was broken by Worth. "But he can't do that! He can't walk away from an accusation of cheating without answering it."

"No matter what Bottersley attests to, I can oppose it," Bernell said. "And with your accusation, seconded by Mrs. Beecham . . ."

Except, Rosalyn thought, Mrs. Beecham is considered by many to be deranged. What judge would believe her against the mighty Marquess of Whitbourne? Her eyes turned slowly to Worth. She ought to be angry with him for throwing away their future. Yet all she felt at this moment was anxiety that out of a stubborn pride he would refuse to share that future with her.

"Worth . . ." she began.

But Worth's eyes were still on the door. "He can't do that," he repeated. "Someone needs to show him . . ." He glanced briefly at Rosalyn. "The duel isn't over after all, my sweet. I'm sorry." Swiftly he brushed her forehead with his lips and was gone.

⸛ EIGHTEEN ⸛

Rosalyn, following his passage through the corridor and taproom of the London Inn, reached the entrance just in time to see Worth, on horseback, vanish up the street toward the westerly outskirts of Ashburton. She turned anxiously to Bernell, who was on her heels. "Was Lord Whitbourne on horseback, too?"

"Yes, I believe he was. He had met Bottersley here earlier this morning to go over papers, and said something about not wasting time with a carriage."

They stood on the stoop together while Lady Harriet, her face a study of bewilderment, joined them. Mrs. Beecham appeared last, her expression serene and uninterested. The rain had ceased and a pale autumn sun was struggling through scattering clouds, but Rosalyn's mind was not on the weather.

"What does he think he'll do?" she cried out. "What can he expect . . . ?" She was utterly frustrated. She had been so sure this morning that everything would at last work out for Worth, and now the situation had become impossibly, frighteningly muddled. "Bernell, I don't under—"

She was interrupted by the proprietor, who came out of the inn with a concerned frown. "Miss Archer, Mr. Mayhew, I must warn you about the river, if you're goin' home. It rained heavy up by Postbridge in the night, and the ford may not be safe. Be sure to cross up at New Bridge."

"You might wait at my house until you know the ford is safe," Lady Harriet suggested. "We could take some lunch. I confess I'm famished after all this."

It surprised Rosalyn that Lady Harriet's expression was no more than a mask of polite concern for her safety, that she seemed not to recognize the danger in the dispute between Lord Whitbourne and Worth.

"Thank you, Lady Harriet," she said, "but I'm much too anxious about Mr. Forrester to eat. Bernell, couldn't we go after him in the barouche? Where has Donald gone?"

Bernell, promising to look for the footman, left them immediately. Lady Harriet frowned at her. "My dear Rosalyn, it may be best to leave the men to their own doings. I doubt your interference . . ." But then she recognized Rosalyn's distress. "Well, do what you think you must," she finished gently. "But I fear I must say goodbye to you now."

As she turned toward her house, only a street away, Bernell returned, saying he had found Donald in the inn's dining room, drinking white ale, and had sent him to fetch the horses and carriage, which waited in the courtyard. Rosalyn nodded her thanks with a brief, tight smile, and continued to look impatiently in the direction Worth had gone, as though a steadfast gaze would bring him back. Then, gradually, she became aware of Mrs. Beecham.

The old seamstress had seated herself on the stoop before the inn door and was now rocking back and forth, humming to herself. Finally she broke into a recognizable melody, and Rosalyn caught the words of an old nursery rhyme.

> "Run John, run John
> The gray goose is gone
> And t' fox is run out of the town, O."

She sang it over and over, rocking back and forth. Rosalyn turned a questioning gaze to Bernell, who put his fingers to his lips to warn her not to interrupt. Finally the singing and rocking stopped, and Mrs. Beecham rose heavily to her feet.

"Are you all right?" Bernell asked her.

"Aye, young Mayhew, I be well enough. But some there be who ain't."

The carriage arrived from around a corner of the inn, and Rosalyn went up to her and said, "Get in, Mrs. Beecham. We'll take you home. As soon as . . ."

But Mrs. Beecham shook her head. "Noa, my work iss done. Get along naow, if 'ee'd not be too late."

An unexpected thrill of fear gripped Rosalyn. "Too late for what? Where do you expect us to go?"

Mrs. Beecham continued to shake her head and, at Rosalyn's questions, simply began to wander away from them. "River of Dart, River of Dart," she crooned. "Every year 'ee claim'st a heart. River of Dart . . ." She sang it over and over as she walked away.

Rosalyn turned alarmed eyes on Bernell, who was frowning after the old woman. Her urgent touch on his arm seemed to mobilize him. "Yes—get in." He guided her toward the barouche. "She must be talking about the flooding river." He helped her into the carriage, climbed in beside her and called out to Donald, waiting on the driver's box. "To the ford, Donald. And drive like the very devil!"

The river was indeed swollen. The mild shallow stream they had forded that very morning was now a raging torrent, the dark brownish water surging against the river's banks as though feverish to break its bounds. Tendrils the ivy that crept along the land's edge had been tugged into the waters and now danced crazily atop churning rapids like a drowning person struggling to stay afloat.

Donald halted the horses and looked back for instructions. Rosalyn's eyes searched up and down the banks of the angry river while its roar echoed in her head and its wild moor scents filled her nostrils. Even then she might have missed the evidence, had not Donald seen how the mud at the bank of the ford was freshly churned by horses' hooves.

"Yes, I see," she responded to the footman's observation.

Bernell said quickly, "They must have been here less than ten minutes ago. But did they manage to cross or did they go down to the bridge near Buckfast?"

Impossible to cross the torrent now and examine the ground on the other side for evidence of a safe crossing. "To Buckfast, Donald," Rosalyn decided quickly, pointing him toward the route to Blackroy Manor. "And look sharp for any horsemen on the road ahead."

She herself could not tear her gaze from the river, which was visible from the road in the frequent breaks between the trees and bushes. Lord Whitbourne's angry, evasive eyes as Worth seconded Mrs. Beecham's accusation burned in her mind. How he would have loved to challenge Worth to a real duel with pistols then and there! Now, without the restraining presence of two lawyers and three women, she could almost imagine what he might do, should Worth accost him and demand satisfaction. The terrible image of Worth helplessly wounded or killed by the marquess's pistol (possibly hidden under his frock coat) was beginning to plague her. She could even picture his ravaged body being swept downstream in the flood.

She dared not express her fears, but wondered if Bernell, silent beside her, eyes darting everywhere, might not be thinking the same thing. She remembered anew Worth's retelling of how Mrs. Beecham's husband had met his death. Lord Whitbourne was not a man one crossed lightly; possibly, not a man one might cross and still live.

What they all finally saw, at almost the same instant, was the horse Worth had been riding, reins hanging free, browsing serenely along the road past a curve that had been obscured by bankside willows and alders. Her heart in her mouth, Rosalyn ordered the carriage to continue more slowly. Soon after, along a treeless, rocky stretch of the riverbank, she caught a glimpse of blue cloth, similar to Worth's new-made serge hunting jacket, caught between two rocks.

"Oh, no!" she cried out. "Stop, Donald!"

Not waiting for Bernell's help, she jumped down from the barouche, nearly falling when her right ankle threatened to buckle from the jolt. But she recovered and half ran, half limped, to the bank. It was indeed Worth's jacket, ready to break loose and float free down the river. She rescued it just in time and held its water-sogged fabric tightly to her breast. Not drowned, no, not Worth!

Obsessed and unthinking, she followed along the bank, through wet ferns and bracken which had already received the crest of the flood, her eyes straining for some sign of him. She did not hear Bernell's calls to wait for him. She continued over stones and slippery moss and around rocks, skirting the wild torrent's hungry lapping tongue, with no memory, much less sensation, of a handicapping limp.

And then she caught a glimpse of his pale hair, shining with water in the indifferent sun, nearly hidden by the tall ferns. He was kneeling above something, motionless. As she approached him, she saw he was streaming wet.

"Worth!" Breathless with trepidation, with relief, her voice barely exceeded a whisper, but he turned his head slowly toward her.

His face shocked her. It was haggard with exhaustion, his hair matted down on his forehead, rivulets of dirty water dripping from his nose, his chin, his ears and hair. He was on his hands and knees, breathing heavily in huge, body-shaking gasps. His eyes acknowledged her, but he did not return her greeting. She saw he had not the breath and expected him to collapse at any moment into the foliage.

She ran to him, crying, "What happened, my darling? Are you all right? Oh!"

The soaked fabric of Lord Whitbourne's dark frock coat was suddenly visible beneath Worth's hand. And then she realized it was not just his coat, it was Lord Whitbourne himself, stretched out and motionless, his face to the sky. She fell to her knees beside Worth and looked from the marquess's lifeless face to Worth, whose eyes registered an anguished helplessness.

"Tried . . . to save him," he managed at last. "Wasn't . . . quick enough."

Then his big body simply collapsed toward her. She caught him in her arms and cradled his dirty wet form tightly against her breast until Bernell and Donald found them.

Worth's story had to wait until evening, until he was back at Torview Hall in clean, dry clothes, rested, with hot food in his stomach and a bandage on his forehead where a rock had cut it. An attentive audience sat expectantly about him in the upstairs parlor. By then the news was all over the Dart Valley that the Marquess of Whitbourne had been the latest victim of the raging Dart River.

Rosalyn occupied a stool next to Worth's chair, her hand locked in his, as he told them what had happened. He had come upon Lord Whitbourne some hundred feet from the ford, and had called out at a distance that he must stop and face his accuser. Lord Whitbourne had turned enough to identify him, Worth was sure, but had not replied. Instead, he had reined his horse toward the river, hesitated a short time, then forced the animal ahead, into the water.

Mulling it over with his listeners, Worth concluded that the marquess, perhaps even noticing the swell of the water bearing down on them from some distance away, had expected to reach the opposite shore in time and might have hoped that way to lure Worth into following him across so that he would be caught in the sudden torrent. But his reckoning had been off. The marquess was only slightly past the middle of the ford when the high crest of water caught him. He tried to ride it out, but his horse was quickly swept out from under him, and soon Lord Whitbourne had disappeared under the water's surface, only to reappear, fighting for breath, some distance downstream.

Spurring his horse, Worth had endeavored to close the distance between them. Finally, in what seemed his last chance, he had leaped from his horse, thrown off his coat, and dived in. He had managed to reach the marquess, but the ocean-breaker force of the current had swept them both down the stream. He had fought to keep both their heads out of the water, but it had been useless; by the time the water receded enough for him to make for shore, he knew he was rescuing an already-drowned man.

"You bloody fool," Captain Fortescue exclaimed in admiration, fingering his mustache. "To risk your life to save your worst enemy. Not another man in a hundred would've had the strength to pull himself out of a flood like that, much less another."

"As I thought earlier today," Rosalyn said, smiling at him, "Worth Forrester, you are honest but sadly foolhardy."

His eyes went to hers as she spoke, and for long moments she forgot everyone else in the room, as she thought how close she had come to losing him entirely.

"Is it too great a fault for you to try to mend?" he asked softly.

"If you give me leave, I shall do my best."

"I think I shan't mind in the least being mended by you, Rosalyn."

Lord Clifton cleared his throat rather loudly, but none save Olivia paid attention. It was Bernell who brought them back to reality.

"Lord Whitbourne admitted to me this morning that he never made out a will. So now, Worth, not only do you become Marquess of Whitbourne by natural succession, but, after examining the evidence you presented to establish your identity today, I should think his majesty's courts will name you heir to all Lord Whitbourne's land and business interests as well."

Worth looked up as if the significance of such a result had just occurred to him. "All of them? Great Jehoshaphat, Bernell, I don't know if I'm ready for that!"

"Some of us may be happy to educate you to your new position," Lord Clifton said grumpily. "Provided, of course, you stand forth like a gentleman and declare your intentions concerning my granddaughter."

"Grandfather!" Rosalyn reproved him, her cheeks flushing. She lowered her eyes to their clasped hands, but when Worth's fingers squeezed hers she looked up again to his face. His startlingly clear gray eyes searched hers, as though he apologized for not having settled it all with her privately first, then silently questioned his right to do so now. She smiled back, an intimate smile that gave him her unqualified assent. Satisfied, he raised his head to Lord Clifton.

"With pleasure, sir. As you can see, your granddaughter and I have developed an immense admiration for each other. I know that when my mother at last arrives in England, I could give her no better gift than a daughter-in-law such as Rosalyn. So I hope you will consider it appropriate if I . . . ask for her hand in marriage."

Lord Clifton harrumphed mightily and searched for some way to have the last word. Finally he looked down at their still-clasped hands. "It seems you already have it, my boy," he said.

About the Author

After raising three sons and two daughters, Marjorie DeBoer turned her writing hobby into a career with the publication of her first historical novel in 1983. A graduate of South Dakota State University with a major in English-Journalism and a minor in Music, she has taught piano, violin, and public-school music. She continues to divide her time between piano and choral performance, and writing. She and her husband share their St. Paul, Minnesota, home with a Siamese cat and, on occasion, a hungry college-student son.

SIGNET Regency Romances You'll Enjoy

Delightful Regency Romances from SIGNET

*Prices slightly higher in Canada

**Buy them at your local
bookstore or use coupon
on last page for ordering.**